Sunshine
Degrees of Freedom
Emma Ellis

This book is written in British English.

Cover by Miblart

TRIGGER WARNINGS.

Please note, this book mentions domestic violence, child abuse, substance abuse, miscarriage, and infant death.

Chapter 1

Part 1

'Do not train a child to learn by force or harshness; but direct them to it by what amuses their minds, so you may better be able to discover with accuracy the peculiar bent of the genius of each.'

Plato

***

Harriet scrolls through the catalogue, casting her eyes briefly over each design. *Design* is the company's choice of word—not hers. *Design* is a word she would usually use for clothing or home interiors. This catalogue is nothing of the sort. Page after page of smiling six-year-olds stare back at her with wide, needy eyes. She stiffens, tightens her cardigan around her body, and hardens herself to their expressions. These images are not of children asking to be loved. They are merely faces. Soulless and inanimate. She certainly could never love such a thing.

'This is just the Caucasian catalogue.' The assistant's voice is laced with the kind of smarmy confidence she used to know from men when she worked on film sets years ago. She was easily swayed by such tones back then. Now they make her bristle. 'We assumed this is the catalogue you'd prefer. But, of course, you can have whatever you like.'

Harriet avoids his stony glare and keeps looking. She doesn't need more choices. She doesn't even know what she's looking for. Some semblance of a likeness to herself, perhaps. That's the arrogance of humans, isn't it? People bond more with those who look like themselves. As if her face is something that deserves to be loved more than any other. She shakes off that thought and reminds herself again: these faces don't need love. They aren't people. They are robots.

Not just robots. Top of the range MechaniKids, as they are more formally known. Her job will be to raise it, to educate it, to prepare it for its next stage of being. A little more involved than owning a washing machine or microwave, but she's sure she'll manage. The salary that comes with the job will iron out any inconveniences. She's still not sure how she breezed through the interviews so well. Competition was fierce, as the interviewer reminded her several times. 'To raise a MechaniKid well, we need the perfect example of a human parent.'

As if there is such a thing.

But she acted the part, as if she were back on the movie sets and West End stage. She might not earn a living in front of the camera anymore, and she's certainly less photogenic than she was in her twenties, but she can still play Miss Perfect if she needs to. When her application came back as successful, she hid her glee, bottled up every fizz of excitement and carried on with her dull day as normal, though a little lighter, knowing today would soon come.

She stops on a page, and her breath hitches as she gazes upon the face of one of the kids. Her chest swells with a feeling she's known only too briefly. She swallows and tightens her features, blinking as her eyes mist over.

'This one.' She points to a picture of a little boy with the bluest eyes and scruffy dark blond hair, the kind of hair that would never look tidy. Next to the picture is his name. Oliver. Like the little orphan boy from Dickens. Lost in the world, trying to survive. Little Oliver speaks to her before he's even uttered a word.

'Excellent choice,' the assistant says. 'Please remain seated. I'll be back soon. Your MechaniKid will be ready in twenty minutes.'

'Twenty minutes? Is that all?'

'The specimens are ready to go. It's only the aesthetic touches that need to be completed.'

She nods, then leans back in the rigid plastic chair as he leaves. The room is like a school classroom. There's a kid-height table covered with colouring books and a stacking game, and even a pinboard decorated with crayon drawings of a family. Mother, father, child written in clumsy writing under stick figures. There's a sign saying to remember to wash your hands. Do MechaniKids need to wash their hands? She can't imagine so. It would probably cause a short circuit or something. Oliver will surely come with a manual explaining that. Such details she can worry about later. She bounces her knees, folds her arms, then chews the inside of her cheek.

The doors open and a little boy walks out, dressed in blue jeans and a T-shirt with a dinosaur on the front. His expression is blank while the assistant holds his right hand. The little boy looks all around the room a moment, his eyes fixating on the pinboard for a few seconds before facing Harriet.

'Hello, I'm Oliver.'

Harriet swivels in her chair to face the boy. Not boy. Robot. 'Hi, Oliver. It's a pleasure to meet you.' Harriet smiles.

Oliver cocks his head to the side, his wide eyes watching her expression. He blinks a few times, then his cheeks twitch, as if he's just discovering his facial muscles and, after some trial and error, the corners of his mouth curl up to form a smile. His first smile.

'It's a blank slate,' the assistant says. 'It may look like a six-year-old boy, but it's more like a baby. It will learn everything from you. It will learn to mimic emotions and expressions. This is why we prefer them to spend these five years with a family, like they're regular children. Then, when they're put to work as adults, they'll understand empathy for humans.'

'Fascinating,' Harriet says as she leans forward to inspect Oliver's face, stroking his rosy cheek with her forefinger. His skin is supple and warm to the touch. She brushes her thumb over his silky eyebrows, his eyes twinkling as she does. His pupils dilate and constrict as he inspects her face in return.

She takes his hand, turns it over and presses on his skin with her thumb, observing the colour change from the pressure. 'How?' she asks.

'Genetically modified bioluminescence weaved through the outer biosheath. It reacts to touch and temperature. It's quite something, isn't it?'

Goosebumps creep up her arms. He's so real. There must be a seam or screwdriver point somewhere. He can't be this perfect.

'We'll see you every two months for its assessments,' the assistant says. 'It'll learn quickly. By the time you return it in five years, its mental age will be much more mature. How mature? Well, that's up to you and your training.'

It. The word makes her wince now she's met Oliver, though she's unsure why. *It* is the correct pronoun. Oliver is a robot, not a real boy.

'Download the app as soon as you can. It'll tell you about its battery level and any errors in its system. Now for some paperwork.' The assistant sits on one of the low plastic chairs, creaking under his weight as he holds out a tablet to sign. 'This confirms you will be living at the address you registered with, which is . . .' His eyes widen when he reads her house number, and he clears his throat. 'Swan View Apartments, 107th floor.' His bulging eyes look her up and down, though she shrugs off his surprise.

She lacks the glamour such a high up apartment implies these days. Her clothes may be expensive, but her unstyled hair is tied back with a single band that will snag when she takes it out later.

She can't remember the last time she wore makeup. She'll let him assume she's the maid or cook for a wealthy couple. It's not so far from the truth.

She signs where he indicates as he carries on giving instructions. 'It's fitted with a tracker. Please consult the online handbook if you have any problems or concerns. Here is a bag with the charging cable. Eight hours every night to maintain full charge. Charging should be done at the residence. If you are overnighting elsewhere, please email the support team ahead of time so as not to create an alert.'

'Thank you. And — ' She pulls her sleeves down and tugs on them, crumpling the fabric. 'What happens if I find the task too gruelling? If after a few months or a year, it's just too much? Not that it will be, I'm sure.' She backtracks at the end and bites her lip. She can't screw this up. But she always screws up everything.

'We have other people willing to take them on so you can return it whenever you like. Competition to take one was fierce. You are incredibly lucky to be chosen!'

Harriet smiles. Luck for her is well overdue, and she allows a little pride to warm her insides.

'But be aware, the pay increases every year. The entire five years is preferable for us, and lucrative for you. Although as someone who lives over a hundred stories up, you probably aren't worried about the mon—' He laughs awkwardly, and Harriet eyeballs him as he tries to dismiss his indiscretion.

Her little flush of pride dampens as she remembers now. The five-year pay is not an even spread. Still, a year should be enough, if she's careful with her money. A year should pay her enough so she can have a chance at a fresh start.

'That's wonderful,' she says. 'I'm sure we'll be great. What a fantastic enterprise Truly Realistic Intelligence is.' She smiles sweetly at the assistant. That smile won her awards years ago. It dazzled agents and scriptwriters, and judging by the assistant's blush, it still works.

'Oliver,' she says to the MechaniKid. 'Shall we go home?'

His eyebrows raise, as if considering the word, and he repeats, 'Home.'

'See!' the assistant says. 'It's learning already!'

Harriet takes Oliver's hand, and they exit the building of TRI. The MechaniKid offices are on level 10, the highest level for vehicles and far below her usual address. The air this low is thicker and leaves a residue on her bare arms.

It's been years since she lived so low down and even then, it wasn't for long. She was born below ground with all the other paupers and nobodies. Below ground was the term coined by the press decades ago. Never underground. Below. Beneath those who live above. They selected the term to be demeaning of course, but those below took ownership of it. They wear it with pride. At least, some of them do.

Her latest address is something she never imagined possible once. It's amazing what ambition and a pretty face can do. She squeezes Oliver's hand a little tighter. Years ago, she longed to live so high up. Now, when she's saved enough money to escape her current life, she dreads how low down she'll end up.

Oliver doesn't react to the change in freshness. He follows close to her side and turns his head one way, then the other. His steps are slow and rigid, as if on puppet strings. Exactly as a robot would walk. Outside, there's no view of the sky. The next level is a few metres above them, yet a thin ray of sunlight cuts a course through the high-rises, the particulate matter dancing in the beam. Harriet squints in the glare and lifts her other hand to shield her eyes. After a second, Oliver does the same. *Fascinating.*

She hails a ride with one of the many autonomous taxis, encouraging Oliver inside. His stiff little legs take a while to find their way over the step. When inside, he stands in front of the seats.

'Sit down, Oliver,' Harriet says with a gentle voice. Does her tone matter? Somehow, even though he's a machine, she speaks to him as if he could feel upset. 'The taxi won't leave until you're sitting and belted in.'

He turns to face her and observes her posture, her bent knees and backside on the seat. He tilts his head to each side, as if calculating the angles needed for his joints, then sits. She reaches across him, then pulls the seatbelt over his body and clips him in, clicking her tongue at the silliness of it as she's aware she's putting a seatbelt on a robot.

'Hi, I'm Oliver,' he says again as she sits back down, and she realises she hasn't introduced herself.

'Hi, Oliver. I'm . . .' She pauses a moment, wondering what to call herself. 'I'm Harriet.'

'Hi, Harriet. It's a pleasure to meet you. May I call you Mother?'

Her body freezes a moment before the temperature in the taxi soars and the air turns stuffy. She swallows and clears her throat. 'Sure, Oliver. If you like.'

She isn't smiling but Oliver is, making the same expression he copied from her earlier.

Mother.

She rolls her shoulders back and looks away from him, out of the window at the city whizzing by.

It's only a word. He's only a robot. He needs plugging in and maintaining, not parenting.

Yet she struggles to draw breath as the word repeats again and again in her head. Mother. Mother. Mother.

But he's not a son. He's not a real boy.

Chapter 2

Harriet's apartment is in one of the most prestigious buildings in the south. She refers to it as her apartment, since she lives there, cleans it, and maintains it in every way. Being married to the man who bought it should be enough to make it feel like hers. But in a relationship dynamic such as hers and Anthony's, he owns the apartment, and Harriet might as well be another of his possessions.

As a child, she thought the high-rises soared so tall in the sky they touched the moon. Now, living on the 107th floor, she might as well be on the moon, she's as much of an alien. It was a silly thing for a child to imagine but of course, back then, she'd never seen the sky.

As they exit the taxi, Oliver raises his hand to shield his eyes again, though when Harriet doesn't do the same since the sun is now behind them, he puts his hand back to his side. Harriet tries not to stare, though what exactly is wrong with staring eludes her, since Oliver won't mind being gawked at. It'll teach him bad habits, possibly. Observing manners in front of him still seems important. So, she steals glances only occasionally and finds every observation equally as fascinating. As they walk towards the entrance, Oliver's steps are already a little smoother. He could be mistaken for being a human with a slight stiffness in a muscle, perhaps a club foot. His hand is still in hers, soft, fingers curled, his pressure adapting to hers.

The lobby always has the scent of oiled wood, as if it's just been built. She's sure it's some air freshener they use. The gilded floor and light fittings look like something out of an old movie. When she first set foot in the place years ago, she was blown away by its opulence. Now she finds it gaudy and obscene.

The concierges on the desk dip their heads and say good morning to Harriet. She holds her head high as she walks past, playing the part of someone who deserves to live in an apartment over a hundred storeys up. The staff will be replaced by bots soon, once Oliver's generation are older, humanised, and ready to be put to work. Such jobs have little legs these days. Humankind is meant to aim higher, so say those from the top, with little regard for the force of gravity on social mobility. Harriet is an exception. But then, she did quite literally sleep her way to the top.

She returns their greeting and Oliver smiles at them and introduces himself. They dip their heads to him too and he copies. To them, he must seem polite and respectful. Harriet doubts they have any clue he's not a real boy.

The lift is smooth, whirring up to 107 silently and in seconds. The door opens straight into their apartment, their private exit.

'We're home, Oliver.'

He blinks a few times, turning his head to one side, then the other, and repeats, 'Home.'

They walk inside and she lets go of his hand, then he carries on taking a few steps without her. In the expansive hallway with its high ceilings and brutish furniture, he appears tiny, even smaller than a standard six-year-old. She crosses her arms over her aching chest as she wonders for a moment if he'll need toys. She pictures toy dinosaurs littering the floor, stray Lego bricks hurting her bare feet and muddy shoes bringing in the dirt from the local park. These are all the things a real little boy would do. These are all the things a real mother would have to tidy up.

She unpacks the charging cable and makes a note of the handbook web address, then takes Oliver's hand again and shows him around the house. He won't judge the waste of space the high ceilings are, the overly spacious living room, or expensive furniture and excessively stocked kitchen. In this apartment, the lights all work with a flick of a switch. There's never been an outage the whole time she's lived here. When Anthony's home, he doesn't even bother turning lights off when he leaves a room. He has no concept of waste. Each over-sized room is equipped with more light fittings than an entire street below ground. The place always has a subtle smell of packaging, since everything is replaced so frequently. The television is two months old. The dining room set just over a month. The sofa is positively archaic at seven months old. Anthony will moan about that later, scream at her that he's sitting on some crusty old thing, and she'll think the same when she sits on him. A thing past its best. She wishes disposing of him was as easy.

She proceeds to show Oliver various items around the house, calling them by name and he repeats them each back to her. Chair. Table. Kitchen. Window.

The window covers the entire wall of the kitchen-diner. It tints automatically if the glare is too bright, and the triple glazing keeps the temperature insulated. Oliver stops by the window and stares at the panoramic view of the entire town's upper floors, and the tips of the glass lifts that lead up so high. The Hel-E commuters take off from the top of the buildings, flying like bugs into the city. Oliver's eyes follow them, and he presses his index finger into the glass to trace one's route.

The highest public walkway is on 99 and looking down from here, there's a beautiful view of parks and play areas, the flowers in bloom colouring the park borders. There's even a clear view of the adverts on the light-up billboards. Some new coat design is this week's craze, the advert telling everyone to throw their old one away and replace it with this latest model.

From this height, it's not just the town of Reading that can be seen. The air is clear enough this high up that, to the east, there are the peaks of London skyscrapers catching the evening sun. The vehicle levels are way below. This high up has the benefit of receiving the lion's share of sunshine and being far above the dirt at ground level. There's no landfill site in view at all from up here, no stench of waste or soot to breathe in.

The evening rays beam through the window from the west. When Oliver looks towards the west, he shields his eyes again, then takes his hand away when he faces the east.

'That's the city of London.' Harriet points. 'And all the buildings close by are the town of Reading. Top levels.' She loves this view, never tiring of it. She can spend hours of the day watching the clouds morph from shape to shape, then disappear and be replaced with the brightest blue. Up here, she doesn't need to reach for the sky. She's in it.

Oliver's eyes widen a little as he continues to take in the view, his mouth opening slightly. If she didn't know any better, she'd say he appears in awe. He presses his hands against the window and leans into it, his face millimetres from the glass, his heels lifting off the floor as he allows the window to take some of his weight. When he rights himself and puts his arms back to his sides, the faintest smudge on the glass from his hands remains, though he has no breath to create a steam mark.

The lift pings and Harriet stands upright, facing the open doors with her fingers crossed that he's at least sober. Anthony's walk-slash-stumble out of the lift confirms otherwise, and she steps in front of Oliver, shielding him behind her.

Anthony sniffs, then rubs the white powder off his nose. He's a far cry from the man she met years ago. He was so suave back then. She remembers telling her friends he was dreamy. Was it just his money she found attractive? Looking at him now, she can't imagine it was anything else.

'Honey,' he bellows without even looking at her, dumping his jacket on the floor. 'Why can't I smell dinner?'

Her heart sinks a little at Anthony's obvious bad mood. 'I thought we'd get a takeaway.'

He stops walking, swaying on the spot for a moment as his eyes narrow at Oliver. 'What's the kid doing here?'

'Hello, I'm Oliver. It's a pleasure to meet you.'

Anthony takes a step back and grimaces. 'Shit. It's one of those things.'

'Shh!' Harriet covers Oliver's ears and wonders if that's even where his sound receptors are. 'He can hear you.'

'It's a machine, you idiot.'

She crouches down and faces Oliver. 'Oliver. Remember your room? Go wait in there.'

Oliver turns and walks down the hallway.

'It has its own room? Why? Just stick it in the corner with the vacuum cleaner.'

She faces Anthony again, takes a step closer, then puts her arms around him and presses her body into his portly belly. He smells like a brewery. 'Remember, baby? We talked about this. It would be good for us, for me, to look after him. Chris says —
'

His fingers bite into her back, pinching her flesh. 'And who the fuck is Chris?'

'Chrissie. She's a woman.'

His grip relaxes a little, his exhale coming out with a groan, though his cheeks still ripple over grinding teeth.

'She says that practising mothering skills can help, you know, conceive. She got a cat and she got pregnant. But I know you hate cats, and since your company invests in TRI, we thought this could be worth a go.'

His hands lower to her waist, where he squeezes a bit of skin. 'Perhaps running after a robot might help you get back in shape too.'

She smiles as sweetly as she can manage. 'Sure, baby. Quite likely.'

'With a body like this, everyone will think you gave birth to the fucking thing.' He snorts a laugh. 'All the flab and none of the babies. What luck do I have? Where's that gorgeous actress I met years ago, huh?'

She averts her gaze to the floor, playing the part of meek and demure, just how she knows he likes it. 'I'm sorry. I'll try harder.'

'Good girl.' He steps away, then lies on the sofa, putting his arms above his head and raises his eyebrows at her. 'Now earn your keep.'

Her smile remains fixed, though she can't help her eyes from hardening. She was a decent actor once but she's out of training, and the constant pandering to her husband has been wearing thin for years. Anthony doesn't notice. He never does. If he ever has the slightest inkling she doesn't love him, he punches her until she professes otherwise.

His face wears a smug grin. He may not be the toned and muscular man she once met, but he's still strong. Those arms positioned over his head have chunky muscles and weight that could plough into her like a jackhammer.

She shoots him an admiring look, softening her eyes until they scream at him how sexy she thinks he is, nurturing his ego. It'll be quicker that way. Power gets him aroused more than anything. She walks over, then unzips his fly, doing exactly what he expects of her.

Anthony wants a child — an heir, he says. As if his genes are something to be cherished. There was a time when having his baby was what she dreamed of, too. Together, they were to be a power couple. Beautiful, rich, with perfect children ready to conquer the world. She remembers that as she fucks him, recalls her naive dreams that morphed to nightmares, swallowing back the bitter aftertaste of her stolen years. She fucks him like she hates him. Her groans are of anger rather than pleasure. He likes it, thank God. Such ferocity finishes him quickly.

When Anthony goes for a shower, Harriet checks on Oliver in his room. He's standing there, doing nothing at all. She walks around to face him, and he reaches his hand out, touching the tear that's tracing down her cheek. He inspects it.

'It's a tear,' Harriet says. 'People shed them when they are sad.'

'Sad?' He looks at her, and his blank expression changes. His mouth downturns and his eyebrows knit, copying her expression again.

'Sad is when people aren't happy,' she says.

'Oliver can be sad.'

'No, Oliver. You shouldn't be sad. It's much better to be happy.'

She checks Oliver's charge on the app. He's ninety-five per cent depleted. It says, ideally, he should be allowed to run down to zero before charging the first few times to maintain the battery.

'How about a story?' she asks.

She sits on the bed and gestures for Oliver to do the same. After a few seconds to consider it, he obliges and sits beside her. It's a full-sized adult bed, though the room is decorated like a nursery with yellow walls and a border of painted jungle animals. The cot is still in its box, unbuilt, unused, a layer of dust resting on top.

On her phone, she loads up a selection of children's books and selects a picture book with few words, one that should suit his current mental age. She sits next to Oliver to show him the pictures. They're all bright colours with sunshine, bubbly clouds and colourful flowers, just like life up top.

'Mummy and Daddy take the baby to the park.'

Oliver points at the woman in the drawing. 'Mummy.' Then he points at Harriet.

'That's right. Mummy is like Mother.' She scrolls to the next page. There's a drawing of a grassy lawn, birds in the sky and two parents smiling warmly at each other. 'Mummy leaves the baby with Daddy while she goes to get ice cream.'

Oliver's mouth hangs open as he takes in the colourful drawings. He can't have any concept of what ice cream is.

'With mummy gone, the baby cries and cries.' Harriet adds a gasp for dramatic effect.

Oliver's hands go to his cheeks and his chest rises, as if he too is gasping.

'Mummy returns and the baby is happy again.'

Oliver grabs Harriet's arm, his grip tight and his chest lowers, as if releasing a slow exhale. Harriet watches him, at his enthralled little body's responses to the story.

'Happy again,' he repeats.

The app beeps to say he is ninety-seven per cent depleted. The short story has worn him out. Harriet smiles. Robot parenting is going to be easy.

She pulls his jeans down a little to find the charging port on his right hip, tells him goodnight, then plugs him in. His eyelids blink slowly, his long eyelashes fluttering. *Adorable.* Then he closes his eyes completely and his head drops down. His hands are at his sides in loose fists. She unfurls his fingers and inspects his palms. Smooth skin encircled with lines that would fool a palm reader. His nails, pale and clipped, have an uneven edge. There's a hangnail at one cuticle. Perfectly imperfect.

She lays his body down on the bed, then puts a blanket over him. It's a silly thing to do. It's not like he'll feel the cold, yet it seems so inhumane to leave him without a blanket. Though how can it be inhumane when he isn't human? She considers this as she watches him sleep. Not sleep. Oliver is charging. Sleeping is what humans do. It twists her mind like some puzzle or paradox. She steps out of the room before she can dwell on the topic for too long.

'Goodnight, robot,' she says, and turns off the light.

When Harriet gets into bed that night, she lies awake until Anthony starts snoring, then creeps to her dresser and takes her contraceptive pill from its hidden compartment. She swallows it and closes her eyes and invites a tingle of excitement to flow through her. A year looking after Oliver and she'll have saved enough money. Enough for a taxi or two, some rent, so she can get away and reclaim her independence.

Anthony's snoring from the bedroom jerks her from her daydream, yet her self-worth doesn't dissipate. She can do this. She can be free of the prick.

Chapter 3

Harriet met Anthony five years ago. She'd just turned thirty-two; he, ten years older. Past her prime for showbiz, so her agent told her many times. But she still had the fresh dewy face of youth. Somehow, the traumas of her past hadn't left their mark on her complexion.

The movie she was shooting when she met him was a period romance, as most of her other roles had been. Harriet had that sort of face — featureless and innocent. Straight out of a renaissance painting. She was cast as a wealthy single woman who falls in love with the stable boy. It was her most significant role to date, not the lead, but a close second. She was making a name for herself. A few weeks prior, she was recognised in a bar on the 5th floor. 'Hey, I saw you in that film . . .' the guy said, and Harriet nodded, then used her TV voice when she said goodnight after she signed her autograph. It wouldn't be right to sound like she was from below ground. Her actor persona was one from better places, accustomed to finer things. Her past didn't matter now. She was going places.

She was attractive, photographed well, and was naturally thin, which pleased the casting directors, though it was unlikely she would ever be a superstar. Pretty, but not striking. She had that girl-next-door vibe, though was getting a little old for that. She was clocking up enough roles to provide her with a reliable salary and had managed to move above ground into a proper flat for a few years. Before that, she was squatting in a warehouse on 2. The real joy of acting was that it kept her above ground. Movies were never filmed below ground, or hardly ever. Being on camera meant time above, with the sun and natural air.

The grimy life below ground was all she'd known for most of her life, with an abusive father and a negligent mother. She was going to be better than that. She was talented enough to make her dreams come true.

The movie was being filmed in a stately home in Oxfordshire. An ancient place at ground level, though the fencing at the perimeter kept the landfill from overspilling. Huge fans at the fence kept out the smell and smog. Harriet recognised the fans as being a much-upgraded version of ones used in the cities below ground. Down there, parts were salvaged from dumps by scavengers sorting through piles of trash the above grounders deemed as disposable. Scavenging is a lucrative trade, though usually short-lived. No one survives in the dirt at ground level for long. Those fans around that stately home were built from brand new parts. They were untarnished and spun with the faintest purr. The resources spent on protecting the old building for the sake of antiquated nostalgia was breathtaking.

It was a palace of grand rooms, priceless ancient art and regal furniture, set in acres of land where deer roamed for the sole purpose of being shot by aristocrats with little else to do. Anthony was hiking the grounds with such people, rifle in hand, ready to shoot some poor creature to impress his company's latest financiers. One of them owned the palace and a movie being filmed at his place of residence is the kind of showing off few can resist. The group of them stopped behind the cameras to watch a scene being filmed. Harriet, in character, was playing the shy and coy part. She could blush on command and make her eyes water as easily as blink. She acted the scene of her life, and the crew gave her a clap when it was done. Her chest swelled, and in a corset that was not easy.

She walked to the marquee to get some shade and a glass of water. This film was going to change her life. The butterflies swirling in her stomach told her things would never be the same.

'Hi,' Anthony said and stood closer to her than a stranger normally would. His face wore that smug half grin she'd grow to hate.

Harriet looked over one shoulder, then the other, not believing such a man would mean to talk to her. Anthony was the kind of wealth she could never imagine talking to. His accent was similar to hers in the movie, not hers in real life. He was so dashing and well-presented, she could easily imagine the stately home was his.

When it became clear he was talking to her, she blushed, naturally this time, not acting. 'Hi,' she said, maintaining her on-screen voice.

'Weren't you in that movie about the Royals, set years ago? You played the maid to the princess.'

Harriet nodded. 'Yes, that was me.'

'You're very talented.'

'Thank you.'

'Maybe I could take you out for dinner one night, if you're free?'

She could have sworn her corset tightened as her lungs couldn't inflate enough. She took a sip of her water as her throat ran dry. 'Sure.'

She'd never met anyone like Anthony before. He was all chiselled jawline and smooth, tanned skin. Had the kind of physique that told her he'd never been hungry. She noted his muscle definition through his shirt. He could afford to waste calories at the gym.

Growing up below ground with her father's aggression had almost put her off men entirely. People, in general, were hard for her to feel any sort of attachment. The good ones never lived long enough and the bad ones couldn't be trusted. No one could ever love her enough and she was the same with them. That's what her last girlfriend told her anyway. Like all the rest, she told Harriet she was cold, distant, a closed book. The latter was undoubtedly true. As for being cold, that may have been the impression Harriet gave, which it so often was. But for someone who had never known the warmth of love, how was she meant to be any different? She never learned how to give such emotion nor how to accept it.

Anthony, though, was a man. The gender her agent said would be preferable for her career. 'No one wants a dyke in period dramas and rom coms,' the agent said. And since those were the only significant parts destined for Harriet, someone as manly, as successful, and as determined to cultivate some affection from her heartened heart as Anthony was the match of her dreams.

The dinner was divine, as was Anthony's apartment, his wine collection, the gifts he showered her with. Every moment of those early days was intense, smothering but not in a way that had red flags. It was years later Harriet would see how obvious the signs were. He uttered words in her ear that she never imagined she'd hear. 'You enchant me. You're the most beautiful girl in the world. I want to spend the rest of my life making you happy.' Then the classic, 'No one will ever love you like I do.'

No one ever had, and she was sure he was right—no one ever would again. She usually was so unlovable. Fanciable, fuckable, sure. But lovable? Until Anthony, she genuinely believed the answer was no.

A month later, he watched her film another scene. Harriet was to make love to the stable boy among bales of hay. No nudity on film. It was all discreet under a horse blanket, but it was passionate, forbidden love coming to fruition. She dry-humped the actor under the blanket and groaned in a way that Anthony had made her in real life. Her glossy dark curls fell from their updo as she moved to take her position on top and their feigned orgasms arrived together. It all went exactly as choreographed. Under the blanket, she was still clothed.

At his apartment that night, Anthony paced the hallway, bit his nails, punched one hand with his other fist, then wept in her arms. 'I love you. I can't watch you do that.'

'It's just acting, baby. I'm all yours.'

He cupped her face, his eyes boring into hers. 'You're mine, Harriet. Stop this acting. I can't have another's hands on you. Marry me instead. I'll look after you forever. You'll never need to work again.'

Harriet wanted to act for the money, not the fame. Fame is only good for admiration and finding a perfect partner. In Anthony, she had all of that. She didn't hesitate for a moment when she said yes and with their hasty vows, he purchased himself his favourite possession yet.

She should have known better. There should have been a voice inside screaming it was too soon, to slow down, that she's been building a career, and she should continue. That's what her flatmates were telling her. They begged her to stay, not just to cover her part of the rent, for her own good.

But she'd just turned thirty-two, lucky to make it to that age given her upbringing. Those born below ground didn't often live that long, and her agent said her career would be short. Why turn down Anthony for the sake of a few years of unreliable work?

She had friends then. Not all the kind of long-term, would-do-anything-for-her friends, but people who cared. The kind of friends who would have a drink together and give sensible advice with a giggle and put the world to rights. And they all said the same thing.

Don't. Just don't.

And she said the same thing every ditz says: Anthony is different. Trust me. I know what I'm doing.

It makes her cringe now and her gut knot with shame. *Idiot.*

Her own mother ended up tied to an abusive man, unable to escape. Harriet always swore to herself she'd maintain her independence. But at the time she thought, no, she *knew,* Anthony was the real deal. He was going to look after her, protect her. They would make a life together, he promised. They'd have a family.

He would love their children.

Chapter 4

'Mother, Mother, Mother!'

Harriet drops her laundry and runs to Oliver's room. Anthony left for work an hour ago and with her relief at his retreating footsteps, she'd forgotten all about Oliver.

He stops crying when she enters and he sits upright in bed, his hands clutching the blanket, the rosy glow gone from his cheeks.

'Oliver. You're awake.'

He turns his head in her direction, then tilts it up and down to take in her shape. He blinks a few times as his gaze rests on her face. He doesn't make eye contact but looks at her as if making a mental note of her features. His knitted brow relaxes after a moment, and his downturned mouth flattens to a more stoic expression. 'Hello, Mother. I am so pleased you're here.'

She walks to him and unplugs his charging cable. When she does, she jumps as he wraps his arms around her neck in an embrace. She takes a moment before hugging him back, spending that moment wondering if he was intending to strangle her. Impossible, she tells herself. MechaniKids learn from humans and Oliver has no concept of causing harm. When she reciprocates his hug, his rigid arms soften and his face nuzzles into her hair. If she didn't know any better, she'd think she could feel his breath on her neck.

She rubs his back. 'This is a lovely cuddle, Oliver.'

'Cuddle,' he repeats.

She uncurls his arms from her and looks at his face. Some colour returns to his cheeks. How that's possible from just some bioluminescence, she can't fathom. His eyes have red rims like he's been in distress. The colour change is subtle yet remarkable, and she gazes upon it. She can't imagine ever not being amazed.

'Were you upset, being on your own?'

'I wondered where my mother was.'

'I was right here, Oliver. You don't have to worry.' She keeps her tone gentle, though struggles to maintain a relaxed expression as she thinks a clingy robot could be a nightmare. The story last night was a mistake. Even that level of peril is too much for Oliver's impressionable mind. Not mind, programming. She really needs to stop anthropomorphising the robot.

The TRI assistant said Oliver learns from other people, so he probably needs a little time to adapt. She'll teach him some routine and fill his learning desires with happier things.

She checks his battery level on the app, which confirms he's fully charged.

'How about we go for a walk? Do you want to explore the park?'

'Ice cream?'

'No. No, ice cream.' Well, she might have an ice cream. Her waistline is Anthony's concern, not hers. If he found her exceedingly unattractive, that would be perfect. She piles on the pounds as much as she can. She was always skinny, so it's not easy and she's still not overweight, just not the size six she was years ago. Another stone and she might be safe from his clutches.

Oliver's clothes have creased at the back. She probably should have undressed him before bed. He could do with a few more outfits. She grins at the thought. It's like having a doll. She could dress him in a cute denim jacket and jumper, some dungarees, or a little suit with a tie. Some fluffy pyjamas for bedtime and slippers. There's a kid boutique a few levels down she's momentarily glanced at before. She ruffles Oliver's already messy hair. His natural bed head look is adorable. It reminds her so much of her brother's hair.

She takes a breath and forces that sad memory away. It was a lifetime ago. She has a future to think about now.

She grabs her jacket and attempts to smooth down her hair. It's less well-groomed than it was years ago. Her once silky curls are now a frizzy swirl of ex-brown. Silver grey already weaves through from her scalp, and she hasn't the self-care to bother dyeing it. No makeup, and clothes that fitted better a few pounds ago. The odd time she'd made an effort to lose some weight, Anthony accused her of cheating, yet looking as unkempt as she does, he moans she's not as attractive as she once was. Given the choice, she always opts for the latter.

They take the lift down and stroll out of the building to the busy street on the 99th floor. It's the highest level with public access and modern walkways that lead to other high-rises; only the best buildings have scaled up this high. With the lower density of buildings, there's so much more outside space than on the lower levels, the walkways filling every inch.

There are plenty of parks, clean and spacious, with a clear view of the sky above. Not like the shaded and dilapidated streets of the lower levels. For years, towers have expanded upwards to escape the piles of rubbish below. Up on 99, they're so elevated above the landfill it's as if the rubbish doesn't exist.

Above 100, it's all private gardens only. Her apartment has its own outside space, but Oliver needs to mingle, and she needs to get away from the square footage that Anthony owns.

The paths are wide and open every few metres to sprawling outside spaces, all level and smooth, not a pothole or piece of rubbish in sight. If anyone needs to discard anything, a food wrapper or baby's nappy, they throw it over the six-foot fences that line the walkways. It'll fall most of the way down and then get tossed over again until it finds its way to ground level where it can be forgotten.

All the way to the park, Harriet tells Oliver what things are. Sky. Walkway. Shop. Park. Children. He repeats every word.

At the sight of other children, Oliver cranes his neck as they walk past. He has no boundaries when it comes to staring and Harriet wonders how she'll teach him manners. Perhaps her observing him has already made an impression.

When they arrive at a park, she tells him other words. Swing. See-saw. Bench.

On that bench is a mother with a toddler wriggling on her lap, the kid crying. Oliver stops and watches, then his mouth drops open and he starts to wail.

'No!' Harriet says and spins him around, then kneels beside him. 'That's crying, Oliver.'

'C . . . c . . . crying,' he says as his torso jerks, like he's gasping for breath between sobs. There are no tears, but he sniffs and she wipes his eyes with her sleeve as a real parent would, sure it makes her appear less bizarre to the passersby.

People are looking. There's the odd tut from childless people, and sympathetic looks from parents. Harriet's face heats. 'You don't need to cry, Oliver. Crying is for when you are sad. Are you sad?'

His torso stills, and he closes his mouth. His sniffing stops and he focuses on Harriet. She smiles, and he mimics her facial expression instead.

'I am always happy when I am with my mother.'

Okay. Tantrum averted. She exhales a steadying breath. Oliver's mouth forms a small O, his chest deflating as if doing the same. When the guy at TRI said Oliver learns by copying, he wasn't wrong. She's going to have to be careful about what Oliver sees.

Across the perimeter of the park are real grass verges and flower boxes. Oliver bends to pick up a dandelion, its yellow bloom matching the pattern on Harriet's top.

'Flower,' Harriet says. 'It's a yellow flower. It's pretty.'

Oliver looks at the dandelion and repeats, 'Pretty.' He then looks at Harriet and says the word again. 'Pretty.'

Harriet laughs, Oliver following. His laugh is a perfect giggle, smooth as pearls. He hands the flower to her. 'Pretty flower. Pretty mother.'

Harriet's lungs fill as the weight of the world lifts off her for a moment as she looks at Oliver's face. So sincere. So kind. So . . . real. She cups his face, her thumb stroking his cheek. It's a sunny day, his skin warm under her touch. She'll need to get him a hat.

She leans forward and gives him a peck on the cheek, then picks him up, her arms encircling his back. He leans into her, his fingers entangling with her hair, his cheek resting on her shoulder. She thought he'd be heavier, but he's the weight she'd expect from a child his size.

Walking around the park, other parents smile at them, looking at them with envy in their eyes at the bond they observe. It's a little while before Harriet puts Oliver back down, only when her arms ache too much. He needs to improve his walking, not be carried. He needs to learn about the world, not just about hugs. It surprises her how much she misses carrying him as soon as he's down. His little body pressed into hers was somehow satisfying. Her arms ache more when empty than full.

They sit on a bench, Oliver remembering exactly how much to bend his knees and hips, and he leans on her again as they watch the other kids play in the park. Some parents scold their children, others show signs of impatience, or the children are naughty. Oliver sits perfectly still, smiling, holding his mother's hand, and she thinks, this is her doing. He's already perfectly well behaved. She's raising him to be a good little boy.

She corrects herself. Robot. Not boy.

The swings and climbing frames all seem a bit much for him right now with his current coordination. The balls make noises when kicked and bounced off the hard ground, each sound making Oliver jump a little, though less each time. He looks at the climbing frame the most. The tangle of rope and wood must be such a confusing thing for his unworldly eyes. Harriet can picture him up there, doing the monkey bars and getting her to watch as he does the same trick for the millionth time. Her little brother used to do that sometimes, when he was well enough. Her stomach knots when she remembers telling him she'd seen it enough times and he'd beg her to watch once more. What she would give now to watch once more.

She leans into Oliver and speaks quietly. 'Soon you'll be able to climb and kick a ball, Oliver. Would you like that?'

He nods and keeps watching. He has the appearance of a six-year-old but the faculties of a toddler. Harriet imagines what he'll be like when he's chatting and running and playing with other children. Will he make friends and go to school? How long will that be?

She shuts down her imagination again. She won't have Oliver for that long. She only needs the money for a year.

They walk to the shops and he skips alongside her, able to do so now since his gait is already more fluid. He stumbles occasionally, his feet not keeping up with his mind, but each time he corrects his mistake, skipping higher and smoother the next time.

A mother is singing to her baby, and he copies the song.

Every day, the sun shines for you. Every day, you are my sunshine.

The lyrics perfectly suit life up here where the sun really can shine. She can't imagine such a song would have made sense to her when she lived below ground. It's the kind of song Harriet imagined she'd sing to her own children once. Before Anthony took those dreams from her.

She needs to keep remembering that, to keep hating him, to feel the bruises he leaves in places where others can't see. She never wants to be as poor as she once was, but a wealthy life, she knows, just isn't worth it.

'Are you okay, Mother?' Oliver asks, as Harriet's mind is occupied with hate for her husband.

She doesn't answer for a moment, drawing her chin in as she realises it might be the first time in years anyone has asked how she is.

'I'm fine, Oliver. Now that you've asked, I am just fine.'

Chapter 5

A month after Harriet married Anthony, her period was late. She felt her breasts, tender to the touch. When she ate her breakfast, she ran to the toilet to throw it up. Her hands went to her tummy, flat and smooth, but her palms tingled and a warmth fizzed through her.

She cleaned the apartment until it gleamed, put on a new dress she'd just picked up, and made her face and hair tidy and perfect. The dress had little flowers on it, and it looked just like the thing a mother would wear. She cooked lasagne, Anthony's favourite, baked fresh bread and buttered it with garlic, then set the table. He arrived home from work on time, sober, and greeted her with a whirlwind of a hug. As he tucked into his food, he commented on how good it all was, how he didn't deserve such a good wife.

Then, she told him. 'I think I'm pregnant.'

He dropped his fork, and his mouth hung open. There was a second where she was sure she saw dismay on his face, then his expression erupted into joy. He jumped off his seat, but his knees gave way and he bent down to hug her waist. He buried his face there and sobbed happy tears. 'You make me so happy. When this little one arrives, our lives will be complete.'

She stroked his hair, still dark and full then, and cried happy tears with him.

She'd been working in a school, part time, giving drama lessons for the pupils. They were all good kids from wealthy families, mostly well-mannered with a strong desire to do well. Some recognised her from the movies; some of the parents certainly did. She loved that job, encouraging the children's creativity, applauding them, their adorable little bows at the end.

When she was pregnant, she glowed during those days, imagining her child making up plays and singing and dancing. Would the baby take to the stage like her, or prefer business ventures like Anthony? She didn't care either way. It still amazed her that her child would have a choice of the kind of life it wanted to live.

She lost the baby at twelve weeks. The cramps came and she knew. There was no doubt in her mind. She just knew.

As a child, she had seen the same in so many women. Those who lived below ground were rarely blessed with healthy pregnancies. Harriet knew then that she was stupid to think hers would be any different. Her short time living so high up was nowhere near enough to rid her veins of the pollution of her past.

In the hospital, she and Anthony held each other, crying, but listened to the doctors and despite their sadness, they were undeterred. It's normal, they were told. Just bad luck, try again.

And they did.

When she fell pregnant again, the joy was the same, though Harriet's anxieties nibbled at her constantly. She'd never told Anthony she lived below ground. Ever since they met, she'd maintained her accent from the movie. Plummy, well-to-do. Not from the filth and grime of the down below. Anthony assumed she was from the upper levels, and she never corrected him. It was easier to act the part than reveal the shameful truth. The fact he never enquired about her past should have been a warning.

She sweated through sheets at night and said little during the day as she imagined her baby being born sickly, deformed, like so many she'd witnessed in her childhood. In her hands, she saw dirt under her fingernails and scrubbed them until they were raw.

She didn't revel in Anthony's excitement, instead imagining his saddened face when she'd let him down again. People like her don't get to know true happiness. Happiness is reserved for those who were born under a real sun, breathing real air.

When her stomach began to swell, they enjoyed each of her body's changes and as she passed the early dangerous months, she scrubbed her hands less. When her baby moved inside her, for a moment she could picture its face, hear its cry, feel the weight of a newborn in her arms.

Anthony spoke to her bump and bought a cot for the nursery. Every day, he told her how much he loved her.

Bit by bit, she let go of the darkness of her past. Anthony had changed all of that. He'd taken her up to the light. He would love their child as he loved her. And it would all be perfect.

Chapter 6

In Harriet's bag is a book on dinosaurs wrapped in dinosaur-themed paper. It's been a year since Oliver came home with her. Most parents take their children out for ice cream or to the water park for their birthdays. Celebrating with a MechaniKid is a lot more limiting.

Oliver loves picture books on animals and his reading has advanced quickly. He gobbles up facts like a normal kid does chocolate. Along with the dinosaur book is a copy of *Charlotte's Web*, Harriet's favourite book as a child. She remembers it being about the right to survive, to live, about one species caring for another.

This anniversary is bittersweet. She's grown quite attached to Oliver, more than she thought she would, certainly more than any other electrical device. He looks at her face more intently now and his eyes light up when he sees her. Whenever they walk through parks and playgrounds, he's well behaved. That's the true tell, she thinks, that he's not a real boy. He lacks the naughtiness of other children. He's never destroyed clothes with grass stains or talked back. A blessing, most parents would say, though to Harriet such perfect behaviour makes her smile falter. There's soul in misdeeds. It's so incredibly human to be mischievous.

The wages have been coming in, and Oliver has passed each of his bi-monthly assessments with ease. Harriet has enough money now to start her free life. Today is the day she returns Oliver to the company.

She shivers a little. The altitude above 99 often leads to intense sun but chilly winds. Oliver watches her shiver, then does the same, his little body vibrating. In her bag is a cardigan for each and she dresses Oliver in his, then puts the other on herself. Oliver would be fine in any clothing but the aesthetics would not. There's the threat of rain ahead as grey clouds collect from the west. In the direction of the city, the sky is clear so they should avoid any downpour on their way to TRI. Her chest sinks as she imagines her journey back from TRI without Oliver.

She has a handbag packed with some essentials, that's all. She'll text Anthony goodbye, then throw her phone away. There's cheap accommodation a little further north and much lower down. On the 5th floor she can manage for a while until she finds some work. She pushes her sleeves up, then holds her arms out to the sides as the warmth of the sun hits her skin. God knows when she'll be this close to the sky again. She jumped too many stages to get here. From below, to 5, and then over 100. It was never going to end well. She was foolish to think otherwise.

They stop at a bench close to a duck pond and sit. Oliver, next to Harriet, takes in the scene.

'This is a lovely spot, Mother. I like the ducks.'

'Yes, Oliver. It's lovely.'

'And look!' He points to an insect crawling along the bank. 'It's so tiny. How amazing!'

He has an affinity and curiosity for all tiny creatures, Harriet often wonders if his eyes see detail she can't. He pays little regard to whatever the billboards are advertising, the one next to them showing an advert for a new Autotaxi toy every child should have. He much prefers to look at the living creatures.

She never noticed the complexities of emotions before, not until she started scrutinising the intricate movements of his face and posture. Not just the easy emotions like happy and sad. But confused, worried, awe, fear. It's sometimes the subtlest of twitches, a light that shines less brightly. He notices everything in her, like she has the words written above her head describing her innermost thoughts. He's impossibly perceptive, seeing her in a way no one has before. Not just looking at her but seeing her so deeply it's like he can read what's written on her bones.

'I got you a present.' She reaches into her bag and hands him the books.

His mouth opens, then his whole face smiles. 'A present for me?'

She nods. 'Open it.'

He's seen children unwrap gifts before, though he's never received anything wrapped. He fumbles around the edges for a few seconds before his deft fingers rip at the wrapping, then leaves it in a neat pile on his lap, not chucking it on the floor or over the fence like other children would.

When the books are revealed, he holds them up, as if he has won a prize.

'It was my favourite book as a child,' Harriet says. 'About a spider called Charlotte.'

'And a dinosaur book!' He drops his arms, pressing the books into his chest as he leans on Harriet. 'I love them, Mother. Thank you.'

Love. She wonders where he's picked up that word or how he knows what it feels like. He must have heard it from other children. His ears are finely tuned to words depicting emotion. He says it flippantly, like he would've seen the way a child covets a new bike or device. Love, he must think, is something visible, tangible, and materialistic to a child.

She puts the books in her bag and lifts him onto her lap. He wraps his arms around her, his cheek pressing into her neck. She's not going to cry. He's only a robot. He won't miss her. He doesn't love her. It's only programming. She squeezes a little tighter, forcing herself not to imagine what could have been, what a future would look like for her and Oliver if he were a real boy. But such a future isn't what's in store for him. In a few years, his personality module will be placed in a teenage body where he will live in an institution with other MechaniTeens. Then, five years after that, he'll be switched into an adult body and will be assigned a job. There will never be any place for Harriet. She was only ever a temporary guide for him. For her, he was her ticket out. She sniffs back a tear and tells herself, mission accomplished.

She places him back on the chair next to her, pats his head, then ruffles his hair a little. She's been styling his hair with this cute wax for kids. It has cartoons on the packet and smells like vanilla.

Harriet runs through her plan again. Take a taxi to TRI. Drop off Oliver, then find a hostel somewhere between 1st and 10th. The electricity that low down is patchy at best, with frequent blackouts and poor lighting. She can't think about how much she'll miss her luxuries up here. She'll seek out some old friends in the poorer quarters to find work. Themed bars would do, or some acting job that involves enough costume she can hide in plain sight. She's never seen any of her old acting friends in the big movies. A few adverts and minor film roles is the most she's noticed so they can't be earning much, but unlikely any would have resorted to living below ground. Below ground is off limits. She cannot, will not, go back there, whatever it takes. There are too many shady corners there for a woman on her own. She's forgotten how to navigate down there. She's been away too long.

Across the pond, a laugh snags her attention. There's a woman she hasn't seen in years. Michelle. A good friend and brief fling from years ago, from just before she met Anthony. One of the many who fell for Harriet, yet Harriet never returned her heart so openly. Harriet watches her. She's aged, though less than Harriet. Her once tight curls have dropped, despite her hair being shorter. Her skin is darker. She's lost the pallor from life in the shady lower levels.

'Mason, Tulla! Come here, please.'

Two children wearing wellies run to her, skirting the boggy edge of the pond on their way. The water and mud splash up their legs and they kick more at each other. Michelle puts their jackets on. The rain clouds are inching closer.

'Your parents won't be happy if we arrive home completely soaked.'

So, she's a nanny. That makes sense. She always loved children. Harriet recalls a night they spent together, Michelle saying how she'd like to have a child with Harriet. It was just before Harriet was cast in that period drama movie and her agent's words rang like warning bells in her mind. Same-sex relationships don't cut it in the movie world. Harriet needs to sell her entire existence, not just her acting skills.

She shouldn't have left Michelle like that. She should have been kinder. When she gave up the movie for Anthony, Michelle told her she was an idiot and Harriet retorted with something even less kind. Harriet shifts her weight on the bench, uncomfortable however she sits. There's an ache in her hip from where Anthony belted her a few nights ago.

Karma's a bitch.

Harriet stands, takes a breath and readies to say something but instead, Michelle walks away with the children. It's for the best, Harriet thinks as her shoulders slump. She needs friends from lower down than Michelle. Some bonds are too broken to fix.

She keeps her focus on Michelle and reaches for her bag, then for Oliver's hand, but finds only air. The bench is empty.

'Oliver?'

The splash comes from her right and sends a jolt through her chest. Her heart freezes for a moment, then pounds in her ears.

'Oliver?'

Sweat breaks out across her brow and shoulder blades. Her breath comes out in shudders as she steps up to the pond. The surface of the pond ripples with silky concentric circles that hit the bank, then ricochet back again.

'Oliver!'

She spins around, looks behind, around the pond, anywhere else but down. 'Oliver!' He always comes when she calls. He's such a good boy. 'Oliver!'

She looks down at the pond again as the last ripple flattens, the water smooths, reflecting the clouds above.

Oh God oh God oh God!

'Oliver!' A scream this time, from the deepest place inside her where her worst fears lurk. She tears off her cardigan, drops her bag, then without another thought jumps in. The cold water makes her gasp before she dives down. It's murky, a brownish soup with clear patches through the weeds. She thrashes around in the icy gloom, her hands searching and grabbing but finding only slimy weeds.

She comes up for air, spits out the muck and screams his name again before diving back down. Her hands are in front of her, fingers outstretched and grasping for the limbs she knows so well.

She needs a breath and strains to control her lungs as her chest convulses but there, in a clear patch, is his dinosaur T-shirt.

She comes up for air once more, sucks in a final lungful before she dives again and finds his little body unmoving in the same spot. She grabs him under his armpit and hauls him up, kicking her legs frantically to get to the surface. When she reaches the bank, her panicked lungs gasp for breath as she grabs onto a fence post and heaves herself up, not letting go of Oliver before pulling him clear of the water.

His eyes are half closed; his head dipped down.

'Oliver!' She shakes him. Like a fool, she presses her fingers into where his pulse should be and listens for breath. 'Oliver!' He's pale, a ghostly white. She opens his lids and beneath reveals only the whites of his eyes.

There are onlookers now. One says he knows CPR.

'No!' she says. 'He's breathing. I can feel it.' She can't. Of course she can't feel his breath. There would be no harm in telling these people he's not a real boy. But she would look a fool, a hysterical human panicking over an electrical device. Her reaction is only justified if it were for a real son, by a real mother.

Phoney. Fake. That's what she'd hear from them.

She wraps his arms around her neck, then rubs his back. 'There, there, Oliver. You're okay.' Her voice is tremulous, etched with raw fear of a mother for her child. The cold wind smacks her wet body and her whole body shakes. She picks up her cardigan from the ground, but rather than put it on, she drapes it over Oliver, as that's what a real mother would do.

She smiles and nods at the crowd. 'He's a bit upset. I'll call his dad to come and meet us,' she says through her shivers. 'Get him checked out at the doctors.'

That's enough to make the passersby continue with their day.

She stands, her shoes squeaking, clothes clinging to her skin. She squeezes him tightly, continues to rub his back as if he's the one who's freezing. His limp arms rest on her shoulders. He still hasn't made a sound.

'There, there, Oliver.' *Please wake up!*

It's a long walk to their building, so she opts for the nearest lift to take them down to the vehicle level. As soon as they're in a taxi, she holds his head in her hands, then prises his eyelids open with her fingers again. 'Oliver! Please, wake up.'

She checks her phone. They're meant to be leaving for TRI now, but she can't turn up with Oliver broken. He must be okay. Surely, she can fix him.

She clutches his shoulders and shakes him gently. 'Oliver, darling, please wake up!'

The taxi arrives at her building, and she picks Oliver up again, nudging his arms around her. She talks to him all the way past reception, stroking his hair, as if consoling an upset child.

As soon as they arrive at her floor, she hurries through to Oliver's room then fetches towels to dry him. She strips off his wet things and rubs his limbs and torso, as if he needs warming up. Perhaps that's all it is. Don't batteries deplete quicker in the cold? She's sure she's read that somewhere.

Her stomach knots, her throat is occupied by a lump, and she hacks up some pond water. She still hasn't stopped shivering and her teeth clatter as she repeats his name. Her fingernails are tinged blue, and she checks Oliver's to find his are the same. His cheeks are pale and she is sure he must really be cold.

He's in his fluffy pyjamas now with ducks on the front and she lies him down, then piles blankets on top. She continues to dry his hair with a towel. There are weeds in it and some brown sludge. She uses a comb to remove the debris. There's a little buzz from his inner workings somewhere, but he still doesn't respond.

Her freezing hands are shaking, but she manages to load up the manual on her phone and searches for what to do if there's water damage.

A MechaniKid is fine in a rain shower. A MechaniKid can even wash their hands! A MechaniKid should not go swimming. In case of an accident, a MechaniKid can last up to two minutes under water. Submersion under water may result in the MechaniKid going into standby mode. Do not charge until dry.

She loads up Oliver's stats on the app. It shows water has been detected. His battery is at seventy-five per cent.

She runs to the kitchen and finds an old electric radiator, then plugs it in under Oliver's bed. She places her hand on his forehead as if he has a fever and speaks to him.

'You're going to be okay, Oliver. I'm sure of it. If you can hear me, know that you're going to be okay.' She sniffs back some tears, takes his hand and kisses his palm. The radiator is warming and she shuffles closer to it, her shivering easing a little.

From her bag, she takes out the copy of *Charlotte's Web* and starts to read to him. She does the voices as best she can, a snuffly one for the pig, Wilbur, a soft motherly tone for Charlotte. She reads the whole book. The ending is so much sadder than she remembers, and her tears flow freely as she reads the final chapters.

'Mother,' Oliver says as she reads the final page.

Harriet drops the book and grabs his hands. 'Oliver!' she cries, then sobs. 'You're okay!' She weeps into his hands, trying to silence her emotions and calm her shuddering body. 'Thank God you're okay.'

His facial muscles twitch, and he looks at every part of her face. 'You're crying, Mother. Are you sad?'

'No, Oliver. I'm not sad. I'm so happy you're okay.'

He looks at her then. Not to her or inspecting her. *At* her. His eyes are locked on hers. His face is expressionless but not the wooden, emotionless face she's seen so many times. He is solemn. His eyebrows draw in slightly and he blinks.

'You are happy I am okay, as you would be sad if I wasn't.'

She smooths back his hair, then kisses his forehead. 'Yes, Oliver. I would be very sad if you weren't okay.'

She wipes her eyes on her sleeve and checks the time. It's too late to take him to TRI now. She emails them and apologises for their missed appointment, saying she'll bring him for his assessment tomorrow instead.

He takes her hands. 'I would be very sad if you weren't okay, Mother. I want nothing more than for you to be happy.'

She chokes on her breath. 'Oh, Oliver.' She doubles over, her hands still holding his, her forehead resting on the mattress a moment. She looks up at his face etched with worry. 'You always make me happy.'

She leaves him to rest, then changes into some warm and dry clothes. Her hair is a mess, a tangle of weeds knitted through the frizz. There's some expensive bubble bath on the bathroom shelf and she dollops a generous amount into the bath and runs the hot tap. The steam clears her sinuses and she sits on the floor for a while, just inhaling the herbal scent. It smells better than the pond sludge she's covered in.

While she waits for the bath to fill, she pours a glass of wine, sits at the dining room table, then reads some more of the handbook.

The asset must be returned in working order or else the client may be fined for damages.

She nearly broke Oliver today. How could she have been so stupid to get distracted when next to a pond! No decent parent would do such a thing. But Oliver never wanders off. She took it for granted that he stays close. The other children don't. They run off all the time. Oliver's learned bad habits and she's a bad parent.

Not parent. Robot carer.

She checks his stats again on the app and besides some damp still being reported, everything is normal. He's okay being in the water for two minutes. It was definitely less than that, she thinks.

She gulps back some wine and her phone pings. TRI have emailed back.

No problem about missing today, but we are now fully booked. Please fill in the form attached to complete his assessment at home and we will see him for his next in two months.

Her body sinks into her chair, heavy and spent. She can't return him for another two months. That means she has two more months with Anthony.

But also, she gets to spend two more months with Oliver.

She shakes that thought away. He's programming. A computer dressed as a human. She should not value his company so much. It's testament to how few friends she has. She's none now. None she kept in touch with. Being 100 levels above them made keeping in touch too much bother, too difficult to excuse when Anthony was so set on them creating a life together. But that image of a life together is up here on his level, in his apartment, while he goes to work. It was never going to be a life together. She's nothing more than an accessory to his current.

That must be why she feels such an attachment to Oliver. Any bond they have is a symptom of her loneliness.

She scrolls through the assessment form. It's the usual. Identifying animals, asking about his relationships, what he's afraid of. Questions he can breeze through as well as any child. She can do that with him tomorrow. Right now, she has to wash, prepare dinner and be ready to face Anthony again. He'll be back in a few hours, and she was hoping to never have to see her husband again.

She takes the rest of her wine into the bathroom and soaks in the tub, washing her day away.

At least Oliver is okay. That's more important. Oliver has to be okay.

Chapter 7

Oliver's batteries completely die before he's dried out enough to charge. For an entire day, Harriet is without him. She could use the day to enjoy some free time, to go to the gym and do things she can't do while caring for him. She should go clothes shopping for herself instead of just Oliver. Anthony's never begrudged her buying expensive clothes, as if a well-stocked wardrobe is compensation for everything. But Harriet can't motivate herself to do anything. Instead, she sits indoors, paces, bites her nails and hopes for Oliver to fully recover. Every ten minutes she checks the app or goes to Oliver to inspect his body, his temperature, his charging port. She combs the last of the weeds from his hair, then sponges pond muck off his limbs.

That night, she stares out of the window at London's top levels. A fog creeps in just before sunset, blocking her view of the walkways and parks that lie a few levels down. Some of the streetlights break through, like fireflies in the mist. Besides that, it's the darkest night she's known. No moon, the endless stars above merging with the twinkling lights from high-rise windows. She'd never seen the night sky before she moved in with Anthony. She'd never seen the moon and never known the warmth of real sunshine. Below ground, there's no sky at all. Below, noise governs sleep cycles. On 107, there's no noise. The apartment walls are thick, the windows triple glazed. Up here, noise isn't part of her circadian rhythm but a warning. She waits for the noise of the lift ping, for his heavy footsteps to fall, his brutish and demanding voice echoing down the hallway. She waits for the sound of her heart pounding.

When she escapes, noise won't frighten her anymore, but her stomach drops as she knows she'll also lose the sunshine.

***

When Oliver is fully charged the following day, she runs to his room as soon as Anthony's left for work.

'Oliver! You're awake. How are you? Feeling okay?'

'I feel great, Mother.' His voice is clear, his eyes are bright. He sits up and moves his head around without any rusty creaks or snags.

Her posture slumps with sweet relief and she sits on the bed beside him, then pushes back his messy hair. 'Why? Oliver, you're not in trouble, but why would you go into the pond?'

'Other children were walking in the pond. They had different shoes on. Should I have worn different shoes?'

The children Michelle looks after, splashing in their wellies. Harriet palms her forehead. Oliver has no concept of water depth at all. She'd never explained swimming to Oliver since she knew he'd never be able to swim. She's a terrible mother.

'The other children, Oliver, well . . . they can do some things you can't. There are some things I can't teach you.'

'Perhaps I could make friends with other children and they could show me?'

He has a longing in his eyes, a faraway stare as if he is visualising times that will never be. Does Oliver have such an imagination? If not, he does a good job of seeming so. For the first time, Harriet realises Oliver desires friendships besides just her, and she wonders then, with a pang of sadness in her chest, if Oliver knows he's not a real boy. It never occurred to her before. He's spoken briefly with other children in the park, kicking a ball with them a few times or sitting on the see-saw. He's so real, the other parents don't notice. The thought sits heavy in her stomach, and goosebumps prickle up her arms. She looks at him, his face that sucks up knowledge and learns so quickly. He's noticed so much about others and the world around him. Could it be he's not learned anything about himself?

She clenches her jaw and rolls her shoulders back. Oliver is only going to live with her for another two months. She'll let them enjoy their final two months together and will leave that conversation to TRI.

Oliver shuffles closer to Harriet, his arm resting on hers. 'The other children in the other shoes, I think, they were brother and sister.'

'Yes. I think so too.'

'It would be nice to have a brother or sister.'

That knocks the wind out of her. It's normal for children to want the company of a sibling. Oliver must have noticed that in other children, observed sibling bonds and games. He speaks with a tone of longing without the bitterness of envy, and Harriet's heart crushes a little to know she can't give him all he desires. 'It would,' she says. 'But that probably won't be possible right now.'

'Oh.' He lowers his chin, her arm taking more of his weight. 'Do you have a brother or sister?'

Harriet's eyes flit up to one of the framed photographs on the shelf. The boy, ten-years-old in that photograph, has the same messy dark blond hair as Oliver, the same crystal blue eyes. 'I had a little brother once,' she says. 'He's no longer with us.'

As if he can sense her unease with the conversation, Oliver gives her hand a little squeeze, then gets out of bed. 'Well, at least we have each other now,' he says and gives her a kiss on the cheek.

She squeezes her eyes shut. The cheek he just kissed has a lingering warmth and she touches it, savouring it. 'Yes, Oliver. We have each other.'

Chapter 8

Harriet walks to the supermarket with Oliver, wishing she'd taken the lift down to the vehicle level and hailed a taxi. Her right leg aches with its most recent bruises, swollen and angry, hidden under her jeans. She busies her mind to distract her from the discomfort. Her thoughts are lost in a world of housework and shopping, trying to think of practical things to distance her from any upset.

Oliver's pace is slower, she's sure. He's slowed himself on purpose to help her. He was in bed when the beating came last night. Since Oliver learns from other people, it's a wonder he hasn't turned violent. Instead of witnessing Anthony's drunken rages, she's filled Oliver's days with happy memories, playing and reading and time outside. It's only when the dreaded evenings come that she has to worry about what he sees. Some nights, she puts him to bed early, making sure he's out of sight when Anthony comes home. She can't handle the thought of Oliver ever copying Anthony's behaviour. She hopes she's raised him to be a better boy.

Tomorrow is Oliver's fourteen-month assessment. Just one more day and he'll be returned to TRI and she won't have to worry about such things. Not long now and Oliver won't have to worry about her anymore. Because he does, often asking how she is, noticing a sadness in her, asking if she's happy. It's the most attentive anyone has ever been towards her and it's a burden, really, to conceal the truth from a being as perceptive as Oliver. Her sadness shouldn't be felt by him. Her mistakes are hers alone to endure.

Some tension across her shoulders dissipates when she thinks she won't have to feign happiness in front of Oliver anymore. There's some freedom in knowing that no one will worry about her. No one and nothing.

'Are you all right today, Mother?' he asks. His eyes lock on hers, as if he can see right through to her thoughts.

'Yes, Oliver. Thank you for asking.'

'I had a bad dream last night.'

This slows her pace further. Since when did Oliver dream?

'There was shouting and smashing, like Anthony when he's angry.'

He's never called Anthony father. There's nothing fatherly about him and, if she thinks about it, he was never introduced as such.

'That's not a nice dream,' she says. 'Were you frightened?' She searches his face for signs of fear, but he shows none. He's telling her facts without emotion, as if recalling some TV show. Did Oliver hear their row while he was sleeping? Not sleeping. Charging. Is that possible? Maybe she'll check the manual later.

'I don't think I was frightened,' he says. 'Only, when I woke, I was worried about you.' He stops walking now.

Harriet tugs on his hand. 'Come on, Oliver, we've a lot to do.'

He still doesn't walk. It's the first bit of disobedience he's ever shown. His lips curl back, revealing clenched teeth. 'He's a bad man, isn't he? Did he hurt you?'

'Shh!' She puts her fingers to her lips, Oliver copying her gesture. 'Keep your voice down. This is a private matter.'

'Why do this?' He puts his finger to his lips again. 'It doesn't stop me from talking. Look, I'm talking now and my finger is there.'

'It's just a gesture, an instruction. Please keep your voice down.'

He takes his hand from her grasp and folds his arms. 'I know you're not telling me things. You think you're protecting me, but you're not. It's not me who needs protecting from him.'

She puts her full hand over his mouth now. 'This is grown-up business, Oliver. You need to be quiet.'

He shakes his head to remove her hand, then leans in closer. 'The thought of him hurting you makes me hurt, too. The thought of him hurting you makes me want to hurt him. If I wasn't sure you were okay, I'm not sure what I'd do.' He leans back, his mouth softens but his forehead is furrowed and face pinched. 'It's strange, this lack of control. Like my arms and hands are so tense they want to do their own thing. What is this feeling? This emotion?'

Oliver has been learning from Anthony then. This is how it works with families. Violent parents lead to violent children. Only Oliver isn't a child. He's more perceptive and harder to hurt. She pulls him in for a hug and he holds on tight. When she releases, his glassy eyes bore into hers.

'When you feel like that, Oliver, you need to take a deep breath, like this.' She inflates her chest to show him how. 'You need to think of your happiest times and let that bad feeling go away.'

'Why does it ache here, when I'm worried about you?' He presses his hand to his chest.

Her eyes sting and she swallows. 'I don't know, Oliver. That's just how it is.'

She stands and takes his hand, a little giddy as she walks. She wonders if anyone has ever cared for her like Oliver does. It's clever programming. The people who built him must be really, really clever to be able to replicate a bond. It sometimes almost convinces her that Oliver really loves her like a son would. Sometimes, when she watches him sleep or marvels at his progress in the playground, she mistakes that swell of pride for something entirely more motherly. Sometimes — often, if she thinks about it — she gets a pang of euphoria when he calls her Mother, and when he runs to her arms and laughs at the voices she makes when she reads him a story. Oxytocin is the hormone. She read about it. The happy hormone mothers experience. Somehow, Oliver's programming taps into that. It's very clever engineering.

It's been a satisfying journey, raising a machine. And if she didn't know any better, that pang of euphoria could be mistaken for something more natural and innate. Something a real mother would feel for a real boy.

Hormones are silly things. She dismisses her thoughts.

They take a detour around the supermarket, as she needs to find something to cook for Anthony tonight. Her meal the day before wasn't up to standard, he said in much less polite words. She's been batch cooking for weeks, loading the freezer for when she leaves him tomorrow. Frozen pies and lasagne. She does a mental stock take of how many meals are there for him. She's ready to leave him, but leaving him without any meals prepared would add to her guilt. Her chest tightens at the thought. Why does she feel guilty about leaving a man who has been cruel to her?

'Wait here a moment,' she says to Oliver, and she darts back to the cheese aisle.

She'll cook another lasagne, his favourite, and put another spare one in the freezer. That'll keep him going for a while. She's sure he's less likely to come after her if the freezer is well stocked. There's nothing like an empty belly to make a man more angry. She remembers that from her father. His rages were always worse if they had no food.

She picks up a bottle of Anthony's favourite whiskey, so he can also drown his sorrows, then pays, loads up her bag and walks home.

She's in the lift of her building before she realises she's forgotten Oliver.

Her hands go to her mouth and her heart races. She dumps the heavy shopping bag with the concierge, apologising, running, sprinting all the way back to the supermarket, her wide eyes searching for a taxi to hail to shave off a few seconds. Any pain from her leg bruises has vanished, adrenalin replacing discomfort.

How long ago did she leave him? How could she have forgotten him? He'll be okay. Surely he'll still be there.

She races through the supermarket door, barging past crowds and pushing past trolleys. No time for apologies. She has tunnel vision, her eyes like lasers through the crowds searching only for Oliver.

'Oliver!' she shouts at the top of her voice as she approaches the counter where she left him. *Oh God oh God oh God!* 'Oliver!'

He's there. Exactly where she left him, a little worry etched through his face, but he's fine.

'Mother.' He smiles at her and she pulls him in for a hug.

Tears stream down her cheeks and as she shivers, she holds him tighter.

'You're shaking, Mother.'

'I'm okay.'

Her cardigan is on top of her handbag, and he reaches for it, then drapes it over her shoulders. His action is so gentle, so caring. 'I don't want you to be cold.'

She cups his face with her hands. 'My sweet boy.'

There's a hand on her shoulder and she looks up to see a woman smiling, deep crow's feet lining her eyes, grey hair pinned back with some spiral locks making a bid for freedom. 'I left my son in the supermarket once,' she says. 'This young lad was as good as gold. You're a good mum.'

Harriet chokes back some tears. 'Thank you.'

Oliver reaches out and strokes Harriet's cheek, catching a tear with his finger. He tries to mimic her expression.

'Tears, but you look happy.'

'Tears can be happy, too. I am happy you are all right.'

'I am always happy when I am with my mother.'

Mother. She's heard him call her that so many times over the last year. He's said it so much it almost feels normal, but rarely has she felt deserving of the word. Why is it now, after making such an awful mistake, she feels like more of a mother than she has before?

Her limbs are heavy. The ache that ripped her heart years ago has never abated, but as she gives Oliver another hug, she's a little lighter. Like there's a little inner glow inside her, a deep gratitude for Oliver, for making her feel like a mother, a job she wanted so badly yet was never blessed to have.

She smiles at him and he reciprocates with his perfect face, full of warmth.

'And I am the happiest when I'm with my son.'

Chapter 9

Harriet stopped working as soon as she found out she was pregnant the second time. Anthony said it was for the best. He didn't want her to have anything else to think about. The other children might carry germs, cause her stress, make her worry. She was to rest, take gentle walks, to think about no one's child but theirs. If he could have wrapped her in cotton wool, he would have.

Her days stretched out ahead of her. Anthony hired a cook to prepare their meals, all healthy and nutritious. A cleaner came around daily, using natural products. Harriet didn't need to lift a finger. She watched TV, read books, slept, gazed out the window at the view of the city and counted the minutes until Anthony came home.

What a good father and husband. Protective. A provider.

She was fifteen when she ran away from her parents. For years after, she lived on the fringes of above ground, and often still below, wherever she could find a bit of work and food. There was often little choice for someone penniless. It wasn't clean below ground. The excavated walls were contaminated, along with their water and food. Toxins leached into their systems from the landfill sites that smothered the ground above.

But that was years ago, she told herself so many times. She hadn't been below ground in a decade.

Her body changed daily, and she revelled in it, as did Anthony. He marvelled at her growing breasts and hips. Her belly was something to behold. He spoke to it, caressed it, and filled the growing foetus with ambition and ideas. He played all of his favourite music and told her tummy about his family and company, of all that was in store for the baby once it was born.

At twenty-six weeks, her waters broke. Anthony took her to hospital, the best hospital, and raged at the medical staff demanding the best doctors, all the doctors, and he'd pay whatever they needed.

There was no stopping it. Their little boy was born, far too early and impossibly tiny. He managed just a few small breaths in his tragically brief life. Anthony held him at the end as Harriet watched on, broken, her arms cramping with her loss.

They named him Freddie. It wasn't a name they'd discussed. It wasn't a name that meant anything. Best to save the meaningful names for the children who lived. He had dark hair like Anthony, the same shape to his ears. His perfect little mini-me.

When they returned home, Harriet sat alone on the sofa, and Anthony opened a bottle of whiskey.

Harriet was no stranger to grief. For Anthony, it was the first time his money hadn't delivered what he wanted. It was the first time he wasn't in complete control.

Harriet stayed on her side of the sofa, her skin crawling with guilt. Her body was poison, and from the sharp line of Anthony's brow, the way his chin jutted out, she was sure he blamed her. There was not a word of consolation from him.

Harriet cried silently into a pillow as Anthony drank.

She fell asleep on the sofa when Anthony went to bed, then to work the next day, leaving her alone.

Chapter 10

It's as if Anthony knows tonight is their last night together. He arrives home early and when the lift pings to announce his arrival, his greeting comes through with joviality. Harriet pauses in her cooking a second to gauge his mood. He hangs his coat. His footsteps are light, walking as if he's barely drunk.

'Where's my gorgeous wife?'

'Just about to serve up.'

His arms wrap around her waist, startling her.

'Good day?' she asks.

'The merger went well. Better than well. Your husband is a genius, you know.'

She can smell it on him as he presses his body into hers. Perfume. Not her brand. More flowery and sweet than she would choose. A younger woman could give him the child he wanted. Anthony won't fear being ensnared by some accident. He would take control of that baby as he had Harriet. No doubt he's falling into the gleeful arms of younger women, ones without the resilience to his gifts and vacuous words. Anthony having a mistress suits Harriet just fine, and she's suspected it before. Raging jealousy only comes from those cheating themselves.

'Glad to hear it, baby. You're so smart.'

'I love you so much. You know this, don't you?'

She puts her utensil down and faces him. 'Sure, baby.' She kisses his cheek.

She knows he loves her. He loves her too much, so much it suffocates her. If he didn't, he would have left her years ago when their attempts to have a child failed, when she became a shell of the woman he married.

This is how he likes her. Empty. Broken. Obedient. There's manipulation in love. It's the most violent of emotions.

But if he has a mistress, that's a good thing. That might make him less likely to look for her. Though she pities the woman. No doubt he's swept her off her feet like he did with her. He was so pleasant back then, so generous and gentlemanly. He lived a lie before she did.

He sits at the table and watches her serve up, his eyes roving over her body. She tries to walk normally, to smile sweetly, for her movements to not disclose her plans. It's her grand finale in the performance that has been her marriage.

She pours him a whiskey, then sits next to him.

'How was your day?' he asks.

She pauses, her fork millimetres from her mouth as surprise stills her. He hasn't asked about her day in years. Her heart race picks up, and she exhales as the steam from the food heats her face even more. She swigs from her water. 'Fine, baby. The usual.'

She glances at Oliver. He's standing in the corner watching, his mouth a straight line, his eyes darting between the two of them.

Anthony starts to talk about his work and Harriet takes another mouthful, chew chew chew, and listens for the intonations in his voice, watches for the swell in his temporal vein, for all the tells that show her his good mood has hit a wall. He finishes his whiskey and pours himself another. She concentrates on her food, her eyes low, being small, subservient, and nods along with his dialogue. She grips her fork tighter. Everything that comes out of Anthony's mouth smells like the turd she flushed down the toilet this morning.

'What is this?' His change in tone makes her jump. Anthony picks a bit of mushroom out of his lasagne. She notes the tension in his jaw, a flinch of his biceps. His whiskey glass is empty. His good mood was all too brief.

'A mushroom.'

'I don't like mushrooms.'

'Since when?'

'Since you make them taste like bits of snot.' He brushes his arm over the table, the plates flying off the edge and smashing to the floor. She jolts back in her chair, her hands gripping the seat. 'Mushrooms are the filthy food for those below ground. After the day I've had, I have to come home to a plate of snot.'

She tries to smile, for her face to be soft and pleading. 'I'm sorry, baby. I'll make you something else. I'll—'

He yanks her up by her hair and pushes her into the wall, his forearm pinning her by her neck. He pushes his mouth on hers, then pulls away and rests his forehead against hers. His forearm still pushes into her neck. 'You do love me, don't you?'

'Of course, baby.' Her voice is barely a whisper under the pressure of his arm.

He loosens his grip and takes a step back. 'I have a work event. The company is going on a retreat with some big new customers. It would be good if you came.'

She rubs her neck and gasps for air. She won't be here by then, but she can't let him know that. Act natural, concerning, say all the things he expects her to say. 'Okay, baby. I need to know the address to let TRI know where Oliver would be.'

'Just leave the microwave here.'

'He needs looking after.'

Anthony's fist slams down on the table and Harriet yelps. 'I am your husband. Do you hear me? You do what I say, not what the fucking microwave says!'

If she doesn't look after Oliver properly, she risks a fine from TRI. Anthony knows this. 'Of course, baby. Let me find a sitter. What date?'

His top lip curls up like a snarling dog. 'Why do you need to know? Want to let your bit on the side know you're not going to be around?'

'What? No, baby. There's no one but you. There could never be anyone but you.' She steps back, but there's no further retreat she can make. The wall presses into her back.

He steps closer, raising a fist. 'If I ever hear about anyone else—'

'Don't hurt me in front of the boy!'

'Boy? What boy? You mean the microwave? The toaster? That thing is no substitute for our son!'

His knuckles blanch as his fist tightens, and he pulls it back further. She turns her head to the window, that vast window looking out on the glinting high-rises and seamless sky. Her reflection is faint, but it's there, faded, like a vague impression of who she used to be. Actor. Mother. Wife. All blurred and un-recognisable. It's raining now. She watches the raindrops trace lines down the pane as she braces, expecting the full force of Anthony's fist.

'What the fuck?'

Harriet's eyes snap open wide at Anthony's cry. Oliver is holding Anthony's wrist.

Oliver's face is fixed in a tight grimace, his soft little boy features have morphed into hate and wrath. 'Don't hurt my mother.'

Anthony tries to shake him free. 'Get off me!' He lifts his leg and kicks Oliver's chest.

Harriet's hands go to her face. 'Don't hurt him!'

'You stupid fucking cow!' With his arm now free, Anthony lifts it again for a punch.

'Ow! Fuck!' Anthony's hand collides with Oliver's arm instead. There's the clang of bone against metal. Oliver is standing between them, both arms raised up above his head, shielding Harriet. Anthony grunts, then takes a frying pan from the side.

'No!' Harriet jumps between them, pushing Oliver behind her. 'He's programmed to protect humans. It's what he does. You don't want to teach him bad habits. The company will suffer. Your company invests in TRI, right?'

Anthony's nostrils flare as he looks from her to him.

'You don't want to damage their equipment,' she says, wishing she sounded more authoritative than pleading. 'How would I explain that?'

'So, I'm being ganged up on in my own house? By my wife and the goddamned toaster?'

She steps closer and paints a sweet smile on her face. 'You don't want to hurt me, baby. You always feel so bad when you do. Come here.' She puts her arms around him, lays some kisses on his neck and his taut muscles loosen. He drops the frying pan. 'Let's have a good time. Just you and me. Come on, baby. Let me make you feel good.'

His eyes go to her chest, and she licks her bottom lip as he pushes the weight of his torso against her, pinning her again to the wall. His hands hold her wrists to the sides.

'You're going to give me a child. I will fuck you as much as needed. I will fuck you until you are ripped in half, if that's what is takes.'

'Of course, baby. I know what you need.'

'That thing is not our son.'

'I know, baby.'

He releases her then and she takes a breath, inflating her lungs fully, as if she may never inhale a breath again. She smiles at him, then takes his hand and leads him to the bedroom. Before she shuts the door, she calls back to Oliver. 'Oliver, go to your room.'

Oliver hesitates a moment, then does as he's told, keeping his eyes on their bedroom door for as long as he can.

When Harriet checks on Oliver later, he's sitting on his bed, his little hands still in fists at his sides, his eyes narrow and glaring into the mid-distance.

'Oliver.' She sits on the bed beside him.

He turns his head slowly and meets her gaze, inspecting every contour of her face. 'Are you okay, Mother?'

'I'm fine. Thank you for protecting me.'

'You also protect me.'

She lifts his arm and pulls his sleeve back. His skin is crumpled a little. There's a tinge of blue-grey over the folds. She traces it with her fingers. 'Does it hurt?'

He shakes his head. 'No.'

'We're going for your assessment tomorrow. TRI might ask about this. I'm going to say you were clumsy and fell. Okay? If they hear about Anthony, they might take you away from me.'

She's leaving him there tomorrow anyway, but she doesn't mention that. She doesn't know if she can explain that to Oliver.

'Why do you live with him, Mother? Why not just leave?'

'It's complicated. Please, will you tell TRI what I said?'

'I'll say whatever you want me to. I'll do whatever it takes to make you happy, Mother. That's all that matters to me. There's this feeling here.' He presses his hand into his chest. 'When I think of looking after you and spending time with you. It doesn't matter to me if you do things I don't like. Anthony goes mad over some food, but you could never upset me like that. I don't care if you get things wrong. I still have this warmth. A lightness. It's pleasant, when I think of how lucky I am to have you as my mother. What is that feeling?'

She holds her hand to her chest, her heartbeat making a little dance. 'That's love, Oliver.'

He's said love before, but he spoke of objects. To understand love for a person is something she didn't imagine him capable of. Oliver climbs on her lap and gives her a cuddle.

'I love you, Mother.'

A tingle spreads through her extremities and she recalls Freddie, the brief moments she held him for, the giddy feeling of love so intoxicating, she thought she would die when he did. She squeezes Oliver a little tighter, inhaling the vanilla scent of his hair. Can he know such a feeling? He's copied some familial love he's seen at the park somewhere. He's describing some human bond he's observed. It's adorable, fascinating, a feat of engineering.

Her life was never about love. It has always been about survival. Love is messy and awkward and leads to grief. She can't explain this to Oliver. She can't explain all the sadness his love for her will bring when they have to say goodbye.

Her job is to teach him empathy over five years and in little over one, he's grown to understand love. When she returns him tomorrow, she can be proud of the work she has done. Oliver is the one thing in her life she hasn't messed up.

Chapter 11

Her physique didn't spring back after losing Freddie. She stayed plumper, rounder, as if her body was still leaving room for a baby. She stroked her residual tummy, imagined he was still in there, yearned to feel him move, and in her moments of acceptance she mourned the memories they would never make.

The post-birth aches lasted months. Her arms cramped, longing to hold a child that didn't exist. Anthony never asked how she was. He scowled at her rather than looked at her with the adoration he used to. He looked at her as if she were made of dirt, as if she were filth lodged in his shoe. If she couldn't give him a child, she was useless to him.

She was sure he would leave her then, kick her out and turf her back out to a life of poverty. They'd signed a pre-nup. Everything in their life was his. She would leave as penniless as she arrived.

That thought clamped around her throat, made her struggle for air. Below ground, every inhalation was laced with soot. The ground was soft underfoot. Spongy grime squelched and sapped energy. Muffled sounds of pain and moaning snaked through the tunnels. The damp air reeked of despair.

She never longed for the wealth that Anthony bestowed, just enough to keep her a few storeys up. Anthony stopped her working and controlled all their finances. He could track every pound she spent. Her place was at home, to serve him, enslaved. He had a leash around her neck.

She and Anthony used to make love. Now, sex was a chore of determination, an endgame. She grimaced through it, his foetid drunken breath coating her face.

'Pregnant yet?' he asked almost daily. She shook her head.

'Well, what the fuck is the matter with you? Your insides must be rotten if the baby didn't want to stay in there. Your own body kills children.'

She curled forward, shame trembling through her. 'I'm sorry. I'll see a doctor. Let's both see a doctor.'

That was the first time he hit her. 'There's nothing wrong with me, bitch.'

They did eventually visit a doctor. The best one in the city, Anthony said. In the waiting room, he squeezed her knee so tight it left bruises.

They visited that doctor three times, had all manner of tests, and the doctor told them it was just a matter of time, that they were both healthy, despite her past. She'd revealed that she lived below ground when the doctor asked. As she said this, her cheeks burned red, so hot with shame even Anthony's icy glare couldn't cool her down.

When they arrived home, he threw her through the front door and kicked her. 'Keeping secrets from me! Dirty underground whore! You knew I never would have married you if I knew that! You've poisoned us. Everything!'

'The do . . .' She coughed and wheezed. 'The doctor said I'm healthy. That we are. We can try again.'

He pulled her up by her hair and screamed in her face. 'I'll make sure you're buried deeper below ground than you've ever been. There should be a whole new level dug out for bitches like you.'

'Please, baby. I love you. I want your baby.'

He released her hair, and her body sagged to the floor. She rested her forehead on the cold tile, her tears pooling beneath her. They were both grieving and their griefs turned them against her. Her body, her past, her fault. He couldn't hate her enough, for she hated herself more.

Anthony knelt on the floor, his back bowing and put his face in his hands. 'I'm so sorry. I didn't mean to hurt you.'

She pushed herself up, crawled over to him and took him in her arms. 'I know. It's okay. I'm okay.'

'You still love me?'

'Of course, baby. I love you.'

He grasped her shoulders, his fingertips biting, and spoke to her through his teeth. 'If you ever stop loving me, that's where you'll end up. You understand? I'll make sure you're dumped in the worst bit below ground. You'll never see daylight again.'

She then saw what kind of father he would be, and she knew she could not allow a child of hers to suffer such a fate. As month after month passed with no pregnancy, and Anthony's rages became worse, Harriet was aware she could not carry his child, and she started on contraceptives.

That was years ago, and those words still keep her awake at night. Anthony has never been below ground. He can't comprehend how awful it was to live there. He had every right to hate her. She was toxic. The doctor's test can't tell everything. She was sure it was her body, her dirty, wretched body cursed with heartache and grief.

Someone like her isn't meant to be loved. Someone like her isn't meant to experience the joy of being a mother.

Chapter 12

The crumpled skin on Oliver's arm has smoothed but there's a larger patch of greyish blue. It looks like an ink stain. Harriet inspects it, holding it up to the light and presses it gently with her finger. It blanches under the pressure, then turns dark again when she releases. Oliver must have some sort of fluid in his mechanics that's escaping from the trauma. She blots it with some tissue, but none is leaking. Oliver says it doesn't hurt, but does he know what physical pain is?

Harriet dresses him in a long-sleeved top, then packs his favourite books and a couple of dinosaur toys in her bag. She squashes it down to do the zip up, her own things filling most of the space. She's packed some spare clothes and a toothbrush. That's all she's escaping this life with. She drapes her jacket on top of her bag and shoulders it. After a quick glance around the apartment, a lingering gaze on the view outside, she mentally says goodbye to the place. Then, she shuts the door behind them.

The taxi ride to TRI is quick, too quick. She holds Oliver's hand the entire way. Usually, she doesn't. Every other time he's had his hands pressed against the window and has been captivated at the view of the lower levels, the other vehicles whizzing past, the busy narrow pavements and lit up shop frontages that dominate the vehicle levels. This time, rather than stare out of the window, Oliver watches her face.

'What's wrong, Mother?'

'Nothing, darling.'

'You have a sadness about you, and your face is trying not to show it.'

She forces a smile and strokes his hair. 'I'm just happy I got to spend this time with you.'

He returns her smile. 'I am always happy when I am with my mother.'

Her chest tightens, it's hard to breathe in the taxi. She cranks the air con higher, and goosebumps creep up her arms. When the taxi stops outside TRI, she takes a moment before alighting, needing a few extra breaths before stepping foot inside TRI for the final time.

Oliver's eyes are still on her. He tilts his head one way, then the other, his brow wrinkling, his mouth twitching as she knows hers does when she's lost in thought.

They take the final few steps towards the building. There's no sunlight, just the shade of the building and the cold inches over her bones. The automatic doors slide open and she lifts her chin, then they step inside.

The assessment centre isn't at all like the room where she first collected Oliver. It's cold and clinical, all white and chrome, as if they don't want to use anything cheerful or homely to make an impression on the MechaniKids before their assessments. Harriet approaches the desk.

'We are here for Oliver's fourteen-month assessment,' Harriet says to the receptionist. The air con is up too high and she shivers, rubbing the top of her arms. Oliver looks at her quizzically.

'Just a bit cold, Oliver.' She takes her coat and puts it on.

Oliver shivers too, and she zips up his jacket.

They take their seats at the far end of the room. The chairs are different from last time. They often are. Like everything, they're replaced frequently. These new ones are less comfortable and clang against the floor when Harriet sits. The place smells like fresh paint. A new shade of white. There are no magazines or TV. Only a blank wall to stare at. Harriet has often wondered if this is part of the test, to see if the MechaniKids have patience.

After a few minutes, they're called through. It's a different assessor. A man in a white coat with the sort of booming voice and presence that makes her want to cower. A blunt and charmless fellow with aftershave so overpowering she wheezes. Her smile tightens to disguise her instant and blatant dislike of him.

'My name is Colin. I'm head of MechaniKid development here at TRI.'

'Hello, I'm Oliver. Pleased to meet you.'

Colin bends his neck to look down at Oliver, though doesn't shake the hand Oliver offers. He grunts a response. The smug grin on his face reminds Harriet of Anthony.

They follow Colin into the usual shoebox of a room. Three desk chairs and a table are all the furnishings with a window that she assumes is a two-way mirror along the back. It's so drab their voices echo.

They all take a seat, Colin closest to Oliver.

The usual assessor is friendly, welcoming, putting them both at ease. Colin makes Harriet feel they're here for an interrogation rather than a simple assessment.

'Now, it's a little different this time.' The assessor has a tablet and loads up a picture. 'Since it has come such a long way, we want to assess some other aspects of its learning.' Harriet bristles, as she always does at their use of the pronoun *it*. Why can't they just use he, or at least his name? *It* is a table, a cup, a . . . thing. Oliver is so much more than that.

Colin tilts the tablet to reveal it to Oliver. 'Tell me what you *feel* when you see this picture.'

On the screen is a picture of a cat.

'I like cats. I feel . . . excited. Like I am energised. Like I want to run.'

Colin eyeballs Oliver as he says this, as if his eyes can dissect his expressions. There's no praise when Oliver says his answer, no encouragement at all. Colin scrolls through to the next picture.

'Now, what about this picture?' Colin shows Oliver a picture of a child with a grazed knee, crying.

Oliver makes a sound as if he's gasped. He frowns and his hand covers the bruise on his arm for a moment, then he reaches for the child in the picture. 'Is the child okay? Did someone hurt the child?'

'It's okay, Oliver,' Harriet says. 'It's only a picture.'

'I am worried for the child.'

Colin holds his hand up to tell Harriet to be quiet. She huffs and shakes her head.

'Describe that to me, Oliver,' Colin says. 'How do you know you are worried?'

'I . . . I just know I am.' The corners of his mouth dip downwards, and he looks side to side, like he's searching his mind for the answer. 'I need to know the child is okay. That's what worried is. I want to know how this happened. Is someone going to help her?'

Harriet's hands press into her chest and her arms cramp. She needs Oliver sitting on her knee, to rock him gently and tell him it's okay, that he's such a sweet boy for caring so much.

Colin provides Oliver with the smallest of nods to console him. 'Yes, Oliver. The child has someone to help them.'

Oliver sits back in his chair and smiles. 'I am glad. I am especially glad that my mother is okay. I would be sad if I was not there to protect her.'

Harriet fidgets in her seat, unease replacing her pride. Her eyes look at him and widen, willing him not to say anything else.

'Next picture,' Colin says.

The usual tests then commence. Dexterity, tool usage, reading, coordination. For Oliver it is all, quite literally, child's play.

Afterwards, Colin takes Harriet out of the room, leaving Oliver alone for a few minutes. She hasn't given him a hug since the assessment finished. She hasn't told him he's done well.

'It's showing remarkable levels of empathy for its young age. You are doing an excellent job. You obviously have developed a bond.'

This is where Harriet is meant to say that she's returning Oliver, that she can't cope, so that she can get away and take her life back.

'Yes. He's been quite the joy,' she says. 'He really is a very smart and caring boy.' There should be some commendation for Oliver. She's been raising him, but he's also naturally kind and intelligent. Colin's praise should be directed at Oliver too.

'Yes, the home life experiment for MechaniKids is turning up some good results. I noticed there's some damage though to one of its limbs.'

Her stomach drops, her mouth turns dry, and she attempts to clear her throat. 'A tumble. His coordination is excellent, but sometimes he gets it wrong.'

'Naturally. You may notice some bruising, but it's pro-grammed to heal. If anything more significant happens, then bring it back for inspection.'

The coldness of his answer startles Harriet. Is Colin not con-cerned about Oliver's welfare, worried he's in pain? Does he not want to quiz her more in case there is abuse at home, which obviously, there is.

Harriet's hand goes to her own bruise on her hip. She digs her fingers into the welt. How many more injuries would she have if Oliver wasn't there? How much worse will it be when she runs away and Anthony catches up with her? She wishes she could thank Oliver somehow. She wishes she'd taught him to know gratitude.

She goes back to Oliver and sits in the room with him while Colin sorts out some paperwork. She's practised what she's going to tell Oliver so many times. He knows the word goodbye. He just doesn't know goodbye can mean forever.

Oliver gets off his chair and sits on her lap instead. Her heart flutters like butterflies, her stomach unknots and a lightness takes over. He leans into her chest and she gently rocks him. Her Oliver. Her good boy.

She pulls back his sleeve and inspects his arm.

'Does it hurt?'

'No. If you were hurt, then I would feel it more. I would feel it here.' He presses his finger to his sternum. 'I don't know why. But when you're sad, that's where I feel it. I think that's because you're my mother, and I'm your son. Is that why?'

She bites her lip, her smile quivering. 'Yes, Oliver.'

'I love you, Mother.' He places his palm on her chest. 'You have this feeling too?'

She swallows, her breath catches, and she can deny it no more. He's not a real boy, but he is her son. Undeniably. Somehow, this little robot has captured her heart. 'I do,' she says, quietly, the silliness of it making her wince. 'Of course I do. But, Oliver—' She wipes a tear away with her sleeve. '—I need to tell you something.' She looks up and through the open door the reception desk is visible, the paperwork being completed. She still needs to tell Colin she can't have Oliver anymore. She wishes she could keep him, but Oliver needs an address, a reliable electricity source, a home environment. She tightens her hug, trying to squeeze away the hollow feeling she has when she thinks of life without him.

She can't finish her sentence. Her well-practised speech now eludes her.

'Are you okay, Mother?'

Her breath stalls. He's the only one who ever asks.

Her heart pounds, a rapid beat as she grows too hot, yet she can't release him from her arms. She loves him. He may not be a real boy, but he is her son.

She's said goodbye to one little boy whom she yearned to love so much and was never given the chance. Now she has the opportunity to love another, and she's about to throw it away.

She can't. She can't imagine a life without Oliver.

She's resisted this feeling so much, dismissing its silliness. He's not a real boy, but what is the difference when he shows more humanity than almost any human she's ever known?

'Harriet Chapel,' Colin says. 'You and Oliver are free to go.'

She stays seated for a moment, frozen, her limbs stiff and cold. Oliver wriggles back and takes her hands in his.

'Mother, we can go now.'

She still doesn't move. Whatever action she decides makes her stomach churn. She needs to run, but she can't leave Oliver.

'You're afraid, Mother.'

She shudders a breath. 'I am.'

'It's okay. I am here. I'll always be here for you. We can do this together.'

She looks down at him, at his perfect face, his messy blond hair and his wide, sincere eyes, and she realises leaving him is more terrifying than a lifetime with Anthony.

'Yes, my son. We can.'

Chapter 13

Part 2

'The greatness of humanity is not in being human, but in being humane.'

Mahatma Gandhi

***

'Look again, Mum!' Oliver shouts from the top of the climbing frame. He hooks his feet under the top rung, then swings upside down, his arms dangling beneath.

Harriet's breath catches, the imminent dangers more pressing than Oliver's need for attention. But she forces a smile as she clutches her takeaway coffee cup a little tighter. She watches, unblinking, waiting for him to finish his trick and let himself down without getting hurt. 'Well done. Now be careful,' she says, as that's what the other mothers would say.

'Look again, Mum!' Rarely mother these days. Over the years, he's picked up all manner of slang from the other children, as well as a rebellious streak. Just this morning, she found his clothes from yesterday in a heap on his floor.

'Oliver, where are your clothes meant to be?' she asked.

'On the floor?' He stretched out the word floor as if he was really considering it.

'No, Oliver. Where really?'

'Where you can't see them?'

He said it with the cheekiest of grins, and it was impossible to be cross. She rolled her eyes and put his clothes in the laundry basket. Unlike other parents who live above 100, Harriet washes clothes frequently, rather than only wearing them once, then tossing them over the walkway fences to the landfill below. Anthony rarely notices, but when he does, he shouts at her. 'You think I want others seeing my wife looking like trash? I don't own garbage, if you hadn't realised.'

She apologises and throws her clothes away then. It's not worth a beating.

'Mum! Look!' Oliver yells again from the climbing frame, though he doesn't need to tell her to look again. She's always watching. She observes every move, her stomach lurching, her breath bated in her lungs until she's sure he's safe. 'Well done,' Harriet says again, and when he climbs down, she sits back on the bench and sips her coffee.

The playground has a spongy floor, and she's sure even if Oliver fell on his head he'd be fine. But there's a terror that grips her chest when she even thinks about him hurting himself. It's innate, she's sure, a woman's instinct to fear for children, to catastrophize every object and movement, to see hazards everywhere. Poised to react.

'They're such daredevils at this age,' the mother sitting next to her says. Her son, Jason, is bigger than Oliver. He encourages the other children to push beyond their boundaries. He calls them chicken if they don't. It's funny how whenever they meet up with other families, the parents' names slip her mind. The children's names though, she can recall each one they've ever met.

'I suppose it's how they learn,' Harriet says.

'My Jason is going to be a stunt BMX rider when he's older, or so he says. His dad would love that.'

Harriet smiles and imagines what Oliver will be when he grows up. Certainly not a stunt man. Something caring. Nursing or teaching perhaps. She was a drama teacher once. Oliver has the patience, the love of imagination and the company of children of all ages. She can see him as a grown man, still with his messy hair and cheek dimples. He'd be popular in the faculty and really care about his class. That's what sets Oliver apart from other children — his degree of care.

She blinks away her daydream. They're frequent, her mental musings, though pointless. She'll likely never know Oliver when he's grown.

'We're going for a piece of cake after,' another mother says to Harriet. Her little girl Elsie eats too much cake, Harriet often thinks. She's had fillings already. 'Want to join us?'

'We can't,' Harriet says a little too quickly. 'Oliver's allergies.'

That was a clever idea she had years ago. A very believable way to excuse Oliver's lack of ever eating anything. He's never been to a birthday party. Never gets an ice cream with the other children. She keeps a water bottle in her bag with a straw, which she holds to his mouth sometimes so the other parents think he's drinking.

While watching their children, the other parents gossip. Harriet mostly listens and nods when appropriate. She was never a chatterbox. Her parents saw to that in her early teenage years, but now she's even quieter. The more she speaks the more she might slip up. Her life over the last few years consists of threads of lies, and the blanket they form is her gag.

The other parents brag about their children, though Harriet knows Oliver is the smartest, the kindest child of all. She smiles along with them, bitches about neighbours and taxes and husbands. She listens as they speak about their kids' latest milestones. Sometimes Harriet tells them which books Oliver has read. He's so advanced intellectually compared to the other children his size and she feels part of the club. The parent club. It's a role she assumed she'd never get to play.

'Jason has grown three centimetres in two months! Can you believe it? He's starting rugby soon. I have to teach him to go easy on the other kids. They're not all going to have his advantage.'

'Abigail's hair is so long and thick, thicker every time I brush it, I think. It takes so long to wash, but she looks like a princess. I have to take her to the salon every three weeks.'

Harriet keeps quiet when the growth brags come up. The parents never mention Oliver's unwavering appearance, but their brags are like a little stab, like they're singling out the one thing she can't boast about. It's been four years and eight months since she took him home. He's average height for a six-year-old, but his cognitive abilities have accelerated beyond all expectations. His speech and physical abilities caught up rapidly over the first year or two, and now his intelligence is far greater than the other children who appear his age.

'He's off to boarding school tomorrow,' Harriet tells the other parents and wipes her eye. It's an act, of course. A spiel she recites every six months or so, when she and Oliver move their daily activities to a new level, always at least ten levels away from the last. Avoiding long-term interaction is the best way to avoid having to explain why Oliver never grows. MechaniKids are rare, but parents know they exist, and little pockets of hate spring up on social media and in parental gossip in the parks. Like somehow Oliver isn't important, that he's some threat just because he's different. She hasn't told anyone Oliver isn't a real boy, and it's now almost impossible to tell.

Home schooling is commonplace, particularly across the higher levels, each level and zone having their own home schooling parents' clubs. Harriet and Oliver's daily trips to the playgrounds and soft play gives Oliver plenty of social interaction with other children. This latest group meets at a park on 70, and Harriet pretends they live on 72. This high up, there are several metres between their walkway and the one above, the underside of which is well-lit and decorated with fake foliage. Sunlight reflects off the buildings and bounces its way to them.

The upper-middle classes where they still aim high yet haven't forgotten the lowest down, or so they say.

The boarding school is for gifted children, she says. There's one in Kent that she researched online. Oliver would make the grade easily. When she tells the other parents he's going there, they have mixed expressions of impressed and jealousy. Some envy their kid isn't as smart as Oliver and they disguise it by playing on the negatives.

There was a mother in her last area who did nothing but put Harriet down. 'I can't believe you're sending him away. A mother should be with her child. You've home schooled him this far. Why not continue? It's not right.'

Her son, Alfie, was about as bright as a brick wall, but she would insist he excelled in music. He was a sweet boy, though still couldn't even open a Tupperware box without his mother's help.

A few months back, Harriet bumped into a mother she used to see at a park a couple of years ago. The mother greeted them both, then Harriet saw her expression change when she clocked Oliver's height, his totally unchanged appearance. She backed up, as if afraid of some disease, and she shooed her child away from Oliver like he was a monster. Her child once pushed another off a wall and kicked a little girl in the shins. As punishment, that mother slapped her child across his backside. Oliver would never do that. He learns by copying, but he's never learned to project animosity. Even living with Anthony hasn't taught him such behaviours and Harriet would never hit Oliver. Yet that mother thinks Oliver is the monster.

Harriet could have enrolled Oliver in a real school, and she considered it many times. He would thrive, she's sure. But someone could find out. The teacher might notice his lack of appetite, the fact he never uses the toilet. Some MechaniKids do go to school, it's been reported. A waste of public funds, reports said, along with trending hashtags *#NOTreal* and *#fakeKids*. She looked at private schools and even went for an open day. But she couldn't go through with it. Her time with Oliver has always been destined to be brief. She doesn't want to be apart from him. She's often wondered what she used to do all day before Oliver came along. She still keeps the apartment clean and tidy, still cooks homemade meals every night. Before Oliver, she used to do a lot more staring into space, imagining what could have been. Dwelling on the past.

Since having Oliver, her dwellings are more focussed on the future, his future, and what life will look like when the time comes to part with him.

'I'm sure he'll do just great at his new school,' one mother says. 'He's such a bright boy.'

'He'll miss you though,' says another. 'You two have a wonderful bond.'

Harriet smiles and gives a small nod. The bond she has with Oliver is what gets her out of bed in the morning. It's what gives her the strength to face each day. He still runs to her for cuddles, where some other children eschew parental affection. He still asks how she is. Every day, he takes the time to find out if she's okay.

Jason's mother stands to throw her takeaway coffee cup over the fence and offers to take Harriet's also. Harriet declines, lying, saying there's still a few sips left. Throwing her rubbish over the fence is something Harriet has never done. It seems a pointless act of valour to not do it and a strong tell that she wasn't born and raised so high. Everyone high up chucks their rubbish over the walkway fences. Food packets, clothes, year-old electricals. The turnover of consumables is a little less among these families on 70 than those she knows higher up, but still nothing is kept for long or savoured. Even down on 70 no one wants to be seen in clothes they've worn more than a couple of times.

Any rubbish she puts in a bin is still taken down to the landfill sites, so the end result is the same. It just feels less careless. Out of sight, out of mind, is the never-ending human ethos.

Oliver creates almost zero rubbish. He doesn't eat, so there are no food packets to discard. His clothes last ages since he doesn't grow out of them and rarely rips holes in them like so many other children. He's the perfect little boy.

'We'd best be off anyway,' she says to the other parents. 'We need some family time today.'

There are goodbye hugs, promises to keep in touch. Harriet's words are well-rehearsed and sound as heartfelt as they did the first time she said them. There's a pang of genuine sadness in her. This has been one of the nicer groups of parents and, as such, she's been meeting with them for nearly eight months, breaking her own six-month rule. They're the closest she's had to real friends in years. Their farewell messages leave her a little emptier.

'Oliver!' she shouts to the climbing frame. 'Come on, Monkey. Say goodbye to your friends.'

There's a slouch, a sulky rolling of his eyes he does in front of the other children, though she knows that's just a show. When he runs over, his inhibitions melt away and he jumps into Harriet's arms. His embrace is soft and warm, and she hugs him back, his scruffy hair tickling her nose and she smiles. His chest heaves up and down like he's out of breath, one of the many actions he's learned to copy.

'Did you see me dangling on the climbing frame, Mum? Lucas showed me how.'

She puts him down and ruffles his hair. 'I did. You looked very brave. Time to say goodbye.'

Oliver waves and they walk away. He turns and shouts goodbye over his shoulder. After more than four and a half years of having to change friendship groups every few months, he knows what goodbye means.

He runs to catch up, a few skips, then takes Harriet's hand. His steps flow, as smooth and natural as the other children's.

'Goodbye is a sad word,' he says. 'We should have another word.'

'When I was a child, we used to say see you later, alligator.'

Oliver chuckles. 'That's silly. When spider babies leave, they leave on parachutes of web and fly away. I don't think spider babies say goodbye. I think they probably say, fly free!'

'Well, that sounds like a nicer thing to say. We can say that if you prefer.'

Oliver turns around and holds his hands up to his mouth and yells, 'Fly free!' to his playmates.

Summer is just coming to an end, though its warmth still hangs in the air. It's been a dry season, the flowerbeds mostly brown and parched. They haven't seen a bee in a while, but she knows Oliver will be delighted if one appears. He knows how many types and which ones make honey.

A wind whips its way down the walkway, and she buttons up her coat, then bends to do the same for Oliver.

'I like spending time with the other children,' he says as she does up his last button. He could do it himself, but he wouldn't think to. 'But I like it best when it's just us.'

She pecks him on the cheek. 'Me too.'

It's home time for schools and the walkways are filling up with children. As they pass other families, Oliver turns his head to look at them. His gaze goes up and down, inspecting their limbs and faces, the way they move and the jokes they share. Some children are protesting against having coats put on, while others are teasing their siblings. Harriet knows he's always learning, but she also wonders if he's trying to figure out what's different about them.

Harriet strokes his tousled hair as they walk. So many parents say their children seem to grow up too fast. Oliver's intellect may have soared ahead, but visually he's still her perfect, sweet-faced little boy.

'Are you happy today, Mum?'

She smiles at him. 'I am.'

Harriet inspects his leg and notices some of his skin is bunched up from the impact of a fall. She's seen it do that before, knowing it'll turn a blueish colour later, then it somehow always heals. She calls these marks bruises, as it's the most similar word. TRI assessment centre calls them impact marks, but that's too robotic. Too inhuman.

She stopped reminding herself he's a robot years ago. Her original plan of returning him after she saved some money is long forgotten. Oliver is the only person who has ever shown any care for her, the only person in years who has bought her joy.

'I'd like to read the bird book again when we get home. Did you know there are three types of corvid in England! There used to be more. And I saw a magpie again today.'

'That's fascinating.' She has a gleam in her eye when he talks about what he's read. He's such a clever boy.

'Or the book about spiders. Did you know there are over a hundred types of spiders in England?'

'Oh, no. I don't like spiders.'

His fascination with spiders is proof, she's sure, that he forms his own opinions and doesn't just copy. She's never liked spiders, but Oliver gets excited about all of them, coming up with that interest all by himself. Independently. Like a real boy.

He laughs at her, a giggling chuckle. There's something about that sound that always warms her heart. She tries endlessly to make him laugh.

'Or maybe I'll read *Charlotte's Web* again.'

'You must have read it fifty times.'

'Did you know that many spider species have their babies, then die so their babies can live. It seems quite sad, don't you think?'

Her grip on his hand becomes a little tighter. 'Any mother would do that for her children. It's what being a mother is about.'

Oliver looks up at her. He blinks, tilting his head to the side as he inspects her. He often looks at her in a way no one ever has. Like he's trying to read her, like he really cares what she thinks.

They take the lift to 99, then walk across the top-level walkways to their building. Harriet's walk slows as they get closer, her joints stiffening with a chill that envelops her. It's the same sinking dread she feels every day when she arrives home. Her bruises ache as she readies herself for more.

The concierges greet them as they walk through. They're the only ones who must have guessed Oliver isn't a real boy, but they're as polite as ever, and they both smile and return their greetings as they walk past.

'You're scared, Mum. I can feel it in your pulse.'

'I'm fine, Oliver.'

She presses the button for the lift and Oliver faces her, his crystal blue eyes meeting hers. 'You're scared of him. Of Anthony.'

She can't lie to him. He's not even asking a question. 'Yes.'

His lips purse, then recoil as if in disgust. 'Fuck Anthony.'

'Oliver!'

'What? A bad man can swear but a good boy can't? It's only words. And I mean it. Fuck Anthony.'

'TRI won't be too pleased if they know you've learned such words.'

'Yeah, well, fuck the tests and fuck TRI. It's you and me, Mum. What else matters?'

He's speaking quietly, but Harriet still glances up at the top floor reception desk and smiles away her embarrassment. The concierges aren't listening, and she turns her attention back to Oliver, bending to his height. The only warmth she has is from Oliver's hand.

'I know you want to leave him,' Oliver says.

There's so much determination in his voice and sadness and worry. She inwardly kicks herself for teaching him such negative emotions. He shouldn't have to experience such feelings.

Feelings. It is accurate to call what Oliver experiences as feelings, although the assessment centre calls it mimicry. Every two months she has taken him to the centre where he has flown through every test they've thrown at him. The staff there delight in his progress, saying it is their best specimen.

They still call Oliver 'it'. Or 'a specimen'.

Yet every test they perform is designed to see if Oliver can pass for human. And in every test, he does.

'It's a marvel,' they always say. 'It really could fool anybody.'

It.

The lift arrives and they step inside, though she doesn't press the button for their floor just yet. His gaze on her is one of worry, the way she looks at him when he's hurt himself. 'Tomorrow,' he says. 'Let's go.'

Oliver's words fill the space and spin through her mind, making her dizzy. She shakes the thought away. Oliver suggests the impossible. He's so young, so protected. He's only ever known life up here. He has no idea what he's saying.

'Oliver, to hide you would be too hard. TRI. They'll look for you. I only adopted you. They still need you for tests and you have a tracker, so they'll know if we run away. You have to go back and live with them soon.' She hasn't explained the permanence of that or that his body will change. She's sold it more like a holiday, a slumber party with a ton of other children. Like the boarding school she says he goes to.

'Don't I get a choice? Why do I have to do tests? Other children don't. Can't people choose their own lives?'

People can, my sweet boy.

Years of observing other children, and Oliver still doesn't understand he's not a real boy. He's not what so many others would consider *people.*

Of course she has been imagining, wishing, hoping for a way to keep Oliver. When she hands him back in a few months as she's meant to, his personality module will be transferred into an adolescent body, and she'll never see him again. Adolescents, or MechaniTeens, live in institutions with each other. They don't need human families anymore, the company says. Harriet's role will be done. She'll receive her final pay and will never have to look after Oliver again.

Without Oliver, she'll no longer need this address, this apartment, this family environment she promised the company she'd provide for Oliver. She could take her money and run.

Only she won't have Oliver anymore.

At every bi-monthly assessment, she checked again what the procedure is after the five years.

'He will be staying with other MechaniTeens?' she asked, time and time again. 'With no family environment?'

'Yes, we find that best for their next stage, to be only among their own kind and age. You know what teenagers can be like. Now imagine a teenage bot.' It's always been Colin lately, that leering man who treats Oliver like the soulless one. He had a different lab coat last time, a high collared one with a breast pocket. That pocket was empty. It was just for show. Isn't everything? 'So don't worry,' he said. 'We won't burden you much longer with it.'

Keeping Oliver through his next stage isn't something TRI is even considering. As far as they're concerned, Oliver's time needing her is done.

There's the other option, the illegal and possibly immoral one. To take Oliver with her when she leaves Anthony. To steal him. This, she's imagined so many times. A lifetime with her perfect little boy. Their own home, never having to rush back to cater for Anthony and experience the blunt end of whatever rage he's in. It's an impossible pipe dream.

When Oliver suggests such a thing, he does so out of ignorance. Oliver has only known a comfortable life. Stealing him away would mean they'd be on the run from the biggest and richest tech company in the country, most likely resulting in living an asphyxiating life below ground. Poverty, unreliable electricity, and he'd stay a child forever. He'd never grow up.

Oliver deserves better.

'I don't care where we have to live,' he says, pleading. 'I don't care what level or below. As long as I'm with you.'

'But, darling—'

'If I'm not with you, there's no one to protect you from him.'

This isn't the first time they've had this conversation. She'll leave Anthony soon. She's strong enough now and has certainly saved enough money. Every penny from TRI she's squirrelled away in a bank account Anthony doesn't know about. It's enough to get started renting an apartment on a low level. It's keeping Oliver that's out of the question. Oliver needs reliable electricity, and electricity on the lower levels is rationed, if available at all. The lower-level mantra is, 'Electricity is power,' and Harriet is all too aware that the top levels have both in spades.

As if reading her thoughts, Oliver continues. 'If I'm not with you, you'll go back to him. I know it. If I hate where we end up, you can take me back to TRI anytime. But at least then I would have helped. At least then I would have made sure you're away from that monster for a while.'

She cups his face and looks him in the eye. 'When I leave him, it'll be forever.'

'Don't lie to me! I can tell when you're lying. Your voice goes weird, like you're trying to convince yourself as well as me. I won't leave you alone with him. I won't. Let's do this. Together, mother and son.'

She remembers life below ground too well. She's never been able to wash it from her mind. What she smelled she can't unsmell. The dirt still lingers in her lungs. Low levels may not be hidden enough. Oliver is worth too much to TRI. He's their most advanced MechaniKid, so they've said at his assessments. The thought of living back below ground has her clutching her chest, asphyxiated and breathless. She looks at Oliver. His big blue eyes have seen more sunshine in his short existence than she did for the first fifteen years of her life. She can't do that to him. She can't force him into the darkness.

The lift pings as they arrive at their floor and Harriet's breath catches. He's home already. There's a broken plate on the floor.

'Where the fuck have you been?'

'You're early,' she says with a painted-on smile. 'Oliver and I were at the park.'

'The toaster can't walk himself?'

She winces at the word he uses for Oliver. He's been drinking much more lately, so much so, the smell of another woman's perfume has long gone. Even his mistress got sick of him. Yet he still loves Harriet. Too much. Time cast its shadow on her face, sitting her out of the light he used to see her in. But still he needs her, possesses her. His love ties shackles to her ankles and binds her wrists. He'll never let her go.

She knows he's not telling her something. His company is tanking. She's sure of it. It's the only thing that would make his stress levels so high. How he can hold down a board position with the state he's in most of the time is beyond her.

Letters started arriving a few months ago. He's missed payments for something, though she never opens them to check. The big bold letters stating OVERDUE on the envelope is enough of a clue. She plays the part of ditsy, clueless housewife and leaves them neatly on his desk. He paces the apartment often, swearing and raging at the phone, grinding his teeth as he sends emails and texts.

The worse work gets, the more he drinks. It's been a cyclical rage for years now and Anthony hasn't the sense to see it. When he's not taking his temper out on his phone or email, it's Harriet who's in the firing line. He's paranoid about her always, like her bond with Oliver is outcompeting his.

She bends down with a dustpan to sweep up the broken plate. 'I just wanted some fresh air.'

'Stupid cow.' He spits, and as she stands he raises his arm to hit her, but Oliver blocks it and Anthony's fist slams into Oliver's arm.

'Don't!' Harriet jumps to Oliver's defence. 'Don't hurt him!'

'It's a fucking toaster,' Anthony screams and kicks Oliver to the side, cursing when his toe impacts the metal.

Oliver steps away, his back against the wall, his expression blank. His eyes never leave his mother.

'Let me make you something to eat,' Harriet says to Anthony. 'What would you like?'

He pushes her against the wall and his hand goes around her neck. 'You were out fucking someone else, weren't you? Like a fucking whore actress.'

She looks away, removing her eyes from his glare. Across the kitchen is the fridge, covered in Oliver's drawings and she focuses on those instead. Pride overtakes her fear. He draws beautiful, geometric pictures of buildings and taxis, his favourite climbing frame in architectural detail. And faces. All manner of human expressions, perfectly copied from children and parents he saw throughout his day. And his mother. He has drawn Harriet so many times, but most of those pictures she keeps in her dresser drawer. She doesn't want Anthony to know how much he draws her.

Anthony huffs, then releases her and sobs. 'I'm sorry. You know I love you. You know the thought of you being with other men drives me insane.'

She rubs her neck and takes some breaths while she can. Her eyes scan the room for anything sharp or heavy and blunt, anything he might reach to hurt her or Oliver. 'I know, baby. I know. I'm all yours.' She hugs him, though she's rigid in his arms as her body expects a shove or a punch.

The beatings are more frequent these days. Her entire body is coated with bruises. He broke her arm a year ago, and the scar from the surgery left a lumpy line. He showered her with gifts after that. Jewellery mostly. It's all neat in its boxes in her bag, ready to take to sell as soon as she's free of him.

She often lies awake at night, imagining screaming at him. She pushes him off, tells him no, spits in his face, then kicks him. Only ever in her imagination. In real life, she braces and accepts his offerings. She's never been a fighter. She trained in combat for a movie years ago, yet still, when it comes to fight or flight, she's firmly in camp flight.

Anthony grabs a fistful of her hair and yanks her head back so she can stare at his face. His eyes cross, unfocussed for a moment. 'You do love me, don't you?'

She attempts a smile. 'Of course I do, baby.'

'You'd never lie to me, would you?'

'Never.'

He shoves her away, the back of her head smacking against the wall as he goes to the kitchen to pour a whiskey.

Oliver steps forward, his little face full of concern for his mother, but she mouths to him that she's fine.

'Let me do that,' Harriet says to Anthony and takes the whiskey bottle. 'Sit down, put your feet up.'

He stumbles to the sofa and plonks down, the sofa banging against the floor with the weight of him. He had a trim body when they first met, toned and lean. Now his binge drinking and lack of exercise has left him soft and his tummy dollops over his belt as he refuses to go up a clothes size. Yet he still has the audacity to make fun of her waistline.

In her handbag, she grabs a sleeping pill, crushes it up, then puts it in his glass, swirling it around. She hands it to him, and he necks the lot in one gulp.

'Careful, baby. You need to look after yourself,' she says.

He grunts a reply and turns on the TV. She sits beside him, snuggles into him, and waits for him to fall asleep. When he's snoring, she checks on Oliver.

'Oliver, are you okay? Let me see your arm. Where did he hit you?'

'I'm fine, Mum. Don't worry about me. I'm worried about you, though. He shouldn't speak to you like that. He shouldn't hurt you.' Oliver can't cry, but she's sure there's a glint of sadness in his eyes, yet he speaks only of concern for her. 'I'm worried about you. I can't bear the thought of you being hurt or sad.'

'Oh, my sweet boy. Don't you worry about me.'

'We have to leave, Mum. Promise me.'

She rubs her neck where Anthony's hand pressed against it. It's raw and tender, still not recovered from the last incident. Or the one prior. How long before Anthony does something worse? How long before he kills her?

'Mother. We have to go. I can't watch him hurt you anymore.'

You won't have to for long, she wants to say. You'll be back at TRI forever soon.

It's her imagination again, her mind space where she says things she'll never enact. She thought about leaving Oliver at TRI so many times but it was impossible, like cutting off a limb. She looks at his face, ruffles his hair, and she knows she's never going to be able to give him up.

'Mum—'

'Okay, Oliver,' she says. He's right. How did her child become wiser than her? Without him, she's bound to end up back with Anthony, sleepwalking her way into this life. She never left him before Oliver, so why would she leave him after? To run away with him though, is the most motivation she needs. To keep and protect her son gives her the strength she lacked for so long. Another few months and Anthony is bound to really hurt Oliver, and there's no chance she's cutting her time with Oliver short.

They have to leave. Together.

'You're right, darling. Okay. Let's do this. Now, go to your room and charge. We've an important day tomorrow.'

He gives her a quick hug before going to bed. 'Yes, Mum. I love you. We can do this. Together forever.'

She bites her bottom lip and tries to ignore the lump in her throat. 'Together forever. Always.'

Chapter 14

Harriet's jewellery is mostly unworn. She never has the occasion to don such finery. It gleams in its boxes as she takes a quick glance at it all. Chunky gold and blocky stones, the sort of stuff that's worth a lot due to its weight rather than delicate craftsmanship. Investment pieces, Anthony called them when he gave her the apology gifts. He wanted to know he'd earn his money back rather than give her something pretty.

After Anthony leaves for work in the morning, she shoves the boxes in her bag, along with a change of clothes for her and Oliver, a toothbrush, Oliver's charging cable, and a can of mace. She's no idea if the mace still works. It's something she's held on to from her days living in the lower levels, but it might at least act as a deterrent.

She takes a final look out of the window, at the endless blue sky stretching over the top levels. She may never see such a perfect sky again.

Oliver's waiting by the front door, fully charged and ready to go, his face full of the resolve and determination she should be showing, but her cowardice is making her shrivel instead.

She's selfish. She's always been selfish. It's one of her biggest flaws. She could add plenty more flaws to that pile. Taking Oliver, stealing him away, is selfish. Just because she wants him close, she's ruining his chances of growing up, of being safe. He'll be stuck in his MechaniKid body forever and that's something he doesn't understand. Though, somehow, being selfish clouds her judgement. Perhaps giving him up would be the selfish thing to do because it would be less hassle for her. She'd only have to dodge Anthony then, not TRI as well. How much simpler life would be if she had no one to think of but herself and her own survival. But then, what would be the point? Without Oliver, without her son, any life she manages to build would be incomplete.

Her insides cave at the thought of being without Oliver — of never hearing his laugh again or hearing him describe spiders.

'We're leaving, Mother,' he says, as if he's the parent. 'You can't spend another night with him. He'll kill you soon. He'll kill us both.' He lifts his T-shirt to reveal the blue-grey bruise on his torso from Anthony's kick last night. The sight is enough to make her open the front door.

She grabs a scarf and wraps it around her neck to cover up her own bruises. 'Let's go.'

She shuts the door behind them and knows this time, it's for good.

Lying awake last night, she formulated a rough plan. It's one she's been mulling over for years, subconsciously almost. She's watched her old friend Michelle from afar, followed her a few times. She's fairly sure today is her day off, and she'll be out jogging by herself.

Michelle, a friend from her low-level days, a fellow below ground survivor. Michelle was always decent and friendly. She would have kept in touch with some people from the lower levels and below. Down there, someone surely will know how to disable Oliver's tracker. On the lower levels, people have more initiative than they do up here. They fix things rather than throw them away. The techies below have problem-solving abilities to get them out of all manner of scrapes, and the best end up working with scavenged goods in the lower levels where electricity is more reliable than below. Innovative thinking is survival for them. Harriet has until this evening to find out. Or else when Oliver isn't charging at Anthony's apartment this evening, an alert will be signalled by TRI.

She's decided — though doesn't tell Oliver — that if she doesn't get his tracker removed by five p.m., she's taking him to TRI. They don't stand a chance against the company with his tracker. There will be nowhere to hide.

It's just gone nine a.m. and they're already on the 99th floor walkways. The park with the duck pond where she first saw Michelle years ago is just up the road. They walk slowly. She doesn't want to drain Oliver's battery. It lasts a full day, but what if she can't find charge today? Electricity is easily available up this high. The lower levels are in the shade, solar is useless, the air is stagnant as the wind never blows. Like everything, electricity in the lower levels is the top levels' leftovers.

One problem at a time, Harriet.

'Look, Mum. The ducks!'

Oliver's squeal snaps her attention. 'Shh, Oliver. Conserve your energy. Try not to take an interest in anything. Slow down, no running.'

'But—'

'Darling, I don't know when we'll find charge again if we're not going home. Remember what it was like those times when your battery was low, how tired you were, how you couldn't walk?'

His eyes widen, and he nods.

'Well, we need your battery to last as long as possible today. Okay?'

He understands. She sees it in him, a hint of realisation. He can quantify such things better than other children and understands consequences so well. He keeps his mouth closed and doesn't look around at all for the rest of the walk.

They sit on a bench. Harriet removes her jumper and allows the sun to kiss her skin. Oliver is still, silent, not his usual chatty and curious self. He's doing just as she instructed. He's such a good boy.

Harriet does a double take when she sees her. Michelle jogs towards the pond with her curls pinned back, looking as lovely as she did a decade ago.

'Wait here, Oliver. Don't go anywhere. I'll wave you over when I need you.'

He gives a subtle nod, and she runs up to Michelle, sprinting to catch up.

'Michelle!' she pants, already out of breath.

Michelle looks over her shoulder and slows her run to a walk, halting completely when she sees Harriet. 'Harriet? Is that you? No way! Long time no see!'

Harriet catches up and they go in for a hug.

'Sorry,' Michelle says, 'I'm a bit sweaty.'

'It's so great to see you.'

'You too.'

Harriet puts her hands in her pockets and rocks on the balls of her feet. 'I'd love to catch up, but, well, I need your help.'

'Woah! Bypassing the normal pleasantries there,' Michelle says, taking a step back. 'What the hell, Harriet? I've not seen you in a decade and, if I recall, the last time we spoke was hardly friendly.'

Harriet's face burns, and she looks at the ground. 'I know. I'm so sorry, I'm just desperate. You were right. Everything you said back then, you were totally right. I'm so sorry I never listened.' She removes her scarf, revealing Anthony's handprint bruising on her neck.

Michelle's hands go to her mouth, but her gasp is still audible. 'Oh, God. The same guy?'

Harriet re-ties her scarf and nods. 'Yes. I'm leaving. I can't go back there. Not for one more day.'

Michelle glances down at Harriet's arm where more bruises show at her sleeve. She bites her bottom lip. 'Sorry for snapping.

Of course I'll help. Us bottom feeders have to look out for each other, right?'

Harriet's eyes begin to stream, and she sniffs back some tears. Michelle steps closer and puts her arm around her shoulders.

'You can stay with me. Of course. I know of some work. I'll help you get back on your feet.'

Behind her back, Harriet beckons Oliver. 'It's a little more complicated than that. It's not just me.' She leans away from Michelle and reaches for Oliver's hand, and he steps in front of her.

Michelle smiles at him and gives him a little wave. 'He's cute. So, you're taking the rich guy's kid too? Ballsy.'

'Not his. Mine. And Oliver is a special boy.' She puts her hands on Oliver's shoulders and takes a breath. 'The kind with a tracker.' She lifts Oliver's T-shirt to show his bruise, then lowers the waistband of his jeans a little, his charging port now visible. 'He belongs to TRI. But I can't hand him back. I need to keep him.'

Michelle's eyes bulge, she shakes her head and steps away. 'Oh, shit, Harriet.' Her jaw hangs open as she looks at Oliver again. 'You really want to run from TRI? You'll risk everything for that?'

'*Him*. Not *that*.'

'Yeah. Sure. But—'

'I'm not asking you to risk anything. Just give me an address. Someone who can disable the tracker. You must know some low-level techie.'

'Sure. Tons. They're great at fixing tablets and air con units. But this, sorry, *him*.' She puffs her cheeks out and exhales. 'This is beyond most of them.'

'Most? So not all.'

Oliver shuffles away from Harriet's hands and steps forward, his blue eyes staring up at Michelle, his hands interlocked in front of his chest. 'We would be so grateful. It's not safe for us, for my mother especially, back home. She won't leave me, which means it will be my fault if she goes back to that man.'

Harriet chokes on her tears. 'No, Oliver—'

'It's true, Mum.' He looks again at Michelle. 'There must be a way that we can be together, safely. Please, if there is anything you can do. You're our only hope.'

Harriet presses her lips together and looks at Michelle. Her mouth is hanging open, and there's the sheen of tears in her eyes. She peels her eyes away from Oliver to look at Harriet. 'This is really a TRI kid?'

'Yep.'

'Blimey.' She sniffs. 'Okay. Well, there's one woman I know. We were neighbours for a while. She was sacked from TRI a few years ago. Best not to ask why. She's been living on level 2 since. I could call her.'

'Thank you! I'll pay you—'

Michelle waves her hand to dismiss the offer. 'I don't want your money. I've got a good thing going on up here. Just consider it a favour in the bank.'

Harriet goes to hug Michelle, but Oliver gets there first.

Michelle hugs him back, her jaw still hanging open. 'It's just . . . he's just . . .'

'He's my son.'

'Yeah,' Michelle says as Oliver steps away and she peers again at his face, inspecting it in the way Oliver does to other people. She blinks firmly and shakes her head. 'Sure. Anyway.' She gets her phone out and scrolls through to find a number. 'I'll just send a text.' She taps away on the screen for a few moments, then smiles. 'She says to go down and she'll take a look.'

Harriet jumps on the spot. 'Thank you! Thank you!'

Michelle scribbles the address on a bit of paper and hands it to Harriet. 'Just be careful. TRI are powerful—'

'I know.'

'Do you? I mean it, Harriet. You really are risking a lot.'

'The bigger risk is to stay,' Harriet says as she stares at the paper. Her face breaks into a smile, and a glimmer of hope shines within. 'Thank you!'

Chapter 15

Harriet and Oliver take the lift all the way down to 2nd. It's lower than the TRI offices, even lower than the vehicle levels. Here, sandwiched between the landfill of ground level and the vehicles above, the air is a soup of stench and soot. Harriet gasps then coughs as she gets out of the lift. The underside of the level above is so close she could jump up and touch it. It's not the decorated, well-lit ceiling the higher levels have. The dark and grotty surface rains down dust and drips with condensation.

The rubbish piles are almost up to the level 2 walkways in places, having completely overtaken level 1. The trickle of breeze that reaches this low, whips up plastic packaging and fluffy muck consisting of God-knows-what. Her neck sweats and she loosens her scarf, pulling it up over her mouth and nose instead. It's too hot for a face covering, the crackle and heat of furnaces making the air stifling, but the heat is less oppressive than the fumes. She adjusts Oliver's scarf to do the same. Does he take in air at all? She's unsure but the soot and pollution can't be good for him. The face covering also acts as a disguise, not that it's important. The walkways are deserted instead of being the hubbub of life they are up on the top levels.

Pinned to buildings are posters of wanted people, rewards offered. Bounty hunters operate in the lower levels. She's met a few herself years ago. The police down this low aren't trusted by many. Those wronged prefer to take the law into their own hands. They walk past posters of sneering men, tattooed faces and thick neck muscles. Some weedier, with toothless smiles and weathered faces. Harriet shivers at the sight of them. There are no obvious bounty hunters around here, no people at all. The bounty hunters tend to be adolescents with few other ways to make money. Everyone hates them until they need them.

The advertising billboards here aren't even switched on. As they walk around the back of one, it's clear why. Someone has hijacked the electric feed to take into their own apartment. Harriet smiles. She'd forgotten how resourceful people on the lower levels can be. No one high up needs such ingenuity. Everything is handed to them on a plate.

It's a ten-minute walk along the dirty path to the address Michelle gave her.

'Mum, what's wrong with it down here?'

She looks down at him and sees his expression become fixed with worry. Reality must be setting in. He had no idea how bad things are this low.

'Don't pay any attention to it, Oliver. Save your battery, remember?'

The ground is uneven beneath their feet, and the texture is never the same. Harriet doesn't dare look to see what they are treading in. Worryingly soft sometimes, then crunchy, sometimes a gravelly texture. It's the squidgy bits that concern her the most as she tries not to think about whatever it is seeping through their shoes.

They arrive at the address. The bottom floors of the low-rise block look like it'll be lost to landfill within the decade and would be no worse off for it. The facade is blackened with soot, empty bottles and foil wrappers lay in piles either side of the entrance and the drain to the left of the building is overflowing with brown ooze.

It's been too long since Harriet lived this low. She's no longer used to the hardships down here. How quickly she has become a snob. She's become accustomed to all the clean and fine things life up top offered her. She tries not to wince and grimace, tries not to turn her nose up at the state of it. It's too easy to judge the people closest to the filth and assume they cause it, but she knows it's all chucked down from the top. It's the way the system of trickle-down economics works.

Harriet buzzes the number Michelle gave her. Her call is answered by an intercom so scratchy she backs away, sure sparks will fly from the speaker. She introduces herself and an obnoxious beep sounds to let her in.

Inside is not much better than outside. Discarded packets of all sorts of produce creep in through every crevice. The floor is damp and smells like a wet dog. There's a broom by the door with a sign saying 'sweep the rubbish out.' Harriet wonders if anyone ever does.

A door to one apartment opens and they approach, Harriet keeping Oliver sheltered behind her. The woman who opened the door, her face like a bulldog, appears about as welcoming as an incinerator. She glares at Harriet in a way she would eye some off meat.

'Andrea?' Harriet asks.

She grunts in response, her narrowed eyes looking Harriet up and down. Harriet tries to stand still, to not fidget, though she's suddenly aware of her own appearance. Tidy, clean, bedecked in designer clothes. She looks like a tourist.

Harriet lifts her chin a little, remembering when she lived down here that seeming intimidated would do her no favours. She clears her throat. 'Michelle says you could help us maybe remove a tracker?' She tugs Oliver and positions him in front of her.

Andrea's expression morphs, her eyes lighting as she gazes upon Oliver, and she claps. 'You're shitting me! Well, this is the most exciting thing I've been asked to do since forever. Sure, guys. Come on through! Cup of tea? Beer?'

'No,' Harriet says, a little too quickly to be polite. 'No, thank you.'

Inside the flat, the air isn't so bad and Harriet can breathe without keeping her scarf up, and she removes it. They follow Andrea through to a room filled with computer screens, dismembered computers, soldering irons and other things that Harriet can't name. One of the soldering irons is hot and smoking, the smell of burning solder is at least more pleasant than the incinerators from outside.

'Sit it up on the counter,' Andrea says.

It. Harriet tenses but tries not to show her distaste as she lifts Oliver up.

'So, why remove the tracker?' Andrea asks as she sits in a swivel chair and loads up a computer. 'You found a buyer?'

'What? No. I . . .' Harriet searches for the right words, to somehow convey her love for Oliver without sounding crazy. Anyone who calls Oliver 'it' would certainly not understand he's her son. 'I don't want to give him back, that's all.'

Andrea slowly turns to face her. 'You're keeping it? Why?'

'Does it matter?'

'No. You just don't look like the sort. I'm not judging!' She raises her hands and upturns her mouth before facing her computer again. 'I made a bit of money selling these things to folk like you, only, those folks just never looked like you.'

Harriet peers down at her shoes, her jeans, and wonders what a mother to a MechaniKid should look like. 'What do you mean? What do I look like?'

'Not like some kiddy fiddler.'

'Excuse me!' Harriet grabs her stomach like she's been winded. 'That is not why I'm keeping him.'

'Oh, my mistake.' Andrea chuckles, then appears to force herself to stop. 'You're one of them. The MechaniMums. You know, the robo mums . . . ones who think the MechaniKids are real—'

'I have money. I can pay.' She didn't come all this way to be judged and insulted.

'I don't doubt you've got the cash, sweetheart,' Andrea says. Another chuckle, another abrupt stop. 'Listen.' She swivels around and faces Harriet. 'You seem nice. A sensible lady. You could just sell it, make a ton, start a new life.' She eyes Harriet's neck bruises. 'A new life is what you're really after, I reckon. I've got buyers lined up. This is a load of hassle you don't need.'

'Please. Just the tracker removing is all I'm asking for.' Her voice is small, pathetic really. She's always had a stupidly meek voice. She's still speaking with the accent she's been using with Anthony for years. It's become who she is. Has she forgotten the way she used to speak below ground? That's who she was once. It's what's in her bones. All dropped Ts and Gs with shortened words. She enunciates too much to be taken seriously down here. She sounds every bit the hammered housewife.

Andrea sighs and nods. 'Okay. You're the customer. Let me see what you've got.'

Harriet takes a box from her handbag, opens it, and shows her the gold.

Andrea raises her eyebrows and whistles. 'Nice. And?'

'And what?'

'And what else? That's not enough. I'm gonna need more.'

Harriet silently curses. She should have worn different clothes, altered her accent, and presented herself like less of a rich snob. She rummages in her bag and takes out two more boxes.

'Now we're talking. Okay, leave him with me for a few days, and I'll see what I can do.'

Harriet's stomach clenches, and she grabs Oliver's hands. 'No. It has to be done today. By four p.m. If not, then no deal.' She takes out one more box and displays the chunky gold bracelet. That alone must be worth more than anything in the room.

Andrea hesitates, her eyes scanning all the boxes. 'Fine,' she says with a huff. Harriet's sure it's a show. There's no way anyone on 2 would turn down this much gold. 'It's your money to waste.' She plugs a cable into Oliver's charging port.

It's different from the charging cable. The end of it is wrapped in electrical tape, as if she's fixed two cables together. She shakes Oliver to get it to fit, then pushes him to roll him over.

'Gently, if you don't mind.' Harriet says and Andrea glares at her. 'Would you handle any of your computers so roughly?'

Andrea shrugs and continues, though with a little more care.

Harriet rubs Oliver's arm, an attempt to reassure him as she holds her breath.

'Why do I have a tracker?' Oliver asks. 'Do all children have them?'

Harriet's cheeks blush as Andrea looks at her, a mocking smile tugging on her lips. 'Only the most valuable children,' Harriet says. 'And the smartest.'

Andrea tuts, shakes her head, and mutters just about loud enough to hear, 'Jesus Christ.'

Harriet shoots Andrea a look, though she's facing the computer again and doesn't see. If they were looking at each other, Harriet doubts she would have the courage to make such a face.

'Okay,' Andrea says after clicking a few files. There's an image on the screen of what looks like a road map. 'I can see where the tracker is inside. I'll just get a knife.'

Harriet's eyes bulge. 'A what?'

'Knife. Sharp pointy thing.'

Andrea's sarcasm isn't lost on Harriet, though her shock outweighs her annoyance. 'You're going to cut him? You can't just disable it through the computer?'

'No, love. I can disable it, but it'll come back on again. And I don't want TRI fishing around here. I've confused the signal, but now I need to take the thing out. And the only way to do that is to open it up.'

'*Him.*' she says through her teeth. 'Open *him* up.'

'Look. I'll put him on standby mode so he'll be all sleepy and won't feel a thing.'

If Harriet was a little braver, she'd slap the condescending bitch. But she needs this woman, sarcasm and patronising words aside.

Harriet takes Oliver's hands. 'You hear that, Oliver? You're just going to have a little sleep. Okay? It won't hurt. You're such a brave boy.'

Oliver's wide eyes bore into Harriet's, his hands curling tighter around hers.

'I have to be brave,' he says, inflating his chest a little and with a set jaw, he nods.

Harriet, stuck in a juxtaposition of pride for Oliver and anxiety of what is to come, watches Andrea fumble around Oliver's charging point. Harriet had never noticed it before, the faint green glow of a power light, adjacent to it, a pinprick of a hole. Andrea stabs a thin blunt needle into that hole, and Harriet's breath catches.

'Standby button,' Andrea says.

Harriet's vision mists with tears, and she blinks them away. She turns her head. Oliver can't see her worried, can't see her scared, nor can that condescending woman opposite. There's the faintest beep when Andrea puts Oliver on standby and Harriet turns back to look. His eyes slowly shut and his head drops down, the same as he does every night when he's sleeping. She strokes his cheeks, gently massages his eyelids, whispers she loves him in his ear. Sod it if Andrea thinks she's crazy.

Harriet gently lies Oliver on his side, just like she was putting him to bed. There's no hiding the tears now. One traces down her nose as she bends over and kisses his forehead.

'So,' Andrea says. 'The MechaniKid thinks he's a real boy.'

Harriet rights herself and wipes her eye on her sleeve. 'I'm sure he doesn't think that. He knows he's different.'

'But you think you're a real mum. That's bat shit crazy, you know that? He's just wires and coding.'

'Am I paying extra for the judgement?'

'Nope. You're just risking a lot for a machine. And I'm telling you some home truths. You need to understand. His parts will wear out. These things have a shelf life, you know. How old is it?'

'Four.'

'Months?'

'Years. And eight months.'

Andrea's jaw drops and when she can close her mouth again, she puffs her cheeks out and exhales loudly. 'You're risking all of this for an old bot.'

'He's only four. He's hardly old. He's young. He's not going to just . . . expire.'

There's that stifled chuckle again from Andrea, and Harriet clenches her fists.

'Look around you, love,' Andrea says. 'Nothing is built to last. Throwaway culture keeps the great wheel of the economy moving.' She twizzles her index finger in the air like Harriet doesn't understand what a wheel is. 'Trust me, I used to build these things. Your darling little Oliver has a use-by date.'

Harriet looks at Oliver's sleeping body. His perfect skin, his little boy body, his messy blond hair. How dare this woman imply he's old. She rolls her shoulders back and stands straighter. 'Well, I'll get him fixed if that's the case. I'll find him some new parts or whatever he needs. His personality module will last.'

'If you say so.'

Harriet yelps as Andrea cuts into Oliver's skin. Harriet looks away and shields her eyes, as if she's about to see organs and spurts of blood. After a few moments, curiosity gets the better of her and she takes her hand away and looks at Oliver's open wound. It's clean. His peach skin is peeled back, exposing silver-grey wires and discs. There's none of the bluish fluid that leaks when he has a bruise. The smell is the same as a human wound though, metallic and coppery. It incites the same anxieties.

Harriet knows he's a robot, and each of his inner workings aren't going to appear human. But wires or veins, bone or metal, what does it matter? To her, it's all life. What's the difference? Babies are man-made as well as robots. It's only the methodology in the making that is different.

She's often wondered what Oliver would have been like as a baby, with the chubby arms and button nose of newborns. Would he have had the streak of black hair that Freddie had? Or be as fair from birth as her little brother? Her memories of her little brother in his infancy are so distant, but she remembers his fragility, his rosebud mouth sucking on his thumb, the cries he wailed when his teeth came through. There's a helplessness to newborns she never experienced with Oliver. She had to nurture his brain but not watch him grow. She loves him just the same, but there's always been the lingering feeling she missed out, that somehow, there were years of growth she wasn't there to witness. It's a ridiculous feeling, she knows. Oliver was born the size he still is, and now that she's taken him away from TRI, it's the size he'll always be. Her little boy who will never age. It sounds almost perfect, to bypass the troublesome twos and the challenging teenage manifestations. He will forever be this perfect age. Her little boy.

Andrea continues to work, her gaze alternating between Oliver's open chest and her computer. Harriet has often wanted to peel Oliver's skin back to see what he's made of. She fancied herself as an engineer once, a fascination with how things work. But she was too poor for college and too pretty to be taken seriously. She could never have landed a job in engineering by letting men's hands go up her skirt. Qualifications don't come so easily to those born below ground. Life tends to work out how it was meant, she consoles. She grew up raising her brother. She was always meant to care for a child.

After an hour, Andrea grabs a pair of fine tweezers.

'Careful!' Harriet says.

'Really? You think I'm just gonna thrash around in there?' Andrea's tone scolds, but Harriet cannot calm her racing heart as Andrea puts the tweezers in as delicately as if she were making fine jewellery. After a few minutes, she pulls out a tiny silver disc. 'There it is. The tracker.'

Harriet releases a breath, and her chest loosens. 'Okay. Thank you. And you can sew him up?'

Andrea snorts a laugh. 'Sew? Nah. Look.' She pushes Oliver's skin back down, presses on it with a little force and that familiar blue grey colour fills in the gaps. 'It'll heal up by itself. I'll put a bandage on it and tape it up to stop it flopping around. But that's all. Presto. Six hours and the bandage can come off. He'll be as good as new.'

Harriet bites her bottom lip and blinks away some tears. On the table is that little silver disc. The thing that could have ruined all her plans. She rolls Oliver over and searches out that pinprick hole and presses the blunt needle into Oliver's standby button. His awakening is instant, and his eyes flit open.

'Mother?' he says, clear as a bell.

'Yes, darling, I'm right here.' She lifts up his hands and kisses them. 'How are you feeling?'

'Jesus Christ,' Andrea says, shaking her head.

Oliver doesn't notice Andrea's quip. His eyes are for his mother only. 'Fine, Mum. Good. Is it done?'

Harriet looks at Andrea who no longer suppresses her laugh.

'We can go?' Harriet asks.

'Yep. Get out of here.' Andrea pauses her laughing to gesture towards the door. 'You're all done. Be free, you weirdos.'

Chapter 16

As soon as they leave the building and are back on the street, the smell hits Harriet again. She pulls her scarf up over her nose and mouth and stares out across the expanse of dirty streets and grotty buildings. A patchwork of decay and rot. The air is wet and warm through her scarf, but she takes a long gulp of it, Oliver doing the same, both inflating their lungs fully as she realises, as it really sinks in.

Anthony is a hundred storeys away.

TRI can't find them.

They're free.

She squeezes Oliver's hand. The air may be sticky and grimy, but Harriet feels fresh, light, a vast expanse of a future stretching out in front of them. They can now go wherever they like.

'What now, Mum?'

She looks right, then left, then leaves her gaze fixed straight ahead. It's a long walkway to nowhere and anywhere.

'I actually don't know,' she says. 'Getting your tracker off was what I was worried about the most. Now that's gone, we're really free.'

She picks him up then, hugging him tight and spins around.

Oliver laughs. 'What are you doing, Mum?'

'You're mine.' She kisses his cheek. 'I just want to dance. You're all mine.'

She puts him down and they walk, the slight exertion leaving her giddy, or perhaps it's the asphyxiating air of the lower levels.

She really hadn't thought this far ahead. Finding somewhere on the lower levels to stay was what she was thinking, but now she's on second, and is reminded how filthy it is, she knows she needs to be a few levels higher at least. The tracker removal cost a lot more than she thought.

She clutches her chest and catches her breath, a slight swill of panic bubbling her insides. No Anthony. No TRI to chase them. It's just her and Oliver. And now she has to provide for him.

They walk forwards, destination nowhere in particular, back on the ground ridden with debris crunching and squelching underfoot. She needs to find somewhere to rent on a level that has reliable electricity for Oliver. Michelle said they could crash at hers, but that's way too high up, too close to Anthony which is too risky for the time being. There used to be cheap accommodation a few levels up, she remembers from her acting days. Still probably too expensive for them long term until she finds reliable work, but she decides they'll head there, hoping she can get a private room. If lower-level people know about Oliver, they could shun or steal him.

The weight of her decision to flee presses on her forehead, a tightness like an elastic band wrapping around her head, the colours now swirling.

It's the pollution, she tells herself. The smog is bringing on a migraine. As soon as they get a few levels up, she'll feel better, and she'll be able to think clearer. She looks at her son. He has colour in his cheeks, not a hint of worry. He'll have decent charge left since he's been on standby for hours so that buys her some time. He walks with strong, even steps, no sign of low battery fatigue. Electricity is her main worry right now. Oliver needs full charges to maintain his battery, but she concludes a few nights with partial charge probably won't do him any harm.

A sign indicates there's a lift across a park. Unlike the parks higher up, this one is deserted, dark and bleak. No grass grows this far down, no little planting boxes lining the playing area, no bees buzzing around. The remnants of a pond that looks like a slurry pit are dolloped in the middle. There's a broken swing hanging off one chain and a climbing frame with burned ropes. She quickens their pace towards the lift, not wanting Oliver to look too carefully at such a miserable sight. This is not where she will raise her son. She'll do what it takes to give him a better life than this.

Their footsteps scuff on the crumbly walkway, the sound echoing through the park. A crack, like stepping on glass, comes from behind. Harriet's heart skips several beats, and her breath freezes in her lungs.

It's not an echo.

She snaps her head around and squints in the gloom. The figures come from the side, as dark as the shadows. Within a few paces, they're standing in front of Harriet and Oliver before she's had time to think. Two men, easily twice the size of Harriet, stand shoulder to shoulder, blocking the path.

Harriet swallows and tries to project her voice. In the lower levels, the weak are preyed upon. 'Excuse me,' she says as she tries to walk around them.

'Not so fast.' One puts out his arm to stop her. His eyes go to Oliver. 'Is this it?'

The other one's lips curl up into a sneer. 'Yeah, I think so.'

Harriet pushes Oliver behind her. 'Let us pass. Please.' She winces at the last word. Manners aren't going to help her.

'A MechaniKid without a tracker.' The first one chuckles. 'No chance. Worth its weight in gold.'

Andrea. Harriet clenches her fists. She should have raced out of her door rather than dawdled. She should have known someone like her can't be trusted. 'You want gold? Let me get you some.' Panic shakes its way through her whole body and she wobbles as she rummages in her handbag.

'Is everything all right, Mum?'

'Shh, Oliver. Just a moment.'

The second man steps forwards. 'We'll just take the thing. The bag won't be worth anything.'

'I have jewellery,' she shouts now, vibrato breaking through her voice. 'J . . . just a sec. I can pay you well. I have a wealthy husband . . .' she keeps talking, buying time until her fingers brush the cool cylinder in her bag. As she glances up at the two of them, she aligns her finger with the button and pulls out the mace. She sprays them both in the eyes. 'Oliver, run! Go!'

He sprints. She doesn't have time to check where and keeps her eyes half-closed to protect herself. There's a throaty wail from the men as their hands go to their eyes. They cough and splutter as she dispenses the last of the mace. She ducks low to dodge the plume, then kicks each in the balls. One doubles over and the other is on his knees. Half-remembering her combat training from a movie, she kicks them both again, in the guts, the balls again and when they lash out, she dodges their grasp and lands the sole of her shoe in one face and then the other. Their noses crunch on impact.

She runs, eyes wide now, looking right and left, her gaze landing on all the nooks and crannies of hiding places around the park, screaming his name. 'Oliver!'

Her boy, her son! Where would he go? He's so unworldly, doesn't know this place at all, nor does she. 'Oliver!'

She double-backs on herself. There's the silhouette outline of the writhing men, their gravelly curse words, their struggle to get to their feet.

She turns away from them and runs again. 'Oliver!'

Behind a broken billboard she finds him, hugging his knees, his little chest heaving out shuddering breaths. 'Mum.'

He jumps up when he sees her and goes to hug her, but there's no time. She grabs his hand and they keep running. They make it to a further away lift and she presses floor five.

Then, they hug. Harriet's panic seeps out of her, draining from every limb. Her knees slacken and she kneels next to Oliver, burying him in her embrace. She pulls away to look at him, disbelieving he's really there, that they made it this far, that he's hers.

'Are you okay, Mum?'

Gratitude forms a lump in her throat. He always asks how she is when no one else does. He's the son she always dreamed of. She strokes his hair and his cheek. 'I'm fine, darling.'

'Why did those men want to steal me?'

'Because you are such a special and kind boy. You were so good to run so fast.'

She hugs him again and kisses his head. She wants to hug him so tight to squash him, to make him so tiny she could fit him in her pocket, where she knows she can hide him and he'll be safe. It's then her breath catches as she realises, if anything happens to her, what happens to Oliver? She's got no one else. They're alone in this world.

Chapter 17

On level 5, the dirt is below them. The air is still heavy with the undertones of singed trash and sulphur, but Harriet can breathe deeply without her scarf over her face. The outside space is pleasant enough, the walkway above is further away than it is on 2, sporadic streetlights brighten up the space, and the parks and walkways have a few people milling around. Here, like every level higher, people discard their rubbish over the walkway fences for the lower levels to deal with. The rubbish raining down from top levels is constant, the whooshing and clanging like white noise, though the majority flies past the fences with only the odd stray bit landing on the walkways. The occasional kick and shove from a boot and the rubbish is pushed away and out of sight again.

They walk through the park looking for a bench to sit on. Harriet's energy levels are spent, and she curses herself for not thinking to pack any food.

They receive looks of surprise, tuts and shaking heads. Harriet stiffens, unaccustomed to such manners when they aren't hurting anyone. She slows their pace and looks at herself. She's dressed head to toe in designer clothes, tidy and looking brand new. Even her handbag has a little designer motif. Oliver too, is wearing all clothes from the boutique on 99. Handmade clothes that cost as much as a week's rent on 5. They look like every mother-child advert going, like the families on all the billboards advertising products the people this low would struggle to afford. She's a tourist down here, with her well-dressed little boy. *Dammit.* She should have thought of that. She looks like everything people this low down hate yet want to be. She's a walking target.

They find a café, and her stomach grumbles at the display of pre-made sandwiches, but rather than stop and eat, she walks Oliver straight through and makes for the toilet. She locks the door behind them and checks the spare clothes she has for them in her bag. Besides being creased, they're much the same. Expensive looking and too nice for these parts. She takes her top off, turns it inside out, and rips off the label, then does the same to Oliver's. It's the best she can do. When they leave the cubicle, she orders a coffee and a sandwich and as they skulk in a corner booth, she smudges some coffee on her jeans, then stains Oliver's clothes too. It breaks her heart. He is usually so immaculately presented. She takes his socks off as well, but it's not like she can make his clothes appear too small for him.

She checks her watch. Anthony might be arriving home about now. She left a note in the kitchen, a simple goodbye, nothing nasty, letting him know there are meals in the freezer. She shouldn't feel sad and she isn't going to miss him. But the idea of him, what he once meant to her, is something she has missed for a long time. For years, she really believed that one day he'd be kinder to her, that he loved her, that if she had his child she could fix his broken mind.

Oliver was never going to be that child and after a while, she knew that no child could mend what was too damaged. But Oliver did mend her, and she wishes things could have been different.

Her son's legs dangle beneath his chair, and he looks up at Harriet and smiles. He has hope in his eyes, an adventure before him rather than an upheaval. One dream begins as another ends.

She finishes her sandwich and, with her hunger sated, she welcomes more practical thoughts. She needs to replace her phone in case Anthony can track it, but it's synched with Oliver's battery, his health app, and she's not sure if she can log in from another phone. Is it needed? She doesn't often look at it when she knows she can charge him every night.

She faces him, brushes his hair back and puts her hand on his forehead as if she were checking for a fever. She leans in and speaks in a whisper. 'Oliver, you understand what it's like when you're not working properly? When your battery is low?'

'I get tired sometimes. It becomes harder to move my arms and legs. Is that what you mean?'

'Yes. That's it. If you start to feel like that, can you tell me?'

'Of course, Mum.'

Okay. She can cope without her phone. It's the last thing tying her to Anthony, to that old abusive life. Leaving the café, they stroll over to the edge of the walkway. The fence is up to her shoulders, and she takes her phone and throws it over. She smiles and is amazed how much lighter she is without it, like that little device weighed ten kilos.

The tuts and head shakes are absent from the other pedestrians now as they fit in more with their grubby clothes. There are abandoned bicycles along the sides of the walkways, the odd person riding them at slow speed, obviously not using the electric function. Her heart sinks a little as she worries there's no electricity down here besides the streetlights. She may have to try a few levels higher, where rent will be more and she's less likely to know anyone. With Oliver's tracker removed, keeping him charged is her next worry. That and finding work and a place to live.

One problem at a time, Harriet.

She could save Oliver's battery by going up to the vehicle level and taking a taxi, but they're card payments only. Will Anthony think to track her card? She's got some cash and the jewellery, but she'll have to use her card at some point. Not today, though. Not until she really has to and is hopefully settled enough to not be tempted by whatever lure he uses. He'll probably just assume she'll come home of her own accord or else he'll be so drunk he won't even notice for a while.

She watches for signs of fatigue in Oliver, asking if he's okay. She knows she doesn't need to worry yet, his time on standby saved loads of battery, but it's a mother's job to worry.

Another mile and her feet start to ache, though she doesn't let on. They're close to the cheap accommodation she knew of years ago. She had friends who used to live there and hopes they still do. She catches Oliver tilting his head and taking it all in, and has to remind him to subdue his curiosity.

It's another half an hour until they're in a part of town she recognises. It's nicer than she remembers, well-kempt houses where the residents have put in some effort to make them attractive, unlike higher up where the architecture speaks for itself. The streets are busy, that is as she remembers. Hordes of people cram into the same square footage of one apartment above a 100. She pulls Oliver in nearer as some youths who look like they could be bounty hunters or pickpockets scurry through the crowd, and Harriet keeps her handbag close.

She recoils her nose from the smell that wafts from the rubbish below. It's not constant, just occasionally, when a breeze finds its way through and catches her off-guard. In the shade of the levels above, a little hope escapes her. On 107, even on her worst days, feeling the real sun, seeing the clouds and the sky gave her hope and ambition. Down here, it doesn't matter how nicely they paint the houses and how many fake plants they arrange. It's still bleak.

She'll get used to it. She's spoiled, that's all. Oliver doesn't seem to mind. He never whines or complains. It's a tell that he's a MechaniKid. Moaning about every little thing is so innately human.

Harriet scans the crowds for someone she recognises, doubting anyone will recognise her as she's a far cry from the screen-ready fresh-faced actor she was a decade ago. But she used to know lots of people who lived here. It's unlikely they all moved away. She kicks herself for not keeping in touch, for forgetting her roots, for treating friendships like they're as disposable as consumables. Anthony never banned her from social media. She just often found it too hard to face. All those people warned her against diving into such a commitment, against giving up all she'd worked towards for one man. Keeping in touch meant losing face.

'Harriet?'

She snaps her head around and relief washes over her. There's a gap in the crowd and she spots a friend, one she really wasn't expecting to see.

'Theo?' He still has the slight frame, that lopsided smile, the limp he tries to hide. He wears overalls like all techies, stained with rips badly repaired. Can it really be him?

'I'd recognise you anywhere.' He limps over and hugs Harriet before she's even convinced herself it's actually him.

'I can't believe it.' She pulls away and inspects his face. He still looks like the kid she knew. He has all the kindness in his face he always had, so rare for a below grounder. 'You're still up here? You were always afraid you'd end up back below.'

Theo was a friend of Harriet's brother when they were kids. Last time she saw him, he was living a little lower down, maybe on 3, and was scratching out a living fixing old parts from scavengers. He was bright, could repair most things if he put his mind to it. When they were children, she used to watch in awe as he tinkered with old electricals.

'I've alternated a bit,' he says. 'But yeah, fairly comfortably up here now. Living with someone you know actually. Someone you introduced me to ages ago. Monty, remember him?'

'You and Monty?' Monty is an old acting friend. Exuberant and as camp as they come. So loud for softly spoken Theo. Harriet and Monty used to drink together, even went to some auditions. Monty never got far and gave up early on. He found the audition process too demoralising, but he was fun and honest and helped Harriet out with food when she was really low.

He grins. 'We've been together for three years now. I always wanted to thank you for matchmaking.'

Harriet returns his smile. If anyone deserves happiness in this world, it's Theo. He was always there for her and her brother. Their only friend below ground.

'I'm hardly the matchmaker. I introduced you guys years ago. Never imagined you two as a couple, though. I'm happy for you. Monty's a great guy.'

'Yeah, he is. And our friend Shay lives with us too. A fellow below ground survivor. But how are you? What brings you this way?'

'Erm . . .' Harriet searches for words for a moment, wishing her eyes wouldn't water so freely. She blinks away the mist and notes the knowing look in Theo's eyes. He could always tell when things were bad at home when they were kids. She never had to say it out loud. She clears her throat. 'This is Oliver, by the way. My son.'

Theo's hands go to his cheeks before he offers one for Oliver to shake. Theo's eyes stay on Oliver as he introduces himself, and Harriet can see the nostalgia in Theo's eyes.

'He's the spit of Chris, isn't he?'

'Yeah,' Harriet says, a pain in her chest. 'Yeah, he really is.'

'I'm actually running an errand at the moment, but join us for dinner? Please? Monty will go nuts when he sees you.'

Harriet's hand goes to her chest, warmth replacing the pain for a moment. 'I'd love that. Definitely.'

'Great. We're on East Street, twelve Park View apartments.' He takes a bit of paper from his pocket and jots down his address and number, then hands it to Harriet. 'I'll be back in an hour. See you there then?'

Harriet nods. 'Absolutely. It's so great to see you. I'll be there.'

Theo walks off, giving Oliver a little wave before he joins the crowd and is out of sight.

Harriet wants to lift Oliver up for a hug again, an unbound glee fizzing through her. Friends. She has a friend who doesn't hate her, hasn't rejected her on sight for running away and leaving them all behind.

As they walk on, unease claws at her. Did she seem too keen, too desperate? Was the invite out of pity rather than friendship? She doesn't want to be a burden and looking around, people have more here than on 2 or below but still so little.

They find a bench to sit and wait, still aware she needs to conserve Oliver's battery. She shouldn't feel so uneasy. Theo is her oldest friend. After being below ground together for so long, that friendship may have been on pause, but surely it never went away.

'Mother, who's Chris?'

That name knocks the air out of her again, and she takes a moment to answer. 'He was my brother.'

'It must be nice to have a brother. Where is he now?'

Harriet purses her lips and puts her arm around Oliver. It's what made her breath catch when she first saw him in that catalogue. He really does look like him.

She steadies herself before replying. 'He's with the angels, darling.'

Chapter 18

The arrival of new life is never without celebration, even for those who live below ground. So many pregnancies never take, so many babies are born not breathing. Harriet never understood the trauma of that until it happened to her.

When Christopher was born, Harriet was nearly six, and despite his obvious ill health from the start, her parents rejoiced. Harriet often wondered if they celebrated her birth or just dismissed it as flippantly as they did the rest of her life.

Christopher had the brightest blond hair and crystal blue eyes, but he was born sick, as so many below grounders are. If not born that way, then they often become that way. When Harriet first held him, he lay tiny and thin in her arms, his cry not much more than a wheeze. Their parents were sure he wouldn't survive the night. They all sat with him, watching over his cot as they waited for the moment his chest would stop rising and falling. His little hand attempted to grip Harriet's finger, but it was feeble and limp. It was the one time Harriet remembers her parents being sober, not fighting, and showing affection towards her and each other.

Harriet was a rarity. She was healthy and strong, bright at school and lacked the below ground instincts of maliciousness nudging over into greed. She pondered, sometimes, why her parents weren't proud of her or kinder to their child who helped them so much. Her parents, third generation below grounders, were sick in the body and in the mind. In those days, they reserved any love they could muster for Christopher. Harriet didn't require it, she supposed. It was as if they believed their love could make Christopher better.

When he survived that first night, sobriety wore thin and her parents celebrated, necking the home brew as if it was the last party they'd ever have. Even her mother, a day after birth, drank until her glazed eyes couldn't focus on Harriet, until she was unable to hold the little boy they feared they'd lose.

Her parents' love for Christopher ran its course after just a few weeks, when they convinced themselves their doting affection wasn't going to make him better, when his crying disturbed them, and when it dawned on them a child is for life. Like so many things, looking after Christopher became Harriet's responsibility.

Harriet made promises to Christopher that they would escape one day, that they would see real daylight. She told him stories about sunlight like it was a myth or a fairy tale, animating her stories with voices and dance, to show him the wonders she hoped they'd experience together one day. She spoke of wind and leaves and the smell of flowers instead of rot. All rumours she'd heard whispered through the below ground from those who had ventured above. A life of adventure she was surely to have.

She taught him to read, and about the world that he was too weak to explore.

When Christopher's health deteriorated, their parents blamed Harriet. Every cough and fever were her fault. He was rarely out of bed, but when he did manage to walk and his legs gave up, she'd carry him back to his bed and tuck him in and their parents belted her for doing so.

Theo lived next door and was the same age as Christopher. He would bring games for them to play, building blocks or toy cars, the odd book. Theo was also sickly, though not as much as Christopher. He had bad lungs from the damp and mould, like he was slowly drowning in the humid air, but besides a dodgy leg that no doctor could fully fix, his muscles were strong and his cough wasn't too bad. Still, lasting until adulthood seemed a far cry for both of them. The difference was Theo's parents loved him.

Harriet disliked shortening her brother's name to Chris, as her parents and Theo did. No one ever shortened hers, and when he was about six, she asked her brother, what about the rest of your name? Why should that be missed out? What about the 'topher'? she asked, though pronounced it tipher. He laughed and shrugged and said he didn't care, but she called him that from then on. Her little brother. Tipher.

Tipher grew slowly. His clothes hung off his thin frame like he was playing dress-ups. When his milk teeth fell out, no adult ones came through. His eyes remained the brightest blue, and his white hair darkened to a deep blonde. Harriet would fuss over him, do whatever it took to make him comfortable and would sell her own toys and things to buy him pain relief. Yet Tipher always asked how Harriet was. He was the only one who ever did.

Harriet was fifteen when the final chest infection took hold of Tipher. She was by his bedside, holding his hand as his chest became too weak to cough and his face turned grey. She didn't cry in front of him. Instead, she reassured him that he was going to be okay and kept telling him stories of the better life she would give him one day. He was only ten when his feeble grip on her hand relaxed completely. But Tipher wasn't suffering anymore.

Below ground, they don't have cemeteries or funerals. Bodies are tossed above to add to the landfill along with all the rubbish of the world.

Harriet left Tipher there, then ran, bumping into Theo on her way out. He didn't ask. The answer was plain on her face.

'Go,' Theo said. 'Before they come back.'

He knew she'd be in for it when her parents came home. Everyone knew what some parents did to their children, but the culture below ground was to turn a blind eye.

Harriet ran, took the stairs to ground level and then up one more. When she burst out of the doors onto ground level, she expected to be dazed by the sunlight and bright blue sky. Instead, she was welcomed by trash. She took the lift up one more level, and in the shade of all the storeys above, she wept for her brother, for the life he would never have.

She scraped a living in those early days, working in a seedy bar in between auditions for whatever acting roles came up. Voiceovers, mostly. Her storytelling abilities flourished when she was looking after Tipher. Every time she told a story, she imagined him laughing and engrossed in the tale. Every time she performed, she felt him with her, cheering her on.

A few years later, she bumped into Theo on a walkway on a lower level. He had also escaped his own pre-dug grave and made it above. The drier air above had worked wonders on his lungs, though his limp had never totally gone away. He still visited his parents, of course. Why wouldn't he? His parents were great. They used to drop off food to Harriet and Tipher sometimes, even though they had so little themselves. His dad was often ill, yet he'd spare his pain medication to give it to Tipher.

Harriet told Theo she'd keep in touch, but in true Harriet style, she didn't. Harriet shed relationships like a snake sheds its skin. The one relationship she grew up desperate to hold on to, she wasn't able to keep alive.

When she lost her newborn baby, Freddie, too, she believed her touch on a life tainted it.

There wasn't anyone in her life she didn't destroy.

Chapter 19

Harriet tells the abridged version of her brother to Oliver. He doesn't need to know about her crappy parents, the abuse and booze. He's seen enough of that already in his short life. Instead, she tells him about Tipher's laugh, Theo's kindness, and of what a blessing children are. Oliver's bright blue eyes stare at her, engrossed just as Tipher was when she told stories. If Tipher was ever healthy, he would have looked just like Oliver.

'I am so sorry your brother died, Mum. It sounds like you did your best.'

She runs her hand through Oliver's hair and recalls every time he's asked if she's okay. It's as if TRI knew of Tipher and recreated a healthy version of him. It would be easy to believe they are from the same family.

After nearly an hour, they make their way to the address Theo gave her. It's a nice enough part of town for level 5. The parks on the way are wide and spacious, people linger in the streets as they're not too awful to be in. It's cold, shady and dark, and Harriet tightens her cardigan around her. She should have thought to bring something warmer. She remembers the lower levels being stuffy and airless. In her mind that means hot, but the thick air breaks her out in goosebumps and a chill creeps up her spine.

She glances up at the streetlights, only a few are on and she wonders if the rest will come on later. She hasn't seen any other sign of electricity in use yet, and hopes it's just being saved for after sunset when it'll get really dark. If Oliver doesn't get some charge, she's not sure what her plan is.

Theo is walking through his front door when Harriet and Oliver arrive. Harriet picks up her pace to meet him there.

'Hey! You came! Great.'

It isn't said as a dig, she knows this. Theo has never had a mean word to say about anyone. But with Harriet's terrible track record of keeping her friendships means his greeting touches a nerve. She smiles it away.

'This place looks great. I'm just so delighted you're still above.'

'I still visit my parents. They can't venture this far to visit, though. I've tried to convince them to move up here, but they've lived so long below ground, I swear five minutes above ground will make them dry out and turn to dust.'

Harriet laughs. It's an old joke, about how some below grounders have no aspirations to ever get out. She never understood it. Institutionalised, she supposes.

He beckons her through inside and she follows, Oliver by her side. The three-bed apartment is the size of her old kitchen and infinitely more cluttered. Shelves of electrical items to be fixed line the walls and from the ceiling clothes hang to dry so low she has to duck in places. Her place on 107 was always so roomy and bare. This apartment, busy and stuffed full of life and memories, is a home.

Oliver follows her, politely and quietly. He's not shy. He's just keen to learn. She should be reminding him to shut down his curious glances and save his battery, but she can hardly say that in front of Theo. Would he judge, or disregard Oliver as merely a robot and not a boy? She can't be sure that his biological identity won't matter. He's different, and most people regard different with caution.

In the kitchen, Theo puts the kettle on as Harriet and Oliver sit at a table made of bits of old furniture. A collection of wood and metal that should look chaotic but is beautifully constructed and finished. She brushes her hand over the surface.

'That's Monty's work. He's so creative.'

Harriet's jaw drops. 'The same Monty that used to turn up to auditions without even knowing the lines?'

Theo laughs. 'Yep. I guess he found his calling. Anything I can't fix he turns into furniture or ornaments and sells it, some of it he even sells to higher levels.'

Harriet notices his blush. 'You are so smitten it's sickening,' she jokes.

He smiles and hands her a steaming cup of tea, then sits opposite Oliver. 'So, how old are you, Oliver?'

Oliver remains tight-lipped and looks at his lap.

'Oliver,' Harriet says. 'Are you shy?'

He leans a little closer to Harriet. 'You always told me not to talk to strangers.'

She looks at Theo, whose eyes sheen with adoration. 'It's okay. Theo is an old friend. Remember I told you about my brother? Theo was his friend, so he isn't a stranger.'

Oliver then looks up at Theo and smiles. 'I'm six.'

'Quite a big boy then!' Theo says. 'And what do you like to do?'

'Hm . . .' Oliver considers the question carefully. 'I like the climbing frame at the park and reading books about spiders.'

'Spiders! Well, that's just fantastic,' he says. 'There're plenty around here I can introduce you to.'

The front door slams and the three of them jump, then the loud voice Harriet used to know so well rings out.

'Theo!' Monty's voice booms from the front door, and his thumping footsteps get closer. 'What's this surprise you've got for us then?'

Monty stops dead in the doorway to the kitchen, his eyes widening at the sight of Harriet, and his hands go to his mouth. 'No fucking way!' He squeals, then runs to Harriet and grabs her for a hug. 'Girl! It's been years!'

Harriet reciprocates the hug, though a little less tightly than Monty's firm grasp. She'd forgotten this about Monty, his over-powering affection. Years ago, Harriet found it too much to bear but now, rekindled, she feels safer than she has in a long time.

When the hug ends, she wipes her eye on her cuff. Her tears have left a wet patch on Monty's shoulder. His overalls are cleaner and much more snug than Theo's, tailored by the looks of it, no doubt his own handiwork. He always preferred the costume design to acting.

'Hey!' Monty says. 'You need to tell us what's wrong. What happened to the high life up top?'

Harriet hesitates before answering, shame stalling her speech. She knows she shouldn't feel that way, that Anthony's violence is not her failure, yet still, it's tough to admit. After a breath, she braces, and pulls back her scarf to the sound of shocked gasps from her friends. The bruising there is still a deep purple and tender to touch. 'He was going to kill me if I stayed any longer.'

Monty shakes his head, and they all sit back at the table, both their hands reaching for hers. 'You got out,' Monty says. 'And you got this little guy out too! You going to introduce us?'

Harriet watches their faces light up as Oliver says hello to Monty and tells him about his hobbies. They're enchanted by him. It's impossible not to be.

Shay arrives back a few minutes later. She has the hollowed-out eyes of someone who hasn't long escaped from below ground. She's far too pretty to have lived an easy life below and is so thin that Harriet suspects she never got to enjoy any reward for her efforts. The laundry hanging in the hallway is partly made up of sequined underwear and Harriet recognises the signs of a life she knows all too well.

Shay says a curt hello and prepares some food, laying out plates of rice and steamed vegetables. The plates are all mismatched, bashed into shape and repainted, each one unique and beautiful. More of Monty's work, Harriet assumes. She tries to help but Shay tells her not to, like a dog defending its territory, her eyes glaring at Harriet until she sits back down. There's suspicion in Shay's voice and in the way she looks at Harriet, as if trying to force away her natural intuition that assumes Harriet means her harm.

'It's probably not up to Monty's cooking standards,' Shay says, 'but I'm sure it'll do.'

'No food is up to Monty's cooking standards.' Theo laughs. 'But the guy needs a night off sometimes.'

When Oliver doesn't pick up a fork to eat, Harriet tells them he ate a while ago and is a little fussy. She watches their faces for signs of offence or suspicion, but as she tucks into the meal, she sees nothing but acceptance.

They all start to squint as the last of the natural light outside ebbs away and Theo stands to turn the lights on. Harriet exhales the last of her tension as relief washes over her. There's electric on 5. She can charge Oliver.

They chat non-stop, laugh, Theo regaling stories of games they used to play as children, and updating her on the life he and Monty have lived above. Monty's laugh is so loud it could be seismic, and Theo is the strongest she's ever seen him, the happiest, the most content she could have imagined.

Harriet was always so desperate to leave her life below, she never considered the other lives she left behind.

'You can stay for a bit, if you like?' Theo says. 'The spare room is filled with refurb stuff, but we can clear a space for a bit.'

'Definitely,' Monty says. 'You're more than welcome. We'll need the spare room back at some point, but it's yours until you're back on your feet. Then there's a women's refuge place you should check out. It's on 4, but it's meant to be really good.'

Harriet looks at all of them, even Shay nods. 'Thank you. So much. Just for tonight, that would be really great. And I'll visit the refuge tomorrow.'

'You're all so kind,' Oliver says.

'He's a cute kid,' Shay says. 'Really polite.'

'Yeah.' Harriet beams at Oliver. 'Considering my husband, I'm lucky.'

'I had a daughter,' Shay continues with a sheen of tears. She has an angular face, her pixie cut making it appear even more severe, like she's trying to prove her sadness has hardened her. 'Well, you know how it is. Shit, I miss her like mad. I miss being pregnant with her, feeling her move. She was so tiny when she was born. I was lucky, I guess. I had her for a whole year. Some don't get that long.'

Harriet swallows back her own memory of loss. 'My son, Freddie . . . Minutes I had him for. That was all.'

There's a moment of silence, a shared grief and mutual sympathy. Shay and Harriet clasp hands for a few seconds. No one survives below ground without losing someone. They're all born in graves.

'But you have Oliver now,' Theo says, breaking the sadness and grinning at the quiet little boy.

'There's work, if you need it,' Shay says. 'I mean, it's seedy as fuck, but it pays. Just dancing, chatting. No touching, if you don't want. You know the kind of place. There're quite a few places on this level, even more lower down. Turnover is high, so you'll find a job somewhere.'

'Thanks. I'll check it out tomorrow.'

They continue to chat about less serious topics for hours, about their lives down here, the people they know and the places they go until they all start yawning and stretching.

'Well,' Theo says, 'I'll be going to the market early tomorrow.'

'And me,' Monty says. 'Got those chairs and shelves to sell.'

Monty leads Harriet to the spare room, and she helps him shift some things around. He wasn't kidding when he said they'd need the room back. The place is jam-packed with Monty's upcycled furniture and Theo's electrical whatnots. They manage to clear the bed, shake out the dusty duvet, and fluff up a pillow.

'Sorry it's a bit of a mess,' Theo says.

Harriet hugs him. 'Honestly, it's perfect. Thank you so much.'

When they are alone, she asks Oliver if he's tired.

'My arms feel heavy.'

The bed is a single, so Oliver and Harriet will have to share. There's no way she could leave him on the floor. They sit on it, and Harriet takes a moment to get comfortable on the lumpy mattress. There's a little light by his standby button that glows an orangey colour. She never noticed before. She never had to consider it when she had reliable electricity every night. There's a socket next to the sofa and she unplugs the lamp, then plugs Oliver in. With a little flutter of his eyelids, his chin dips and he goes to sleep.

Harriet gets into bed, lying among the gritty sheets and smell of varnish and damp wood. She's exhausted, but they're free. Truly free. Hopeful.

Somehow, against the odds, they've lasted a day and begun a new life together.

Chapter 20

Harriet's eyes open, dry and itchy in the dusty room and she stares up at the unfamiliar ceiling, the curve of the Artex barely visible in the gloom. For a moment, she wonders where she is. There's a window, no curtain, yet morning sunlight doesn't come through. It must be really early. In the far corner of the window, there's an orange flickering streetlight.

Oliver is asleep beside her rather than the snoring oaf of her husband and she rolls on her side, stroking his hair, then traces the contours of his apple cheeks and delicate nose. She's never woken up next to him before, never observed him so peaceful. She thinks perhaps even in sleep, he's projecting her feelings, since it's the most at ease she's felt in years.

'Damn electric is out again.'

The voice comes from outside Harriet's room and still in her sleepy, foggy daze she can't place it.

'I just need to get those chairs for the sale.'

That voice she knows. Monty, Harriet recalls with a smile. They're in Theo and Monty's house. She snuggles deeper under the duvet, cosy and safe.

There's a knock, and the door squeaks open without a pause.

'Sorry to disturb you, Harriet. Sleep in if you like, I just need . . . Oh.'

Harriet rubs her eyes and rolls over to face Monty. 'Please, come in. What time is it?'

'Almost nine.'

Harriet pushes herself up. 'Nine! God, it's so dark still—' She cuts herself off. Moaning about the lack of light down here is top floor snobbery. 'Sorry, I slept so heavily, but I need to get up.'

Monty doesn't move and doesn't respond. He stays hovering in the doorway.

'No hot water, no water pressure even for a cold shower.' Shay. That's whose voice it is. Harriet recognises it now, though she's speaking louder than she was last night, her footsteps heavy, like she's stamping out her frustration. 'There are still streetlights on so it's just us. Typical.'

Shay's face appears next to Monty's and realisation hits Harriet. It's too late. Monty's seen him. He's seen his charging cable.

Shay follows Monty's gaze, then inhales sharply, taking a step back before her face fills with rage. 'Are you fucking kidding me? That's one of them MechaniKids!'

Oliver's eyelids flutter a moment before he opens them, and his face breaks out into his sweet grin. 'Morning, Mum. Did you sleep well?'

Shay and Monty's eyes cut through Oliver's pleasantries. The dusty air grows stuffy and Harriet is momentarily grateful that it's still so dark, sure her flaming cheeks must be glowing. 'I .

. . I'm sorry,' she says as she fumbles with the charging cable, her voice shaking as much as her body. 'His battery was low. He needed charging. I'm sorry, I'll pay.'

Shay steps forward, past the door frame and into the room. Such a small step, yet it makes Harriet recoil and shimmy further down the bed. Shay lifts her lips like she's about to snarl at Oliver. 'You tried to tell us he was real.'

'He is! He is to me. Please.'

Harriet watches Shay's eyes narrow, her hands ball into fists, the tension in her biceps visible through her shirt. She seemed such a tiny, skinny thing last night. Now her entire body resembles a weapon.

'What's going on, Mum?'

Harriet pulls Oliver into her, wrapping her body around to shield him from view, to protect him from whatever blows are coming.

'Get out,' Shay says, her voice tremulous with restraint. Then, louder, 'You hear me! Get OUT!'

Shay doesn't move. Her rigid frame stays standing in front of the doorway as Harriet packs up hastily under her glare, dropping Oliver's charging cable, then spilling her bag. She piles it back in, leaving a jewellery box on the side. 'For your trouble. I'm sorry.'

'Shay,' Monty says. 'Don't be so harsh.' Monty's leaning against the hallway wall. His usual booming voice is weak as he chastises Shay, more like a mewing cat.

'I knew not to trust her.' Shay spits. 'No one comes a hundred levels down.'

There's so much venom in Shay's words, more than Harriet's ever known. When Anthony shouted at her, he was cruel but there was passion there, love disguised as scorn. In Shay, there's nothing but vile hate laced with ridicule. A mocking contempt that punches harder than a fist.

Harriet rounds her shoulders forwards as she stands and takes Oliver's hand, hoping he hasn't been listening. His smile is still fixed, though his brows knit with worry.

'Are you okay, Mum?'

There's a tut, more like a hiss from Shay.

'Yes, darling,' Harriet says to Oliver as she puts on his coat. 'But we have to go.'

She steps past Monty and Shay, dragging Oliver behind her and he says his polite goodbyes. Monty calls after her but she keeps walking, not looking back, keeping her pace quick as if her tears will catch up with her, as if she can outrun her shame.

'Wait!' Theo's breathless call comes from behind as he runs to catch up.

Harriet slows to a stop, her head hanging low, then turns to face him.

'Sorry,' he says as he closes the gap. 'I was at the shop. I just heard.'

'I'm sorry. I really am. I didn't know it would use that much electricity.'

Theo waves his hand, dismissing her concern. 'Don't worry about the electric. It'll come back on later. And ignore Shay. She's not a morning person, especially when there's no hot water. And you know what Monty's like. A grudge never lasts longer than a coffee.' He crouches to peer at Oliver. 'He is really lifelike. I get why you're attached.'

He stands again and gives Harriet a tight half-smile, one of pity rather than wrath, but still, it gets her back up. She never wanted pity. She wanted acceptance. But she can't cherry-pick niceties when they're so few and far between. And Theo called Oliver *he*. Not *it*.

'That refuge,' Theo says. 'I think you won't be the only one with, you know, a kid like Oliver. But probably still keep it quiet. I've got some tech friends who have fixed some parts. If you need anything, then you've got my number. I'll pop by 4 and say hi in a few days. It's really good to see you.'

Harriet relaxes a little when Theo reaches forward and rubs her arm. 'Thanks, Theo. I really appreciate it. And I really am sorry.'

They say their goodbyes and Harriet and Oliver walk towards the nearest lift. She's knotted with tension, a coiled spring. Despite Theo's understanding, shame heats her face. She's sure everyone's looking at her, staring at Oliver, calling her son a fake and her a fake mother. She glances down at Oliver, as sweet as ever and oblivious to her embarrassment. That's one emotion he's never learned to copy. He's rarely observed it. Up on the higher levels, everyone owns it, no one gets embarrassed.

She watches the other children skipping along with their parents, kicking some rubbish and weaving through the crowds, playing tag and getting in a tangle around people's feet. The parents laugh, chastise, pick them up when they fall and quell the tears when they threaten to come.

Harriet forces herself to look away, glowering at the ground instead. Those parents and children aren't humiliated or ridiculed. It doesn't seem fair. Her eyes go to her son, and he looks up at her with his sincere blue ones that light up even the darkest corner of the lower levels. Those eyes reveal so much yet still hide his thoughts. Because he does think, she knows he does. There's a mind and soul behind those eyes that ponders and thinks and feels. And didn't Descartes say, *I think, therefore I am?*

Oliver *is.*

Why should she feel embarrassment or shame? Because Oliver is different? Why should she be judged? Surely, love is love. A parent is a parent, regardless of whether their child is different. She performed Shakespeare for an audition once, more than once, she's always been enchanted by Shakespeare, but one audition comes to mind now, when she chose Helena's speech from a *Midsummer Night's Dream*. She still remembers snippets of that monologue. Helena may have been talking about Demetrius, but the sentiment holds true for a mother and her son. Shakespeare understood all those centuries ago that love doesn't have to comply with rules. *Love looks not with the eyes but with the mind . . . Nor hath Love's mind of any judgment taste.*

A fizz of anger replaces her shame, and she holds her head a little higher, grits her teeth and prepares to glare at anyone who looks at Oliver with anything but adoration. She will not be humiliated by her love for her son.

'Mum,' Oliver says. 'What does lifelike mean?'

Her stomach drops, her mouth running dry. He still doesn't know. Somehow, with everything he's learned, he hasn't pieced the puzzle together. 'It means . . . it means . . .' She searches for the right words, the phrase she could use to explain how special he is, how unique. How much he's loved. 'It means you are. That's all. You are real.'

Chapter 21

There's a time in every childhood where they question what is and what isn't, what comes after and what came before. Self-awareness is something that children grow into, like a wriggling baby discovering his toes, their first dazed stares in the mirror, when they learn that closing their eyes doesn't stop them being seen.

Oliver is just the same, Harriet tells herself. His self-awareness journey is a little off compared to other children. That's all, Harriet reasons with herself all the way to the refuge. Lifelike is a word. Every child asks to have words explained. It doesn't mean that child is any less real. Oliver's hand is warm in hers. His footsteps scuffle along walkways and he smiles at the other children. His place is beside her in this world, just like a son.

Level 4 isn't all that different from 5. A little darker, the level above a touch lower. Uncharged abandoned bicycles still litter the walkways, the parks are busy, and the stench from the landfill below only whips up in clouds rather than the endless fog of rot on 2. The advertising billboards are lit in places so she knows there's electricity somewhere.

The refuge has a high fence with barbed wire around the top. Harriet can't imagine Anthony being able to scale that thing so as malicious as it appears, there's comfort in knowing she'd be the other side of it, penned in as much as he is out. There's an intercom by the gate and she buzzes, waiting. When a woman walks out of the plain brick building and approaches the gate, she smiles at Oliver first, then looks at Harriet with expectant, raised brows but says nothing. Harriet lifts her top to show her bruises. The purple outlines of fingerprints don't require an explanation.

The gates open, the woman looking past Harriet and to anyone in close vicinity, shutting the doors quickly as soon as Harriet and Oliver are inside.

'Welcome,' she says. 'You're safe here.' She has a kind face, crisscrossed with lines that must tell a hundred stories of hurt.

Harriet exhales, a slow breath as if all of her trauma, all of her pain, is being pushed from her lungs. All the hate and violence in the world is now on the other side of a barbed wire fence. She's not going to cry in front of Oliver. She sniffs instead, swallows, then puts her hand on her chest to steady her lungs. 'Thank you,' Harriet says, her weak voice not much more than a whisper. 'Thank you.'

Harriet follows her into the building like an imprinted duckling. Inside, the noise hits her. Laughing children, crying children, a TV on too loud blaring out cartoons, a game somewhere, children's music tinny and high-pitched coming from a scratchy speaker.

Two children, immersed in their game, cut in front of her, laughing an apology as they carry on running.

Oliver's grip on her hand loosens, as if he's about to run off too and join in. She pulls him back, her arms twitching, her heart picking up its pace. All these children, all these parents, they might notice Oliver is different.

Theo said he thinks there are others. She scans the children for signs, for clothes slipping down revealing charging sockets, for the ones obviously not eating, the ones too well behaved. It's impossible to tell, even as a parent of a MechaniKid. That offers her some comfort. If she can't tell, surely no one will know about Oliver.

The woman reassures her the gate is secure, though warns her not to open it unless the coast is clear. There's a panic button that alerts the local police if they need it. 'It's the one thing the police are good for down here,' she says.

She shows Harriet to a bed. Harriet thanks her and tries to hide her disappointment. It's dormitory rooms, since they're so busy. Ten beds share this space. And there's not a plug socket.

'Make yourself at home,' she says. 'Meals are at seven, midday and six. There are snacks for the children in the canteen, tea and coffee. Curfew is at eleven. If you need to be back later than that for work or . . . anything, please let us know in advance.'

Harriet thanks her and before she leaves, Rosa, she says her name is, and she puts her hand on Harriet's shoulder, tells her she's safe, and there's a counsellor if she needs it.

All the other beds are messily made, slept-in sheets hastily pulled over the mattresses, books on the bedside table fanned open at the last page, pyjamas piled up on pillows. On some, women sit with their children, playing with toys or reading dog-eared books. She notes the bruises on the other women, the same fingerprints she wears, the yellow-purple streaks on some of the children too.

The other women give her a nod, and Harriet whispers a hello, before she and Oliver sit on her bed. There's a much smaller one next to hers. A perfectly sized bed for Oliver. She lies down and Oliver snuggles into her, his hair tickling her nose, still smelling of vanilla. She wants to scream and cry, wants to cut and bleed out all the badness inside. She hugs him so tightly he has to wriggle free, yet still she has a desire to squash him, not to hurt him but to shrink away with him, to shrivel up and live among the carpet fibres and dust mites. If they were that small, the world would be safer. If they were that small, they could hide.

How has her life come to this? She once dreamed of bettering herself, of having a family, of being able to do more than just scrape by. Escaping life below ground wasn't meant to be her limit. She was going to be on the stage and in movies. Her dreams shattered years ago, but she didn't see the damage for so long. Up on 107, she was living in the clouds. Now all alone, in a place so full of misery, reality hits like a solid wall. Everything she's touched in her life is broken. She's crushed.

There's a bookshelf at the end of the dorm. It's mostly books too young for Oliver, but she has nothing else to entertain him. She chooses one about a dog and he takes his time, savouring the activity. Harriet leaves it with him while she fetches some water and finds a toilet. The other children are mostly tantruming and chaotic, but as she walks slowly through the dorm and then the living room, she slows her pace and watches the other children a little more carefully. There's the odd child, well-behaved with curious eyes, taking in the scene as if learning behavioural traits from the others, only when they cry, it's all crocodile tears.

Meals are served in a canteen down the hall. On her way there, she scans the walls for plug sockets but sees none. The food is basic, but she can't face going out for food today. She watches for the other children not eating, not turning their nose up as fussy children can do, but not needing to eat. There's a few, she's sure of it. She avoids staring, knowing how self-conscious those mothers must be already and hoping that no one has yet noticed Oliver's traits.

She takes food for Oliver so as not to alert attention, but then eats his share in secret. She'll skip dinner to make up for it, she decides as guilt heats her for cheating the system.

When night arrives, rechargeable lights are lit, offering a dim orange glow through the dorm. There's a torch in her bedside table and she lights the ceiling, showing Oliver how to make shadow puppets. He laughs at her rabbit, loves it when she makes a bat, and tries to copy them himself. All the while she has one thought: how to charge Oliver.

It's a few hours before he'll be depleted, so she grabs their coats and they walk outside into the frigid air. There's already frost forming. In some places, she wonders if it even thawed from the night before. She didn't notice it this morning. She was so riled and hot with humiliation. Now that her mind is tasked with nothing except her son's charge, her whole body shivers as she walks, as if the frost is gnawing at her insides.

She's no real idea what she's looking for. She doesn't dare ask the other women in the refuge in case she's wrong but if she's not, they must be charging their children somewhere. Perhaps there's a bar that has plug sockets or an office building that's left open overnight. There might be some dodgy pylon or an empty house.

People collect around the low wattage streetlights, huddled against the cold, some doing work and reading, others sewing up clothes and fixing gadgets, using the little bit of free lighting that's available. The billboards attract the biggest crowds. It's a clever lure. When people need the light, the only place they can stand is by a huge advert. A type of hat, it says, is this week's must-have. Some fluffy green thing with fleece lining. All other hats should be thrown away in favour of this one.

The shadows cast by the groups shade out much of the pavement and Harriet and Oliver walk in semi-darkness. The odd silhouettes of other pedestrians walking keep her on high alert and her grip on Oliver's hand tightens. She looks at him, checking his appearance, his coordination, for signs he's getting tired. His coat is clean, maybe too clean, but it's buttoned up and his scarf wrapped around his neck as if he would feel the cold. She makes a mental note to crease up his coat later.

Rounding a corner, the streetlights flicker, straining with their lack of electric. The old bulbs probably produce more heat than light. The streets here are quiet. No one bothers to try working under the annoying flicker. Harriet can hear their own footsteps, their echo hitting the walkway fencing and reverberating back. She checks over her shoulders, as does Oliver, and she wishes they could glide, to tread silently over the crunchy walkway.

A million what-ifs come to mind as she dreads so many outcomes. What if the bad men from 2 are around? What if there's no electricity tonight? How will she ever get Oliver charged again if he runs flat? And if he does run out of battery, someone will surely notice he's a MechaniKid and he'll be stolen. Her breath races and her heart hammers to catch up. She holds her chest, as if to squash her lungs and steady herself. She counts her breaths in, exhaling more slowly.

'Are you okay, Mum?'

'Yes, darling. I'm fine. Don't you worry about me.'

Oliver worrying about her fills her with more concern than almost anything. He deserves to feel nothing but carefree joy and happiness. Her filling him with worry makes her heart ache more than her stupid panic attack does.

They pass a strip of bars, all with neon lights and blacked-out windows. The sort of places Shay spoke about. Harriet knows inside there will be higher paying booths where touching is defi-

nitely expected. It's a lucrative enough trade when you've nothing else to sell. And why the hell not? she thinks. She worked
in places before, when she was young and poor and infinitely
more attractive. There's no shame in using what you've got. The
stigma comes from man-centric attitudes of ownership and a
desire for innocence. Despite her lack of judgement in the trade,
she hopes it doesn't come to that. But then, she's been renting
out her body to Anthony for so long, it doesn't even feel like
hers anymore.

She spots it then, in the half-light around the back of a bar.
The shadow of a child. A little girl, same height as Oliver, her
braided hair in ribbons. Harriet can barely make her out between the bar wall and the sacks of rubbish waiting to be tossed
over the fence.

Harriet holds her breath, waits, then takes a tentative step
forward.

'Delilah, you just sit there,' a voice behind the rubbish sacks
says.

Another step forward. Just one, and Harriet cranes her neck
to get a better view around the corner. She sees the white box
with green circles, hard to make out on the dim night but she
knows what it is. An e-bike charging port. But that can't work.
The e-bikes all lie depleted across the walkways.

But she sees it. The little girl sits and leans forward, exposing
her hip, exactly where her charging point would be. There's the
shadow of a woman's hand, the outline of cable.

'Hey!' Harriet says quietly as she skulks over, skimming the wall to avoid the glare of the light.

The woman jolts upright, takes a step back and holds out a knife in front of her. 'Leave us alone!'

Harriet raises one hand to show it's empty, still with Oliver's in her other. 'I'm not going to hurt you. My son, he needs charging also.'

The woman appears like she's lived low down all her life. Her back is arched despite her defensive pose, the dry flakes of her skin catching the light. Her eyes, like black holes in the night, narrow and look at Oliver. 'Well, find another point.'

'I don't know where to go,' Harriet pleads. 'These work? I thought the e-bikes don't.'

'The bikes don't charge, because we use up all the electricity to charge our children.'

Children. Harriet notes the word. Not bot or MechaniKid. The woman's eyes soften as she looks at her little girl, a protective arm hovering over her. She's a mother, like Harriet.

'Are you . . .' Harriet swallows and takes a slow step forward. The woman doesn't retreat anymore and lowers her knife. 'Are you on the run, with your kid? You've taken her from TRI? There are others?'

The woman pockets the knife and bends to finish plugging in her daughter. When the little girl's eyes close, the woman smooths back her hair and rearranges her ribbons. In her face, any animosity is gone. Harriet sees only tenderness and care. 'Some of us are on the run. The rest just need to charge and keep them going to bank the cash. They think they'll give them up like that—' she clicks her fingers '—when the five years is up. But they won't. Most of them won't anyway. They don't yet see how impossible that will be.'

Harriet nods and puts her hands on Oliver's shoulders. She never imagined there were others like her. For years she thought she was going mad or that her bond with Oliver is something unique, somehow sourced from her own history of loss. But these children are loveable, and real, little souls trapped in the inner workings of robotics. Of course other parents would love them as much.

'Yours stolen too?' the woman asks.

'Yep.'

'How long you got with him until he degrades?'

Harriet pulls her chin in, knits her brow, then puts her hands over Oliver's ears. 'Degrades?'

The woman's face mimics Harriet's in surprise. 'You don't know?'

Harriet recalls Andrea saying about parts. But parts can be replaced. Theo said he knew techies who've fixed a few. Surely, Oliver won't just expire. 'I'm prepared to get some parts replaced. I expected that—'

'It's not the parts. You really haven't heard?'

Harriet continues to look blankly at the woman.

'Around five years, they just start to degrade. Some get certain parts fixed, which might help, so you'll need to find someone. My Delilah here is only three and I've had to have some wiring redone already. I'm dreading when she gets to five. These kids, they're new tech. It's not like parts can just be scavenged. They're only designed to last five years. How old is your son?'

'Four and a half,' Harriet says, rounding down a couple of months.

'Shit.' She grimaces. 'Sorry to be the bearer of bad news. I'm sure you'll figure something out. There are techies everywhere working on this.'

Oliver wriggles away from Harriet's hands and rubs his ears. She hadn't realised how hard she'd been squeezing. 'Thank you,' she says to the woman.

'There are other charging ports around. If you put him on standby, he'll charge quicker. So, good luck.'

Harriet takes Oliver's hand again and walks away, each footstep slow and heavy, as if it's her who needs charging. She finds another bike charger a little way down the road around the back of a closed shop. It takes eight hours for a full charge, so she'll be arriving back at the refuge at two a.m. Three hours past curfew. She just hopes that won't cost her their bed.

After nearly five hours of worrying, dozing, and staring into the darkness, she decides being late back on her first night isn't worth the risk, and she takes Oliver back to the refuge, hoping he's charged enough.

They sprint back and after taking a wrong turn, they arrive at the refuge at ten past eleven.

The night worker looks at Harriet with more sympathy than scorn, and reminds her of the curfew as Harriet apologises, promising it won't happen again. Sneaking through to the dorm, tiptoeing all the way, she still manages to disturb some of the other women. They must suspect she's on the game, Harriet thinks, as she struggles to think of another reason why she'd be hurrying back so late.

When she gets into bed, she fumbles in her handbag to find something she can use to switch Oliver on standby again. In her bag, gold chains spill from their boxes and jingle with the sound she can't excuse as being anything other than something valuable. There's a grunt from another resident who turns over in her bed to face the other way. That noise was heard. Could the jewellery get stolen? After finding the clasp of the necklace that she used on Oliver's standby button earlier, she puts her handbag under the duvet, keeping her arm looped through the strap.

Oliver sits on the edge of the bed, so silently, so well-behaved. She kisses his forehead and turns him on standby. His eyelids drift closed and rather than lie him on the cot, she keeps him next to her, snuggling in behind him. His little body is still warm but then, her son's embrace is always as warm as she can be. He's three hours down on charging, but hopefully several hours on standby will conserve his battery.

She runs her fingers through his hair and wills him to be okay. Thoughts of degradation are too much to consider right now. She can only take one day at a time.

Sleep eludes her for some time, and she wishes she had a standby button too. As she lies, she stares up at the ceiling, remembering, worrying, reconciling. Dark thoughts of loss and despair niggle at her mind. When she first moved in with Anthony, his apartment was all grey and dark wood. He didn't protest too much when she bought colourful artworks to hang on the walls. The world needs colour, she said. The world needs light. Snuggling next to Oliver in the bleak room, she can chase those dark thoughts away. Being with Oliver is like being surrounded by colour. 'It's you and me, Mum,' he said to her when they decided to leave. That's the thought she has now to calm her turbulent mind. To chase away the dark.

'It's you and me, Oliver.'

The dorm room is ajar and, making their way to the adjacent dorm are other women just arriving home. It's not just her who's late. Night workers, probably. MechaniKid mums, very likely. She catches the end of a shadow of a child that walks into the next dorm alone. A shadow of braided hair tied up in ribbons.

Chapter 22

The play area of the refuge is busy all day with children. There's a constant cacophony of tears and screams, laughter, and excited yelps. Most of the toys are a little young for Oliver, but he enjoys watching the other children and laughs along with them. Outside the window, a rare beam of light shines through. It must be hot on the top levels, cloudless, with that piercing sun she grew to love.

She sits on the sofa while Oliver picks up a book with mostly pictures, then reads it to a toddler who sits sucking his thumb. Oliver does the voices like Harriet always did. She never reads to him anymore. He's too good for that now. Theo came to visit yesterday and gave Oliver some books and toys. They're now added to the pile in the living area. Oliver never thought to keep them for himself. He wanted all the children to enjoy them.

Harriet leans back on the chair as she watches, the shredded upholstery spilling some of its contents as she does. The room is filled with a hodgepodge of furniture, most weather-beaten and wonky. On a chair on the other side of the room, some more crafty occupants sew up holes as they chat, pausing their work occasionally to sip tea or to stop their children crawling away.

Harriet pushes the sofa stuffing back in. It has crooked feet that cause it to wobble when she leans over and the headrest hangs to one side. Both flaws most likely the result of landing at ground level after being tossed down several storeys when it was thrown out by an upper level. There's a patchwork of stitching down one side where Harriet can imagine it was ripped by more trash landing on top. It's not in bad condition, really. If the below ground scavengers had found it first, they would have snapped it up.

She's spoken with some of the other mothers briefly. There seems to be an unwritten rule about what's not okay to ask. No one mentions what level they lived at before. No one asks about the men they're running from. They mostly talk about the children and any work they've found. The women either have hardened faces or weep non-stop. Harriet assumes one eventually turns into the other and wonders how she fits into that scale.

One woman has twins, two identical little girls with pale blonde hair and eyes almost as blue as Oliver's. Besides that, all the women have only one child, as if having one child with a monster taught them enough of a lesson not to have a second.

There's one little boy whose smile screams mischief, and he has the kind of ears that look like he'll grow into them. His mother despairs of his behaviour, but Harriet laughs and based on the scars and cuts the mother has, it's a wonder the little boy has such a lust for life. There's a little girl who never interacts with any of the other children. She's painfully shy, looking at the floor when another child tries to play with her. Her mum barely pays her any attention, too consumed by her own tears. Perhaps she thinks ignoring her will bring her out of her shell.

Harriet longs to hug that little girl, to tell her she's safe. But that would be overstepping. Oliver tries, though. Children don't have the same boundaries. He has no understanding of taboo. Why do people grow out of such behaviours? At what age do people start to overthink their affection and worry more about others' perception than their own kindness? She hopes Oliver never does. There's an innate goodness to a caring child, in their desire only to fill another with joy and not be concerned about any reward. He hands the little girl toys and books and with her gaze still low, she accepts. She looks about six, the same age as Oliver is meant to appear, but mentally she seems far behind.

When Oliver sits alone, having attempted to befriend all the children with mixed success, Harriet calls him over.

'Shall we go outside, Monkey? We haven't checked out the climbing frame yet.'

He jumps to his feet, his eyes twinkling. 'Yes!'

Harriet still hasn't plucked up the courage to speak to Delilah's mother, but she spots her sitting in the corner as they leave.

'Do you and Delilah want to join us?'

Now she can see her features properly, Harriet notices Delilah's mother is an older mother, perhaps ten years older than Harriet, with the kind of face Harriet wouldn't talk back to. Her brows hang in a natural frown, her mouth almost permanently downturned. When Delilah shows her warmth and affection, that downturned mouth twitches slightly, as if trying to remember how to smile.

She nods and calls Delilah over.

'Hi, Delilah,' Harriet says when she smiles, holding her hand out to shake. Delilah looks at it, tilts her head to the side, then takes hold. Harriet gives it a gentle shake and next time, Delilah knows exactly what to do. She is very much like Oliver was a couple of years ago, when he was still figuring out so many things. He still is, always, but the basics of hand shaking he nailed a long time ago.

On the walk to the park, Harriet learns the woman is called Amber, and she adopted Delilah three years ago.

From Amber, Harriet doesn't find any sort of laughter or easy chat, but a guarded, considered conversation. She's authentic, Harriet notices with admiration. If Harriet wasn't always trying to fake it, she too would be more like Amber. Harriet doesn't ask why she's taken her, or any other personal information. They talk only of the joy their children bring them, and of their fear of being discovered.

'Make sure you take him to the showers,' Amber says. 'Or else you'll either be shunned for having a dirty kid or found out.'

Harriet nods, 'Right.'

'And food—'

'I always say Oliver has allergies.'

'That's good. But some of the others are really nosey. They'll know if you stay in all day and don't feed him. So fake that too.'

The children are on the climbing frame. There's two in this park, one for Oliver's size, and a much bigger one for the older children. At the bottom rungs of the smaller frame, Oliver encourages Delilah to take hold and make it to the next one.

'He's a good kid,' Amber says.

'As is Delilah. She really listens.'

Harriet notices Amber bristle, as if Delilah paying attention is a bad thing.

'She does what she's told. Too easily. I need to make her understand she doesn't have to.'

Goosebumps prickle Harriet's arms. She too was raised to be obedient, subservient, to be a meek little girl who does as she's told. She doesn't ask Amber questions. In Amber, she sees the faraway stare of trauma, of eyes that can't unsee their past. Delilah has the cutest face, round cheeks and a rosebud mouth, big eyes and thick lashes that scream of guileless innocence. She's too young to have known horror, too innocent to deserve it.

Delilah reaches the second level on the climbing frame, and Oliver gives her a clap.

'Well done, Delilah!' he says with animated enthusiasm.

Harriet's eyes are glued on them always, but out of the corner, she notices Amber's gaze isn't solely on Delilah. She scans the edges, the periphery, the faces of everyone else. Harriet's always been on the lookout for dangers that could harm Oliver, but dangers meant falls and sharp objects. Up on the higher levels when she wasn't on the run, danger was a tactile thing, something she could plan for.

Her eyes drift from Oliver as she too searches around. In a place where she's so alone, so poor, trying to hide, the dangers are everywhere.

Chapter 23

Harriet spends a few weeks seeking out work. It's not enough to find a bar. If it were, she'd have found work easily. On 4, there are late night bars but none as late night as on 3. And a level down means she's less likely to get spotted by someone from the refuge. But then, on 3, e-bike charging points are fewer.

Down one level and a little east, Harriet finds the strip of bars where she worked as a teenager. No one will recognise her from those days if, indeed, any of her old punters and colleagues are still alive and local. The people may have changed, but the area hasn't. It's the same strip, with its flickering neon lights and smoky atmosphere, the stench of stale beer and piss. The low-level ground is potholed and gravelly. There's rubbish landing at the edges of walkways that leaves the ground a mishmash of trip hazards of metal spikes, old food packets, and gelatinous puddles.

After weeks of zigzagging around the walkways, searching for the ideal place, she finds a bar less than an hour's journey from the refuge, with a functioning e-bike charging port located behind a pile of rubbish sacks out back. Oliver could charge there while she works nights, her shift late enough that he'll be concealed by the dark. It's a jungle-themed bar and an absolute dive. Jungle-themed is what the management calls it, but that seems like code for fetish bar. Body paint replaces clothes for many of the staff and customers alike. A few squares of fabric conceal what the bar isn't licensed to have on show. Besides that, little is left to the imagination. Harriet was surprised they offered the likes of her a job, but she knows staff turnover must be high. She probably doesn't look as unappealing as she thinks. She's just not what she used to be.

Harriet buys herself a butterfly outfit. A velvet bodysuit that would have looked much more flattering a pregnancy ago and maybe a decade prior, but she squeezes herself into it and a pair of contouring tights. The sequined wings are wide, which should help deflect any wandering hands reaching for her upper body. The bar also isn't licensed for such manoeuvres, though she knows for the right price down on 3, everything is for sale.

She arrives at six p.m. and works until two a.m. four nights a week. There's scope for more nights if she proves herself a good employee. She still has some jewellery left, and she hasn't yet started on her pot of cash from TRI in her account. That's for when she's sure it's safe, when Anthony would have given up looking for her and TRI have written Oliver off as a loss. For now, those hours are sufficient.

At work, she giggles and smiles, putting on a show. She serves drinks to seedy punters and engages in conversation, teasing them for tips. There are the usual hits of recognition. Not from the posters but from her movie days. It's her voice more than her appearance. Though no one ever assumes it's her. They always say something about how similar she looks. Because, surely, such a promising young actress wouldn't have let herself go this much.

She laughs all night, throwing her head back, touching her décolletage as she pouts and listens to their gripes and desires. When punters are inappropriate, she rebuffs them but maintains her flirty face and holds her hand out for cash. Her skin crawls often, a judder shakes her body as if trying to shed her skin, to shake off the filth that crawls over her, to blink away the constant sights of debauchery. She's become a prude in recent years. In her previous life, she wouldn't have even noticed half the sights she now sees.

But none of that is important. A mother must do such things for her child.

The tips are low but plentiful for the right staff who smile sweetly and nurse the punters' egos. It's not all low-level dwellers who frequent bars on 3. Rich men from higher up often travel down to not get recognised or because they 'like a bit of rough,' they often say. Or because they're too tight to pay the entry fees for bars higher up.

Every night when she arrives for work, she scans the faces of the punters for Anthony. She's almost sure he'd never bother to venture so low down, almost sure he won't be bothering to look for her. He'd rather save face than try to entice her back. But just in case, she scans. All her bruising from him has gone now. The lumpy scar from where he broke her arm will remain for life, though, and her mental scars too. Those will never fade. If someone grabs her attention by tapping on her shoulder, she whips around, sometimes too quickly, spilling drinks more than once. Her nerves are in tatters, but she smiles it away and manages to pocket enough each night.

The refuge moves her to a dorm down the corridor specifically for night workers. There's no judgement when she tells them. Why is it she feels she deserves more judgement than she receives? When she was fifteen and first started working in bars, she felt no shame. She was doing what she had to do. Perhaps now, because such work is the result of a drop down from so many levels up instead of the crawl up from below, she feels worse for it. Her high life snobbery still lingers when she looks in the mirror. She tells herself again and again, she is still a woman doing what she has to do.

Her new dorm is a room for ten mothers and their children, same as the previous one. There's a window that's blacked out to stop any hint of daylight coming through and waking those who need to sleep during the day. Underneath the window, someone has ironically written: *It is during our darkest moments that we must focus to see the light. – Aristotle.*

Among the nine other families in her new dorm is Amber and Delilah, much to Oliver's delight. At least that's one family she doesn't have to be careful around.

After work each night, she washes the glitter off her face, changes into flat shoes, then unplugs Oliver and switches him on. His eyelids open and a smile takes over when he wakes and she's there, gazing upon him.

She pulls him in for a hug and stands. 'Blimey! You're as heavy as an elephant!'

'No, you're as heavy as an elephant!' he says with a laugh.

She nuzzles into his messy hair. 'You smell like an elephant.'

'No, you smell like an elephant!'

She tickles him until his laughing reaches a crescendo. The sound of his laugh is what she needs to cleanse away all the seediness of her job. It adds more value to her life than any of the tips she receives. She puts him down and they walk home. At this hour, the shadows stand out more than the light. Every movement and sound makes her jump and spin around. She tries to hide her unease from Oliver, not wanting him to ever know what it is to be afraid, but he watches as always, and his eyes scan the shadows too.

Fully charged and wide awake, he's always brimming with questions. 'Why is it dark?' 'What happens in a bar?' 'Can we go to the park today?' 'Can we play when we get home or read a book?'

His ceaseless questions fill the night with joy rather than fear. On 3, the smell of decay is significant. Smoke from incinerators forms wispy clouds that float over them every few steps. When the streets are quiet, she can hear the fires crackling.

Every night she's afraid, and every night when she gets into her dorm bed and puts Oliver on standby, she's filled with gratitude and relief.

One more day with her boy. One more night being safe.

Chapter 24

Working alternate nights means Harriet can fully charge Oliver, then when she sleeps, he's on standby and with that arrangement, she can just about make one charge last two days. Sometimes she has to tell him to relax or put him down for a nap a few hours before she goes to work. She fidgets with the guilt of it, of how much of his life he's missing out on, but perhaps less waking time will mean he degrades more slowly, though she isn't sure, and the snippets of conversation she manages with Amber don't offer much information. There's so much Amber doesn't know. All MechaniKid mums are feeling their way in the dark. There's no manual for going it alone without the presence of TRI. Oliver and the other MechaniKids aren't simply different from other children. They're brand new as well as different and so there's no certainty.

They settle into their routine, Harriet remembering to do everything with Oliver a real boy would need. She takes him to the shower when she washes, dampens his hair and sponges down his legs so he leaves wet footprints when they leave. He has the most perfect feet. Where his hands were made with uneven cuticles and nails, his feet were crafted to perfection. His toes are like tiny little sausages and when she sponges them it takes all her willpower not to nibble them. He's ticklish there, just like she is, and he chuckles over the slightest touch.

One afternoon, Oliver plays with the other children and one of the little boys spills Ribena all over himself and his mother helps him change his clothes. Oliver stares at the boy's bare backside, his smooth skin, and his obvious lack of charging port, then presses his hand into his own. Harriet is always so careful when Oliver changes his clothes, shielding that part of him from the prying eyes of other mothers. Some probably think she's prude or coddling, but a few other mothers do the same, including Amber. Harriet clocks eye contact with Amber when Oliver's gaze falls on that little boy. He doesn't say anything, but Harriet's sure there's some acknowledgement there. Oliver's starting to realise more and more he's different.

Amber sits on the chair next to Harriet and leans in close. 'You not had that conversation yet?'

'Nope. You?'

'No.'

Harriet swallows and rubs her temples. 'How do I even broach something like that? He's starting to notice. There have been questions.'

'When you do, let me know. Reckon I've got a year or so before Delilah gets that curious.'

Delilah tilts her head as much as Oliver used to, her eyes scanning every scene. It's strange to watch that again, remembering how Oliver used to be. He advances quickly but the day-to-day changes have still crept up on Harriet. Without physical growth, his advancements are subtle, but he's leaps ahead of Delilah.

'Can I ask,' Harriet says to Amber, 'why take her now? You could have had a few years of safety, of having TRI thinking you'll take her back.'

'Because I want to raise her as my own, not what they want her to be.' Amber stretches out her fingers, balls them into fists, then stretches them out again as she tightens her jaw. 'You know they have categories for the children? They're pre-programmed to be a certain way. I had an inkling as to what her programming is, and I want to undo that, to teach her to stand up for herself.'

'Really? I was just told to teach him empathy.'

'Yeah. For the boys, that's the norm. But for the pretty girls, let's just say they're wanting them raised to be meek and obedient. To please. It doesn't take a genius what sort of work they'd have Delilah in once she's older. They wouldn't even let me go in the testing room with her.'

'I was with Oliver the entire time during his tests. Why on Earth—'

'I've no idea what her tests involved but I can imagine. God, I wish I couldn't imagine. I don't want to think about it. I can't. If I asked Delilah afterwards, she'd say she passed, that she's a good girl, and that was the most important thing.' Amber's face reddens as she talks, her eyes bore into her daughter, narrow and fierce, as if she would kill someone who tried to harm her.

Harriet looks at Delilah's pretty, innocent face, tears brimming as she tries to fight away images from her own childhood, her own years where she was expected to please. TRI, the biggest tech company in the world, is capable of such crimes. She inwardly chastises herself for believing anything else. Profit is all they care about. They won't give a toss about the children.

'Delilah is better than that,' Amber says. 'I'm not raising her to lead that sort of life. She should have a choice and be able to stand up for herself. I don't know if I can undo her programming, but I'm certainly not going to condition her to any more of that nonsense.'

'You're a good mum.' Harriet gives Amber's arm a squeeze. 'I know there are people who would judge us, but if the world was made up of parents as devoted as us, this world would be a better place.'

Amber's stern mouth gives way to a hint of a smile. 'Ain't that the truth.'

A scuffle breaks out among some children that snaps Harriet's attention. Unkind words are said, one child pushes another. Harriet pulls Oliver to one side, as the parents of the other children split them up. There are tears and Oliver cries as well, his chest jerking and his balled fists rubbing his dry eyes, and his cheeks redden. Harriet sits him on her lap, rocks him gently, and soothes him.

'There, there, sweetheart. It's just a silly fight. The children are all okay.'

'I...I...I...' His words come out as if he's hyperventilating. 'I'll never understand it, Mum, how some people can be so unkind to others.'

'It's human nature,' she says. 'It's just the way some people are. Not all people, not all the time. Children are still learning how to be kind.'

He buries his face into her chest, holding her as if he thinks he'll fall off. 'But why? I would never do that.'

She rubs his back. 'No, my darling. You wouldn't.'

Chapter 25

Theo is visiting one day with some more books for Oliver. They're all books with only words, no pictures anymore. Books filled with tales of adventurous children and fantastical creatures. Oliver's eyes light up at the covers and even more so when he looks inside and sees how long the stories are. Oliver's reading age is twice that of the age he appears. In the refuge, the other mothers often look upon him with his books, slack-jawed and wide-eyed as Harriet brims with pride at how clever he is.

Oliver calls him Uncle Theo now and Theo picks him up, swings him around, and listens to Oliver's stories of insects and birds and climbing frames. With a little sadness in his voice, he says he's still not tall enough to go on the bigger climbing frame but hopes to one day. Theo locks eyes with Harriet when he says this, sharing a silent conversation as he realises Oliver still believes he's going to grow.

They walk outside, wrapped in jackets and scarfs, the cold air biting. Oliver has a woolly hat with a bobble on top and he runs at full speed when the park comes into view, tripping over and flying forwards, landing on his hands.

'Oliver!' Harriet and Theo run to him. He's standing again before they've reached him, his knees and gloves covered in gravel and dust. His face is reddening and his bottom lip trembles as he tries not to cry. If Theo wasn't here, he wouldn't try to be brave and he'd sob his little heart out. Harriet tries to hug him, but he shuffles away.

'I'm fine, Mum,' he says with a strained voice.

Harriet takes his gloves off. It's not too bad, the gloves must have protected him a little. A small patch of skin on each wrist is bunched up, that inky blue colour seeping through already.

'You're so brave!' Theo says, and Oliver lifts his chin a little higher.

Oliver's never had a male figure to look up to, to impress, or to be brave in front of. In that little bit of pride Oliver shows in himself for being brave, Harriet sees a hint of the grown-up he could become. Determined, not afraid, her little survivor. So different from herself as she's always run away from her troubles. In Oliver, she sees the fighter she always failed to be.

***

Over the next couple of weeks, Oliver trips over frequently. Harriet tries to ignore it, dismisses it as childhood clumsiness, and shuts her mind to the glaring reality.

His perfect little hands are constantly crazed with blue-black bruising. For a while after one trip, he complains of his hand not working properly. One mother scowls at her for not taking him to the hospital so Harriet says she does, buying a bandage at a pharmacy and wraps his hand. In the evening, she holds ice to it, claiming the doctor said it was a sprain.

She doubts the ice helped, but his wrist does recover over a few days.

'I'm sure he's just not getting enough charge or losing concentration,' she says to Amber one afternoon after she's patched up another one of Oliver's accidents. 'He's just a clumsy boy. Lots of kids are clumsy.'

Harriet counts the months off in her head. When did they run away? It must be two months by now. Oliver was four and a half, well, four and eight months actually, when she counts more accurately. So it must be four years and ten months since she first took him home.

'Look, Mum,' Delilah says to Amber as she walks over, Oliver just behind, making a mock sulky face. 'I did Oliver's hair.'

Delilah's hair hangs down to her shoulders, kinked from her pigtails, and Oliver has two little bunches tied in ribbons. Harriet and Amber laugh and clap as Oliver rolls his eyes.

'What a wonderful job you've done!' Amber says.

'Can I do Harriet's hair now?'

Harriet delicately removes the ribbons from Oliver's hair, then runs her fingers through it. 'Sure,' she says and hands the ribbons to Delilah. 'I don't see why not.'

Delilah grins and climbs onto the back of the sofa and pulls on Harriet's hair.

'Gently,' Amber says.

Harriet waves her hand to dismiss her concern. 'Don't you worry. Do what you need.'

Delilah moves around the front, her little feet balancing on the sofa cushions. She sticks her tongue out when she's concentrating.

When she's finished, Oliver laughs so much he holds his tummy. 'You look funny, Mum!'

Harriet strokes her hair to feel the bumps and ties. There's no mirror so she can only imagine the mess.

'Will you wear it all day?' Delilah asks.

How can Harriet say no to a face like that? 'Of course I will.'

Delilah grins and she and Oliver go back to the play area to find some toys.

Amber leans in and whispers, 'You might want to take it out if you go outside anywhere.' She laughs.

Harriet laughs with her, but her eyes are solely on Oliver. He's playing just across the room again now, reading a book to Delilah. He reads beautifully and can pronounce any new word he comes across by sounding it out. That's not the skill of a boy who's degrading.

'Think about it,' Amber says. 'Why would they make them last longer than five years? They're meant to be moved into teen bodies after five years. Everything else will get thrown away. That's what those big companies and everyone up top does. They see his body as disposable. They can charge more for the end product that way.'

Everything Amber says makes complete sense. Everything valuable is disposable. Oliver's perfect little body would likely get chucked into landfill along with everything else. What doesn't make sense is that it will happen so quickly, and what really doesn't make sense is that Harriet would just allow it to happen. They're on the lower levels now, where people are less wasteful and things get fixed. People down here are resourceful and they recycle. She's still sure he's just being clumsy, but if there is a chance he's degrading, she'll find a way. Her son is not some throwaway commodity, nor is her love for him.

***

They're walking through a park. It's Oliver's favourite play park on 4. The climbing frame is the highest and has the best slide, he says. He lets go of Harriet's hand and runs to his favourite spot to start his climb. Harriet watches, biting her nails. A habit she had as a child, but her years of manicures while she lived the highlife put a stop to it. Now, she has broken fingernails and, even worse, hangnails. She gnaws at them whenever Oliver's doing anything remotely precarious.

He hooks his legs around the top beam and hangs upside down for a while, waving at Harriet, making sure she's watching. When he rights himself, his grip falters and he falls.

She gasps and runs to him, but he's up and brushing himself off before she's even close.

'I'm fine, Mum. Stop worrying.' He says this with the kind of laugh that tells her he's all bravado.

'Let me just check you.'

'No! I said I'm fine.' His cheeks are red, and he tries to laugh. He hasn't cried in front of her in ages. It's a boy thing, she tells herself. There are other children around. He's just showing off. 'I don't feel that strong today, that's all.'

She tries to hug him, but he shakes himself free, like her affection would add to his embarrassment. Harriet steps back and gives him some space, though feels a yearning for her little boy. It's the first time he's retreated from her embrace. 'It's normal to be a bit tired sometimes,' she says. 'You're still my monkey.'

Oliver watches some bigger children tackling the larger climbing frame and his jaw sets. 'When I'm bigger, I'll be even stronger, then I'll be better.'

She agrees, though her chest caves in as she knows he'll never get any bigger and, somehow, he hasn't figured this out yet.

A boy, a little smaller than Oliver, jogs over. 'Are you okay, Oliver?'

'Yes . . .' he replies, his voice tapering, his bottom lip wobbling.

She takes his hand, and he doesn't resist this time. She leads him away. After a minute, he stops and she crouches to face him.

'I can't remember that boy's name. My head doesn't feel right. Mum, why can't I remember his name?'

His chest rises and falls quickly, as a child would if they were crying. He makes shuddering noises, then blinks as if clearing tears.

Now out of sight of most of the park, Harriet pulls him in for a hug and he leans on her. He's not embarrassed anymore. Her affection is more important than his bravado. 'There, there, darling. It's okay. You're okay. You just bumped your head.'

'I've upset that boy. That boy called . . .' His little body jerks again.

'Everyone forgets things sometimes. It's normal. Don't worry. Come on, let's go home and get you cleaned up. We can read for a bit.'

He sniffs and walks in step with her, his head hanging low. His hand is warm, gripping hers, his skin soft. He's not like some rusty old machine, not like some frozen computer. Her chest tightens, and she presses her free hand to her heart and tries to steady her breaths. He can't be degrading. He just can't.

She thinks of all the times he's been clumsy or forgetful, all the bruises and sulks. He's had to adapt to so much down here. He has so much less space than he used to, and their life with Anthony must have left him with some trauma. Maybe it's the lack of sunshine down here or his sleep schedule. There are a million ways to excuse his change in coordination and cognition. Degradation is just some rumour. Oliver is two months away from his fifth birthday. She's sure TRI want their products to last a little longer than bang on five years. He's not some disposable product like a carton of milk.

As they walk, she dodges some rubbish being thrown down from levels above that falls the wrong side of the fence. Some clothing, a mobile phone that isn't an old model, food still in its packaging. TRI bosses and their engineers no doubt live many, many storeys up. Her back rounds when she realises how disposable they will think everything is. Keeping anything five years is probably excessive to them, as it was to her once.

They turn onto the busy street. She has to go to work this evening, and he's due a charge. Today has been a bust for him and she notices him tripping a little more, scuffing his feet every few steps.

For the millionth time, Harriet reminds herself that keeping Oliver is selfish. He should have the chance to grow up. There'll be a teen body waiting for him with all the upgrades he needs. He wants to be with his mother, but perhaps one day they can find each other again. He deserves the chance to be with other teens, others like him. Here, in this life, he'll always be an outsider.

She checks the time. She's due at work soon. 'Let's go get you all charged up, okay?'

She tries to sound enthusiastic, but it's impossible when she looks at Oliver's crestfallen face, his grazed hands, and her heart aches with the worry that he really might be degrading.

'Harriet?'

Harriet spins around at the sound of her name. It's a reflex response and, for a brief moment, her heart falters at her own stupidity. It could be anyone calling her name, Anthony, someone from TRI. A little relief makes her heart resume its steady pace when she sees it's only Theo.

'I was on my way to the refuge. Just wanted to catch up. You should get a phone. I could call ahead then.'

Harriet hasn't bothered replacing the one she threw away. It's only Theo who would call, so it seems excessive. He visits once a week at least, and between the refuge and the park there are not many places where she'd be. It's good to have her old friend back. When they were kids and Tipher was sick, the three of them would chat into the night for as long as Tipher had the energy. Sometimes, Theo's parents would drop his dinner around, with extra for her and Tipher, of course, since so often her parents didn't bother. She'd write plays for them to perform and they'd pretend they were on the radio doing interviews with famous people. She'd do all the voices, snooty ones for fancy actors and rough drunks for those who required them. Theo taught Tipher to play cards and chess. She sees so much of his kindness now in the way he interacts with Oliver. It's like he's back with Tipher again.

'Monty says hi. He's hoping to come by next week. He even said he'd bake some cookies. And, guess what! Shay is going to move out!'

'Really?'

'Yeah. We keep arguing. She's always been a nightmare, so she says she's had enough. She's looking elsewhere now, but soon there'll be a room for you, if you like?'

That catches Harriet off guard. 'Theo, I don't know. I mean, it would be great, but Shay would know. Others might know. It sounds risky.'

'Okay. Well, have a think about it. No pressure. I'll let you know when she's gone, and then we can see if she stays away. And if she does, then maybe think about it some more. How's Oliver doing?'

They're in line with the edge of the park. Some swings are empty, still swinging lazily from their last user. 'Oliver, sweetie, go back and play. Just take it easy.'

Oliver goes to the swings and sits. He doesn't push off the ground. He just sits, his hands grasping the chains.

With Oliver out of earshot, she steps closer to Theo. 'He's degrading, I think. Actually, if I'm being honest, I don't *think*. I *know.* He's getting so clumsy. He's starting to forget simple things. Degrading is a thing, apparently. He's nearly five now. His parts are old.'

Theo rubs his forehead. 'Shit.'

'I can't lose him,' she says, and her stomach churns as she does. She has lost so much in her life. Oliver too? No. That's unthinkable. There must be something that can be done. In this day and age, with all this technology, there must be an upgrade. 'Do you know anyone?' she asks, her voice sounding more pathetic than ever.

She thinks of Amber's tone, of her dogged determination. How is it Harriet's always so weak? Her parents and Anthony beat it out of her. Yet it's time for her not to run away but to confront the evils that chase her. She looks at her son, his downcast face, and straightens her back.

She takes her breath, inflating her torso a little and faces Theo again. 'I won't let him suffer. I will not just accept that he will degrade. There must be scavengers or salvagers, anyone in tech who might be able to help?'

Theo runs his hand over his slicked-back hair. 'A MechaniKid is way beyond what I would normally work on. But—' His gaze goes briefly over to Oliver and he nods. 'There are better people than me. Not up here, though. Life's a little too easy, even at this shitty level. No one is so desperate for work they need to risk an injunction by TRI. You'll need to go below, and even then I can't promise anything. If it was a dodgy leg or something, then that would be easy. But his entire system degrading is a whole different thing. But I know someone. If anyone can do it, he can.'

Harriet swallows and shakes off a chill. She tenses her muscles and holds her chin higher. 'Below ground. I can do that. Can you give me an introduction?'

'I'm due to stock up on some parts anyway. I've got some deadlines on a fan regeneration at the moment, I need two days. Then, I'm free.'

'Okay,' Harriet says with an exhale. There's no shudder in her breath now. No more chills, no more shakes. It's only below ground. She's been there before. She can do this. 'Two days. Let's do it.'

Chapter 26

Oliver's clumsiness plateaus over the next few days. He trips daily but appears bothered less as he expects it. He seems a little more shy with the other children, like he's scared he'll forget something. There are babies and toddlers around the refuge, and he prefers to spend time with them than with the bigger children. He hasn't been back on the climbing frame yet. Instead, he gazes wistfully at it when they walk past, but can't summon the courage to climb. He'll sit on the swing sometimes, pretending he enjoys it as much when Harriet pushes him. He's lost so much of his daredevil side.

It's been three days since they saw Theo, and Harriet has almost given up. She should have replaced her mobile phone so she can at least check he's still coming. When she sees him walking towards the park in the morning, she kicks herself for doubting him. Theo has never let her down before.

Oliver stands to run to Theo, and one leg gives way. His knees scuff the ground and Harriet picks him up. He shrugs his arm free of her fussing. He doesn't want her reassurances, pushing her away like a toddler having a tantrum.

'Hey, big guy,' Theo says when he reaches them. 'You okay?'

Oliver folds his arms and pulls his chin in, his bottom lip sticking out. 'I'm fine.'

'Okay. And how are you?' he asks Harriet. 'All ready? Sorry I'm a day late. The parts I'm collecting only just arrived.'

'It's no problem and yes, we're all ready! Isn't that right, Oliver?' She hopes her lilting tone might bring Oliver out of his sulk, but no such luck. Oliver's posture bows, his shoulders dropping as if even the thought of their day is wearing him out. He resembles a grumpy teenager more than a six-year-old.

Theo raises his eyebrows, and his forced smile makes Harriet chuckle and shake her head. 'Will he be okay with the stairs?' He leans in and asks quietly. 'The lifts only go as far as ground level still.'

'He'll be fine.'

'Where are we going?' Oliver asks.

'We're going to visit below ground,' Harriet says. 'There's someone there who can fix you.'

'What's wrong with me?'

'Nothing, sweetheart. But there's someone who can make you strong again.'

Oliver's eyes glint with hope. His chest puffs up like a little soldier. 'I want to be strong! Stronger than ever. Stronger than all the boys so I can look after you and stop the bad men like Anthony from ever hurting you.'

Oh, is it possible to love a child more? It's not. It can't be. It's hard to imagine any other mother could love her child as much or any other son being so caring. As much as she loves Oliver, it's her failures as a mother that make her heart race more, make her palms clammy and keep her awake at night.

That look of hope in his eyes plagues her, makes every step laborious as worry saps her energy. What if Theo's friend can't help? What if she's promised too much? She can jot it down to the other untruths she's allowed Oliver to believe. When she was pregnant with Freddie, she told herself she'd never lie to her child. She wouldn't even let him believe Santa Claus was real. Whereas now, what's real and what's not is the biggest lie of all. She hates herself for thinking that way. Oliver is real. He's just not what other people would deem as real.

She swore she'd never subject her child to life below ground, that she'd do whatever it took to keep them in daylight. Now, the irony with Oliver is to keep him, she has to take him there, to the worst place she can imagine.

It's a frosty morning and they walk briskly to try to stay warm, Harriet's hands tucked under her armpits rather than holding Oliver's. He doesn't want to hold her hand today, not in front of Uncle Theo.

They walk to the nearest lift and ride it down to ground level. It judders and squeaks as they get below 2, as if protesting. Even the mechanical parts don't want to go down so low. Once out of the lift, the stairs are right next door. They step outside onto ground level for only seconds, Theo reminding Harriet to cover her face just before they do. The swarm of flies that make up most of the airspace hits them straight away, the buzzing disorientating Oliver. Harriet takes one of Oliver's hands and drags him the final couple of paces to the door for the stairs.

Even those few paces have worn out Harriet. She hadn't realised how tense she is, how on guard until she releases a breath slowly once the stairs' door is closed.

'Every time I go below, I swear the flies are worse.' Theo says as he swats at some stragglers that have followed them through.

'I can't ever remember it being that bad. It was years ago, though.'

The smell hits her now. Even behind the thick door, the stench from the landfill filters through. It's unexplainable. Like the worst bad eggs and rotten flesh mixed with metal and burning plastic.

'This is the best stairwell,' Theo says. 'It's the furthest from any incinerator. The ones closer are so hot, it's like you're in a soup of garbage.'

Oliver recoils his lips and wrinkles his nose. 'Yuck!'

'Indeed,' Harriet says. 'Are you okay, Oliver? Ready for the stairs?'

He nods and they begin their descent. They take the stairs slowly, one step at a time. Harriet and Theo keep saying well done to Oliver, who huffs at their encouragement. The air is damp, and the humidity turns up a notch every few steps. Harriet had forgotten what that feels like, the constant sensation of moisture, the stickiness of it. Her hair clings to the back of her neck, her clothes snagging on her joints and curves. Damp patches are showing under her armpits and down her chest already. As usual, she's under prepared and out-of-place.

The steps are slippery underfoot and the handrail too slimy to hold on to in places. Oliver is a couple of steps in front of Harriet and she nags at him to walk carefully. He's being careful, taking his time with each footstep, shifting his weight before taking the next step, though her mind's eye still sees peril everywhere and imagines him tumbling, the sodden earth coating him, and she has nothing with her to clean it off.

'How you doing, Oliver?' Theo calls behind him.

'Good,' he says as Harriet tries to smile at his ceaseless bravado in front of Uncle Theo.

She wishes she could feign such bravery, but her footsteps are heavy with dread. She'd forgotten how deep the tunnels go, how endless the stairs seem, what it feels like to be buried alive.

'What part of below are we headed to?' Harriet asks as they get to the halfway point. It's a question that's been plaguing her since Theo mentioned going below.

'E gate. Reading town's western periphery.'

'Do you ever go to the northern centre?'

'Yeah, my folks are still there. They haven't moved.'

Harriet nods and can't bear to ask more. Harriet's family home is in the northern digs of Reading Town's below ground. She scratches when she thinks of it now. It's like watching some crime movie from a time before, all dark and twisted and unjustifiable. It doesn't matter how much time has passed, the stench of it is as fresh in her mind as Anthony's rage.

'They're still alive. Your parents,' Theo says. 'I know you haven't asked, but I figured you might want to know.'

She grasps the handrail a little tighter as her shoulders tense. Despite the humid air, her mouth runs dry. She should have asked. Theo probably thinks she's evil for not enquiring. She'd assumed they're dead and is unsure why she feels any relief they're not. They deserve to be dead. They deserve that fate a lot more than Tipher did.

As a kid, she always told herself that her parents were doing the best they could, that it wasn't their fault that life dealt them a shitty hand. It was just bad luck. Her mother worked on the farms, as so many did, scraping a living tending to cabbages and mushrooms and the occasional squash. Sometimes, she'd take home a few of the matted leaves smuggled in her bag. She'd ferment those in the warmest pocket of their home, selling the cabbage wine for a few extra pennies.

Her dad's main occupation was in extraction, the never-ending chore of keeping the damp out and filtering fresh air in. A council worker, poorly paid and always in demand. But it was steady work. Really, he had no excuse for doing what he did. It wasn't only for the extra money. That excuse was what he told the naive little girl Harriet once was.

'Do this for Daddy, and we can have extra helpings for dinner. You want Christopher to eat a little more, don't you?'

Her brother was a bargaining chip, always. Her dad knew this. He would sneer and lick his lips as if Harriet was the next flesh on the menu. She'd keep her head down and do as she was told. She'd do anything to help Tipher.

When the first blossoming of womanhood sprouted, her father's demands increased. He brought customers to the house, as well as refurbished cameras he'd bartered for from scavengers. He'd give her the dregs of her mother's cabbage wine, telling her it would make it more pleasant, that it would help her see the fun side.

Really, it only made her obedient and too woozy to argue.

She never told Tipher. She knew he'd tell her to stop, and she knew by then that there was shame in what was being asked of her. But living below ground she was, quite literally, cornered. Tipher was too weak to come with her above, and she'd never leave him. All she could do was what was asked of her in the hope it would make Tipher's life a little more bearable.

'They're still neighbours to my parents. I heard down the market that your dad's . . . side business, I guess you'd call it, isn't so productive these days. I'm really sorry. I knew they were bad, but we had no idea quite how bad. My parents were mortified when they found out.'

Harriet shrugs off his concern and his apology. 'It's just the way it was,' she says. 'Nothing you could have done.'

Theo's parents were always so generous, the sort that see the good in people and would never have imagined what really goes on behind closed doors. And Theo was just a kid. There's no way a kid's imagination runs so dark.

There were others who would have known. So many knew what wrongs were being done to her and so many turned a blind eye. From the cries and screams from other homes, from the swollen wounds and pallid faces, she knew, the suffering was almost universal, and she'd be considered one of the lucky ones.

'I haven't seen either of them in years,' Theo continues. 'Though my mum mentioned a while ago they're not in great health.'

Harriet's lips curl up a little at that. Is it wrong to be pleased they're sick? They were always sick anyway, so they're probably no different. With everything they put her through, a little schadenfreude is due. She wishes she had a beer and could drink to their ill health.

'It was just the way it was. Nothing you could have done,' she repeats.

That's how it is below. There are councils and people who run things but no real rules or coordination. People mind their own business usually. When community punishments are dished out, it's violent, spilling over to hurt a lot more than just those in the wrong.

Tipher's death broke her heart, but it wouldn't be in vain. His peace was her release.

'Glad you got out,' Theo says

As she walks down the stairs now, the musty smell of below seeping towards her and, with her broken child and failed marriage, getting out doesn't seem to fit.

Oliver doesn't complain. The walk seems to have got him over his sulk, and he even has a bit more spring in his step. It's an adventure for him. She's never told him the whole horror of it.

She wonders if he has an olfactory sensor, if he's ever learned to experience disgust. The sounds though, he must notice those. His hearing has always been so sensitive, like certain sounds pierce his insides. He shakes his head occasionally but doesn't hesitate.

Each footstep on those endless stairs down squelches in the damp clay and, as they near the habitation tunnels, the din from below gets louder. When she lived below, it was like white noise. It was in the background all waking hours so she barely noticed it. Now returning, it's an onslaught. Grumbles and groans, spits, hissing, shouting, cursing, and crying. The smell of rot, like the old cabbage leaves her mother would bring home, the fermenting sweetness of food gone off, the intermittent squeak of rats.

Her stomach twists as they descend the final few steps, and she's faced with the corrugated iron door to hell.

Chapter 27

Theo pushes open the rusty metal door, watching out for the sharp edges. The door isn't sealed but even so, opening it sends a whoosh of air their way, thick like a steam of condensed puke, and Harriet gags.

'*Eurgh!* I don't remember it being this bad,' she groans with her arm over her mouth.

Theo pulls his scarf up but otherwise appears unscathed by the stench. 'It always has been. You're just not used to it.'

His jibe isn't meant to be unkind, but still it makes her stiffen, her body feeling too tight for her bones. She was born down here and, suffice to say, she's forgotten her roots.

The underground is mostly one level. The parts where the tunnels split into two are reserved for jails and hospices. They collapse too readily to waste any meaningful life there. It chills Harriet's bones to recall that phrase, *meaningful life,* used so flippantly below ground where life is so cheap, everyone is expendable. Expiration dates might as well be stamped into babies' foreheads as soon as they're born. Making it to adulthood feels like cheating the system when so many never get the chance.

It's been a hundred years since the tunnels below ground were carved out of the earth. Every tunnel and cave below was clawed out with desperate hands, weathered and stripped of flesh from the effort. Blood from ripped fingernails still streak the sides. There's the odd plaque pressed into the sludgy walls in remembrance of those who withered away from digging the tunnels.

Everyone below ground celebrates annually, drinking to the efforts of those who persisted, praising their sacrifice. When Harriet lived below, she always cheered and thanked their ancestors along with everyone, but also wondered if those who dug down were really just the ones who ran away. If they'd all stood together against the extortionate prices and impossible regulations of life above, if they'd somehow stopped making the whole of ground level a rubbish dump, they would have had a chance in changing something instead of living like worms and moles.

She laughs at herself when she muses such things now. She's always run away. Cut from the same cloth as her ancestors, clearly.

It's said that Reading is one of the lucky towns. The town above was built on clay and the ground can hold miles of tunnels without losing the integrity of the buildings above. Good foundations, they say. The clay is more waterproof than in many towns. How lucky! Any leaks drip down the walls, not pouring straight on top. The tunnel corridors are wide enough for four people to walk alongside each other in most places, sometimes wider, while still avoiding touching the toxic walls. Everyone knows not to touch them. Hands are kept in pockets always. The argy-bargy of the cramped life keeps to the centre strip of the excavations. Of course, no one can avoid touching walls forever, and what isn't brushed away by contact is evaporated and condensed in the soggy air. Everyone below ground is poisoned, only some are poisoned slower.

In some towns with chalky soil, the tunnels are more prone to leaks. For the poor people in those tunnels, when it rains, the leeching liquids from the toxic rubbish dumps at ground level pour through. Rumours of flooding, submerged tunnels and rivers of septic slurry, would spread to Reading. As a girl, Harriet would listen to titbits of horror, of people drawing in liquidised garbage. 'Bad luck for them,' they would say.

Somehow though, luck doesn't do it justice. It writes off the horror as a role of the dice, the universe's game, rather than something entirely man-made.

Lucky is a word thrown around a lot. Luck is part of the culture. A nation of gamblers, every day was winning at luck. Got some extra food — what luck! Going scavenging — good luck! As if some idea of chance like flipping a coin is all that dictates the outcome. Harriet never understood it. Being born in Reading's below ground rather than above is shitty luck. Meeting Anthony was lucky, her fellow below ground escapees told her. Moving up to 107 was lucky. That's proof to Harriet that luck is bullshit.

The corridors are busy as they always are and they filter in between some excavation workers, far enough back so their picks and axes propped up on their shoulders don't swing into them. The odd drunk stumbles past, going the other way, bouncing from wall to wall, so inebriated that a brush with the walls is the least of their worries. Harriet flinches at the sight of one, then steadies herself. When she lived here, she was cautious but didn't see the hazard in everything. She never felt as scared of the walls as she does right now. What used to seem normal is now a spectacle.

Oliver keeps walking, not staring around. Conserving his battery also makes him look like he fits in, like all this is something he sees every day. Any other outsider would gawp and recoil, but Oliver is polite and doing exactly as Harriet said. She's glad his clothes are dirty, that he has smudges on his face. She swallows back some sadness as she recalls Tipher with that same messy, dark blonde hair walking these tunnels with her, on the days when he had the strength to walk.

She made sure Oliver's battery has been fully charged the last few nights. There's no way she'd be able to charge him down here if it came to it. Electricity is jacked from the dump, the heat the rot produces is turned to electricity, though badly, and the incinerators burn rubbish to generate more. Levels fluctuate more than they do on the lower levels above and sourcing fuel for backup generators is a job for the hardiest of all. It's all stolen from somewhere above. Everyone knows someone who died on that job. But the electric is usually enough for the UV lamps to grow some vegetables in the foetid soil.

They walk past a scavenger doorway. She knows that's where they are before she sees the reinforced door above the heads of the crowd. The smell hits her. The eggy sulphur of the landfill mixed with burning plastic seeps through the tunnel, that reinforced door doing little to keep it out. Beyond that door, the stairs lead straight to the landfill. Adjacent, the tunnel opens up to accommodate the people waiting eagerly to see what has been brought down, to be first in line for whatever they have claimed from the dump. Harriet recalls witnessing times when the scavengers would come down with an unfocussed look in their eyes. Those who did return. Bent double, vertebrae protruding from their spines, and their skin would glow iridescent. Harriet can still see that glow. Her eyes were playing tricks on her, she tried to tell herself when she was older. When she was really young, she assumed it was the sunshine, that they bought a little piece of it down below. No one ever mentioned the glow. It's better not to say. The scavengers are mostly treated like royalty for their short lives as, without the dump, they'd all boil to death or suffocate. The hard hats they wear are nowhere near enough to keep them all alive from the trash raining down from above. The largest items are only meant to be thrown over the fences at night, but so many top dwellers ignore that rule. Their convenience is more important than the safety of those down here.

Harriet remembers the tunnels being roomier, smelling less bad, and her sinuses being clearer. Her eyes still haven't adapted to the gloom and she squints to see. Perhaps it's best not to, she thinks as they pass someone whose face is covered in oozing welts and scars. She wishes her nose took as long to work properly as her eyes. Her gag reflex is too acute these days.

They arrive at an entryway, corrugated iron and plastic sheeting covering the door, and Theo rattles it. They wait. Harriet's head is woozy. She's been holding her breath too much. In her hand, Oliver's grip is still tight. She bends to have a better look at him, resting her free hand on his shoulder.

'Are you feeling okay?'

'Yes. I think so.'

'Not too tired?'

He shakes his head. 'No. Are you okay?'

She gives his cheek a gentle squeeze. 'I'm fine.'

'If Jockey is here, we're good,' Theo says.

Harriet straightens and faces him. His sporadic visits below have obviously kept him accustomed to life down here. He doesn't seem worried or nauseous at all.

'If it's Cheryl, I'll make excuses and come back later. You guys just be quiet. Let me do the talking.'

Harriet nods and stands in front of Oliver. She rolls her shoulders back, lifts her chin, and swallows back a trickle of bile as a fresh wave of putrid stench washes over her.

'Hang on!' The words come from the other side of the makeshift door, masculine, to Harriet's relief.

The iron sheeting wiggles, then slides to the side, followed by the rustling of the sheeting as it's manoeuvred out the way.

'Theo! Long time no see, buddy.' Jockey, Harriet assumes, has a kinder and healthier face than most below ground. His beard is neatly trimmed, and his clothes are mostly clean. He must be making a decent enough living doing what he does, which must mean he's good. A little bubble of hope replaces the bile and her nausea drifts away.

Theo and Jockey shake hands. 'I've got those transistors you wanted last time and a motor. This is your lucky day.'

'Great,' Theo says. 'Also, I've got some more work for you. This is my friend, Harriet.'

Harriet presses her lips together and gives Jockey a nod.

'Best if we talk inside,' Theo says.

Jockey's eyes don't leave Harriet as he steps to one side and gestures into his house. 'Come on in.'

Harriet's skin crawls, every hair on end. It's not a pervert glare from Jockey, but one of suspicion. In a place brimming with dishonesty, outsiders are always viewed with caution. She's forgotten so much of the politics down here. By straightening up and looking strong, she's given herself away as a tourist.

They walk through to a workshop that makes Andrea's on 2 look tidy. Shelves upon shelves line the walls and are jam-packed with whatever's been bought from scavengers above. Rusty metal parts and components mangled with offcuts of wiring, clipped ends of circuit boards, and bottles of solvents. All worth a pretty penny down here. She wonders what's in the closed drawers. It must be weapons. Such a haul needs protecting below ground.

Harriet brings Oliver to the front of her now and he stands very still.

'So, what mess are you in?' Jockey asks.

'This is Oliver,' she replies, holding her hands over Oliver's ears, hoping that's enough for him to shut his hearing off. 'He's degrading.'

Jockey's eyebrows lift, and he looks Oliver up and down. 'That's a MechaniKid? Wow. Well —' he shrugs, '— just take him back to TRI.'

'I've removed his tracker. He's not going back.'

Jockey puffs his cheeks out and exhales with a whistle. Folding his arms, he takes a seat on a workbench. 'So, are you mad or stupid?'

Harriet's cheeks flush and she grits her teeth.

'That thing has got to be worth a mint. And TRI are going to want it back.'

'Not it. *Him*,' she says through her teeth.

'Whatever. But you want to pay me to upgrade some parts, I just feel obliged to let you know what a waste of money that'll be. Tracker or no tracker, they'll find you.'

'We've lasted so far.'

Jockey's shoulders drop, his posture relaxing. 'Well, it's your money. I can do it. A complete system reboot. It'll buy you another few years, if you really want to keep it.'

Harriet's knees weaken as joy fills her, so much so she doesn't even correct the pronoun. 'Yes. Please. Thank you so much.' She kneels and cups Oliver's cheeks. 'Guess what, Oliver? This man is going to make you all better. You're going to be strong again, then everything will be just as it was.'

'Woah!' Jockey holds up his hands. 'Hold on there. You misunderstand. What I can do is a complete system reboot. Basically, a factory restart.'

Harriet stands and looks blankly at him.

'You remember what he was like when you first got him? When he was fresh out of the factory? That's how he'll be. Memories, learning, everything, will start from scratch.'

Harriet's hand goes to her mouth and her eyes blur with tears. She puts her hands over Oliver's ears again, too late to muffle what Jockey just said even though he must have already heard too much. The bubble of hope she had bursts, shattering her insides along with it.

'It's up to you,' Jockey says. 'You can keep him, and I can make him as good as new. Literally, like new. But that's the deal.'

Chapter 28

'I . . .' Harriet's words fail. Her mouth moves like a fish out of water, suffocating. The walls edge closer as her world collapses. She's here to try to save Oliver. What Jockey is suggesting is to delete him, like her son is nothing but a hard drive.

This man can't save her little boy. He can only erase him.

How many parents watch their children grow up and wish they could do it all again? All parents at some stage probably yearn for that. But to delete him, to wipe his mind completely, that's as good as killing him. He'd be a shell, not her Oliver anymore.

But what choice does she have?

She swallows, attempting to summon some saliva to her parched throat. 'I need to have a think,' she says.

'Sure. Take all the time you need.'

Theo buys his parts as Harriet waits, leaning against the shelving unit. At least she can have some support without touching the walls, although, at the moment, she'd have a mud bath in those walls if it would make Oliver better.

They leave the same way they came, past the drunks zigzagging down the corridor and bouncing off the walls. Her parents used to walk like that. Anthony did too. She thinks then, what a blessed relief that must be, to care about nothing except your next hit or drink. Such a simple way to live. Loveless, carefree, doomed to die soon.

How many times has Harriet watched Delilah, her young eyes learning always, more so than Oliver. She's a curiousness about her as she experiences so many things for the first time. She's not yet learned to sulk or talk back, not yet learned to be cheeky. Harriet misses that sweet childish innocence, but she misses it as much as she yearns for the future. She can picture Oliver reading more, getting smarter, and more caring and more worldly, to one day make it to the top of the big climbing frame. Only that last point she knows can never be. As much as she hoped his mind would expand, his body is like that of Peter Pan's. She's already stunted his physical growth. Can she do that to his cognitive advancement also?

'I'm sorry, Harriet,' Theo says as they walk. 'I didn't know it would mean that.'

'It's not your fault. Thank you for taking me.'

'It's worth thinking about, though. I mean, you'll get him back slowly.'

'Like I said, I'll think about it.'

She needs to get above ground. Even on the lower levels she can breathe better than she can here. The temperature has hiked up a couple of degrees. The ground saps what energy she has as each step sinks a little into the clay. She wants to wash, to clean away this place and her disappointment. The air is so damp she wishes she had a hat on as the odd drop of condensation drips down from the ceiling. One finds its way down the back of her neck, and she squirms as it travels between her shoulder blades. Is it just cold or does it sting? It's hard to know, though she doesn't doubt the pH level is likely to be off.

There's a row of hawkers selling hooch and food scraps, past others selling medicines for various ailments and lotions that supposedly protect against the toxins that leach through. She found some change and bought such things for Tipher a few times, desperate to make him well. Nothing worked. It's all nonsense.

They walk past carts and boxes on pulleys where the rubbish from below ground is piled up. The below grounders use the dump just like the above grounders, chucking out what they don't need anymore. The only difference is their rubbish actually is rubbish. It would have been used and reused until nothing more could be done. Wrappers, shreds of clothing, corpses. The odd human limb sticks out the top of a pile. People are mistreated as well in death as they are in life down here. No one wants to dig anymore. Burying a body would be a waste of tunnel and energy. Chuck the dead out on the dump with everything else or serve it up in a stew. Just don't talk about the sadness, write their passing off to bad luck. Calling it fate makes it so much worse.

They approach the landfill exit and stand for a moment as the crowd is too dense to pass. There must be some scavengers on their way down. There's no point trying to get through. They'll only create a ruckus, so they wait.

'I can't do it, Theo. I just can't.'

'I get it. I do.'

Harriet cries, tears falling freely down her cheeks, though she keeps her sobs silent. She doesn't want Oliver to look up and see her being weak and pathetic. She's a bad enough mother already without seeming so pitiful in front of him.

'Hey.' Theo puts his arm around her. She leans on him and heaves a grateful sigh, her tears dampening his top. 'We'll find a way, okay? Even Monty will help. I know he's pretty useless at most things —' Harriet chuckles, '— but together we can figure out something. Put out feelers. Hell, I'll even break into TRI if I have to. Okay?'

Harriet lifts her head and looks at Theo's earnest face. How has she survived so long without friends? She's been so alone. She never knew what she was missing.

'I promised Chris I'd look out for you,' Theo says.

'You never!'

'I did. He wasn't daft. He knew he wasn't going to make it however much he fought to live. He adored you and everything you did for him. Losing touch with you was horrible. I felt like I'd let my old best friend down. You were like a sister to me. But look at you. You're strong, fighting for a little boy to live all over again. And I'll be damned if we don't succeed this time.'

That burst bubble of hope reforms, and she takes a breath. Not suffocating anymore, not weak. The air thins, and she stands a little straighter. She can do this. With friends helping her, together they can save her son.

The crowd moves and they take a step forward. Harriet loses her footing a little but finds her balance, then, again, her ankle gives way and she stumbles. She grabs onto Theo, but he's the same, unsteady, and swaying.

There's a noise, an almighty crash. Lights flicker off, and then on again, and the crowd disappears before her, leaving an expanse of blackness for a second that stretches out as her heart skips several beats.

The lights flicker back on, bright and glaring and in front of her is a gap, a space, where no one stands as if they'd been swallowed up. The smell of putrid damp clay intensifies. There's a wall of it, the air turning hazy.

Then, as quick as they disappeared, a stampede hurtles towards her.

'Theo? Oliv—' The stampede is on her. She spins on the spot, her hands empty. The stampede is screaming, so loudly she can't make out the words.

Her fingers stretch and grasp at nothing, her arms too restricted to move.

Her son! Where is her son?

A chorus of wailing and panic. She can make out the word now. Just one: Landslide.

A thousand people crush her on both sides, her feet sliding on the ground or not at all as the pressure of bodies lifts her, her feet kicking below her. She tries to scream, to shout their names but can't tell if she makes a sound. The din from everyone else drowns her out.

Her arms are wedged into her sides, and she spins again and sees it. The slurry and sludge, the tunnel collapsing by the entrance to above, the landslide as fast as the crowd, swallowing everything in its path.

She can smell it. The river of clay, the burning plastic, the fear. The crowd stays upright for another moment before she hurtles to the ground with them.

The screams die out, the light fades. It's all black and silent.

Chapter 29

She's lying down, one side buried under clay, suctioning her in. Above is dark and her unburied arm can barely move. She calls for Theo, for Oliver, but with her chest half crushed and the debris above, her voice rasps for her ears alone.

There are groans from above and all around. Vibrations of people's agony travel through the ground like a baseline. 'Oliver,' she cries again and again, flexing her fingers, willing his hand to fall into hers.

She wriggles her arm on top, her shoulder. *Think, Harriet, think!* She's not in pain, well, not much at least. She wriggles her toes. Not paralysed then. She's alive. One positive. Keep moving, she tells herself. Stay awake.

She cries their names again, a little more volume this time, adding to the moans and cries of others, the chorus of pain and fear all around her. There's panic in the air, but she's not panicking. She can't afford to panic. Panic is for those worried about themselves. She's only worried about Oliver.

She shimmies her shoulder and whatever is pushing on top of her moves with it, then flops over, and she yelps when it settles face down. A body, pale with death. There's no breath on her face. Its head is half dented. The one remaining eye frozen with his final fear.

Don't panic don't panic don't panic.

Her breath rushes from her lungs and she heaves another, faster this time, then the same, faster again, and faster until her stomach starts to twist and contract. The lumps stream out of her mouth before she can stop it and she chokes on her puke, spitting and coughing it away.

That dead eye stares at her, as if judging, as if mocking, as if now pleased of his release.

She squeezes her eyes shut, grateful for the darkness for a moment, then steadies her breath. When she opens her eyes, just a crack, she hopes for that face to be gone, for death not to be quite literally staring her in the face. No such luck. A dribble of blood from the crushed side of the head dangles its way to her neck. She wriggles her shoulder again, and the corpse moves too. That looseness tells her there can't be anything on top of it, so she's not too buried. She laughs at the thought — or tries to from her squashed position — coughing out her chuckle as hysteria takes hold. Thinking she's not buried indeed! How stupid! She's in a tunnel below ground. Buried is exactly right.

Don't panic don't panic don't panic.

Find Oliver find Oliver find Oliver.

Her thoughts are laser focussed. No pain. No crushing sensation. Ignore the dead body, the screams, and the fear.

One more wriggle and her arm is free from below the elbow. There's the sensation of space around her hand and she splays her fingers. She calls their names again, cries for help, managing to project her voice a little louder this time. She pauses, listening for shouts of Mother.

She can't picture Oliver crushed or buried. That isn't what's happened. It can't be.

Harriet pushes her hand upwards, as far as she can, then waves but it's not high enough. She fidgets some more, the bloodied corpse's face now pressed against hers. She can breathe now but resists as her mouth is too close to his greying skin. She jerks her body to one side, slowly resets, then jerks again. He rolls mostly off her and she inhales deeply, the ceiling visible before her. Her arm is now totally free and she reaches up, waving frantically and shouts with all the strength she has.

'Oliver! Theo! Help!'

There's a hand on her arm. She can't see their face, but they grip her with such force it would hurt if she cared. Another hand and they both pull her arm so hard they could rip it off, but she won't budge. She can hear so little, one ear buried in the clay, the other must have muck in it. Her vision is a blur through gritty and streaming eyes.

The muffled cries of others sound far away and getting further. Despite hardly moving, the room begins to spin and darkness creeps in from the edges of her vision.

No. Stay awake.

She has to find Oliver. A mother wouldn't sleep now. A mother would rip off the buried half of her body to find her child.

And she tries, tensing every muscle she has to cooperate with the tugging hands. There's something cool and pointed against her back, water being splashed on her face. In the chaos, she thinks she hears her name. *Harriet.* The darkness edges closer to her central vision and she can see so little now. There's something cold, a vibration, and in her last moments of consciousness, she imagines him calling for her.

'Mother.'

Chapter 30

Harriet opens her eyes, or at least thinks she does. The darkness remains just the same. She blinks to clear her view but it's unchanged, all shadows and gloom, only now her eyes sting and water.

Questions run through her mind, a thousand in a second, before she can concentrate on the most useful ones. *Am I alive? Where am I?*

She can move both arms and she pushes herself up, a fabric-covered wall brushing against her left side as she does. The smell, she remembers that smell. Herbs and something sweet and—

A light flicks on and she shields her eyes.

'Oh, good. You're up.'

That voice. She knows that voice. She takes her hand away and, squinting in the glare, peers at the kind face of Theo's mother.

'Sylvia?'

Sylvia sits on the bed next to Harriet and cups her face in one hand. There's a mug of something steaming in the other. Harriet stares at the kind woman who helped her so much when she was a child. She has Theo's eyes and chin, his poker straight hair, though hers is now totally grey and is styled back off her face. The same way she always wore it. Her lines from the years Harriet have missed have only added to her motherly appearance. 'It's such a relief you're okay. How are you feeling? Any nausea?'

'No . . . I don't —' A wave of dizziness comes over her and Sylvia supports her as she lies back down.

'You took quite a knock. There's some lemon balm tea here. It'll help.'

Harriet pushes herself up again, fighting through the sickness. 'My son. Oh my God. Oliver.'

'He's fine. Totally fine, so you just relax. Theo cleaned him up. He insisted. I think he quite likes the little fella.'

Knowing he's fine isn't enough, and Sylvia opens the door. There's a short corridor closed off by a curtain but in the gap in the fabric she can see Oliver at the table with Theo, playing cards.

'We're going to clean you up a bit more before he comes in and gives you a hug,' Sylvia says. 'You were half buried. I'm sure you'll be fine, but just in case, let's keep the little soldier over there for now.'

Harriet allows herself to relax a little as she lies back down and takes small sips of the lemon balm tea. Sylvia is a nurse at the health centre and Harriet remembers she always has a tea for every ailment.

Sylvia fills Harriet in with the details. A tower above being ripped down to make way for a new luxury one. The entirety of the old building was chucked down at once, against regulations and without warning, but who gives a shit about the ones who live below ground.

'It could have been worse,' Sylvia says. 'Seventy-eight dead and we've lost access to the dump from that door. But it's all repairable. More could have been killed. You three were lucky.'

Lucky. Harriet huffs at the word. Seventy-eight dead up top would be a catastrophe. Down here, it's expected and written off to luck. She'd grimace if her headache wasn't so bad.

Sylvia leaves and comes back with buckets of hot water. 'Don't worry about the electricity usage for the lights or warm water. We've got plenty at the moment. The most important thing is that you're clean and well.'

Electricity usage. Oh God. Oliver. 'What time is it?'

'Six p.m. You've been out of it for a few hours.'

Harriet's chest tightens, her breaths now shallow. Six p.m. She was meant to be well above ground by now. Oliver's been awake since eight a.m. He needs to be on standby if he's any chance of having enough left in his battery to make the walk up. There's no way there'll be enough electric down here to charge him. Lights and hot water are one thing, but Oliver needs a whole lot more than that.

Harriet tries to get out of bed, swallowing back bile. 'I need to speak to Oliver or Theo.'

Sylvia puts her hand on her shoulder, so gently but it's enough to stop Harriet. 'No, love, you need to get clean and to rest.'

'Please. Oliver has a condition. I need—'

'Okay, okay.' Sylvia leans back and holds up her hands. 'How about this. I'll go get Theo now. Then you clean up. Deal?'

'Yes. Deal. Thank you.'

Sylvia leaves and a moment later, Theo comes in.

'How's the patient?' Theo asks, a warm grin on his face. He looks fine, clean, and unscathed, his limp no worse. Any relief at his health isn't enough to take Harriet's panic away. 'Giving Nurse Mum a hard time, I hear.'

'Oliver? He's okay?'

'He's totally fine. A bit shaken up. We were away from the worst of it. Some others hid his view while we dug you out, but he knows people were hurt. He was really worried.'

Harriet bites her lip. Oliver is such a worrier. He would have been terrified.

'I told him everyone was fine. I couldn't really bear to tell him the truth. But he knows you're fine, and that's who he was most worried about. He has some — what do you call it — bruising, I guess? But he really is fine. He was a bit mucky, but I cleaned him up. I insisted, so Mum wouldn't see . . . you know. He's worried about you, keeps asking if you're okay. But I'm keeping him busy. He's great at Uno. Beat me twice.'

Her heart warms, and she leans back on an elbow. Her little boy really is okay. 'Thank you, so much. But he won't have much charge. He needs to go on standby or else he'll run flat. You need a pointy thing, like a needle. There's a tiny hole by his charging socket on his right hip.'

'Right. Okay, got it.'

'He just needs somewhere to lie down. He can come in here with me—'

'Mum won't allow that. He's a kid and not used to it down here. You got a lot of clay on you.'

'But he'll be fine.'

'*We* know that. You want me to tell mum why?'

Harriet shakes her head, then presses her palm into her temple as the room spins again. 'No. No, I mean. No. I can't risk that. Your mum is so amazing, but she might, I dunno, be angry, or hate him.'

'I'll put Oliver down in my room. You just rest, and we'll get going tomorrow or as soon as you're well.'

Harriet slouches down, unable to argue with Theo. Her entire body feels battered and broken. A night's rest is sensible. The thought of it makes her stomach churn more. An entire night below ground. At least it's at Theo's parents'. Somewhere safe, or safe enough. As Sylvia said, for them at least, it could have been worse.

Theo leaves and through the gap in the curtain, she watches Oliver until he's out of sight. She picks up the cloth and slowly begins to wash the muck off her skin. In all of her years living down here, she was never so filthy. She can't think about that now, though her skin burns as she sponges off the clay. She can't think about how raw and red her skin is underneath. All she can think of is getting above ground as soon as possible tomorrow before Oliver's battery runs out. Before anyone discovers what he is.

Chapter 31

The night-time tea Sylvia brings Harriet knocks her out and she sleeps right through until morning. She feared nightmares of being buried and trapped and never getting out of this place, but her sleep is deep and dreamless. She knows it's morning when she wakes by the commotion beginning outside. Excavators are on their way to work, to repair damage. Farmers leave to tend to their cabbages and mushrooms. The sound was the percussion of her childhood and as she wakes, it's like she's a scared little girl again, wondering what abuses await her, if she'll have a meal today, and if Tipher is well.

Only now, it's Oliver rather than Tipher who's the first person on her mind.

She stands gingerly, her feet finding purchase on the rug below and she pushes against the bed. No woozy head. Her back and shoulders creak as she straightens, her head only wants to turn one way, but she's basically okay. She's only a slight cough as she fully inhales, and her flaky skin is going to need moisturising forever. All small things she can worry about later. She can walk, that's all she needs to be able to do.

Sylvia's left some clean clothes out for her, and Harriet holds them up, pressing them into her chest. As a girl, she was so envious of Theo's doting parents. There are so many bad people on every level, but Sylvia and Theo's dad, Casper, are shining stars down here.

Harriet leaves the room and finds Theo sitting with his parents. Plates of eggs with fried cabbage with radishes and mushrooms on the table. A staple down here but a more luxury one with the eggs. The kind of breakfast she so rarely had. She's pleased to see there's no meat on offer. It wasn't until her life above ground that Harriet learned meat was an ambiguous term. Whatever the chewy and sinewy stuff she ate below ground was, it didn't taste like anything she'd had during her life above.

'Oliver is still sleeping,' Theo says. 'I thought it best to let him rest.'

Harriet exhales and some of the tension in her neck dissipates.

'If he's awake, he's only going to beat me at Uno again and I don't think I can take it,' Theo says and Harriet laughs.

'He's so smart it blows my mind some days,' Harriet says.

Sylvia gestures to an empty chair. 'Sit. Eat.' She speaks with all the authority of a long-serving nurse, then plates up some food for Harriet.

The table is uneven and rusty, with a piece of cloth jammed under one of the legs to make it wobble less.

'Oh, no. That's too much,' Harriet says as she sits and Sylvia pushes the plate her way.

'Don't argue with her,' Casper says with a face of mock fear. 'You know what she's like.'

Casper's whole body slopes to one side. The years have been hard on him. Theo never mentioned his dad's ill health, but he was always a bit sick even when they were kids, like everyone. It's not gossip when it's so common. Casper chews his food slowly, as if in pain. He's skin and bone, the layers of tattered clothing doing little to disguise that. His breakfast portion is tiny, so Harriet supposes Sylvia knows her limits.

'That little boy of yours is a delight,' Sylvia says. 'He looks so much like Christopher, doesn't he?'

Harriet nods and chews her food. Her breakfast is as bland as food always was down here, but it tastes like the best bits of home.

Sylvia looks down at the floor then and fidgets before addressing Harriet again. 'It's not my place, I know, and I know they were awful to you, we never knew how awful until you were long gone. But your mum would love to know she has a grandson.'

Harriet swallows, then grits her teeth. 'No.'

'Okay. As you like. But if you want an update, your dad is basically catatonic now, and your mum, well, she's pretty unwell. The two of them wander the corridors sometimes, delirious. I've found them in here on a couple of occasions, confused and trying to find their house and I've had to take them home. They get lost easily. If you think you'll regret not saying goodbye, or saying your piece, then now's your chance to say it.'

Pinpricks ripple over Harriet's body, like she's ripping off dried mud. If her parents are ever in Sylvia and Casper's house, they're probably trying to rob it. One thing she expressly wanted to avoid by coming down here was her parents.

Harriet swallows another mouthful before she speaks again. The food tastes bitter now. 'I really don't think I can face them. It's been too long and when I left, it was for good.'

Sylvia nods and puts a little more on Casper's plate. 'Well, whatever you like. I know they were the worst sort of parents. The worst sort of people in truth. Down here does funny things to some. I'm just letting you know they haven't long left. They've never been very healthy, I'm sure you know.'

'I told you not to argue with her,' Casper says with a wry grin.

They eat in silence for a while, Casper managing another couple of bites and Theo demolishing whatever's left. There's a plate on the side with some bits for Oliver when he's ready, Sylvia explains.

'It's been so nice seeing you,' Sylvia says. 'I wish I could stay, but we're needed at the medical centre after yesterday. The death toll is over eighty as of this morning.'

She doesn't need to say the word lucky, and Harriet knows she's being ungrateful not to feel lucky. But it wasn't bad luck the tunnel collapsed. It was the top levels and their thoughtless ness for those below, as always.

'I wondered if we'd ever see you in real life again,' Sylvia says to Harriet. 'We watched all your movies, though.'

Harriet's cheeks flush. 'Really?'

'Whenever one came out, I'd come down here to watch with them.' Theo winks. 'That one about the old Royals—'

Sylvia clasps her hands in front of her. 'Oh, that one was my favourite. And what a star you were.'

Before Harriet's face grows any hotter and any more tears can brim her eyes, Sylvia and Casper say their goodbyes and leave for the health centre.

'Sorry about Mum,' Theo says when they're alone.

Harriet wipes her eye on her sleeve. 'Don't be. She's amazing. I can't believe you all used to watch my movies.'

'Local below grounder makes it into the movies? How could we not watch!'

Harriet smiles, though her sense of failure weighs heavy in her stomach. Her life with Anthony took so much from her. She could have had a few more years acting. She could have done so much more if it weren't for him.

She blinks away her sadness. There's no point to the what ifs. 'They never thought about moving above? They're too good for down here.'

'Move? My parents? No chance.' He laughs. 'I gave up asking years ago.'

Harriet smiles. 'God, I never even asked how you are! Are you okay?'

'Physically fine,' Theo says. 'I took a few knocks but somehow dodged most of the slide. That was horrible yesterday. The worst collapse in a decade, they're saying. It's a mess out there. I feel like I should stay and help.'

Harriet finishes her last mouthful and takes her plate to the sink. 'I have to go. You know I have to get Oliver home. Sorry I can't stay.'

'Of course. Totally, I know. And I'll come with you, just in case Oliver runs out of juice and you need help. I'll come back after I've got you home.'

Harriet bends over the counter, taking some deep breaths to stop from crying. 'Thank you. So much, Theo. I really can't thank you enough.'

He stands next to her and gives her a gentle nudge. 'Consider it my penance for being so bad at Uno. I'll wash up. You go get Oliver.'

Harriet laughs, then walks down the hallway to Theo's room. It's been years since she's in this house, but she remembers the way as if it were yesterday. She pushes back the curtain. There's his dresser topped with childhood knick-knacks, a layer of dust covering the old books and games. He's some clothes hanging from a rail, no closet. Some open boxes on the floor are filled with more clothes. It's all as if time has stood still. She walks to the bed, then spins around, checking behind her for another bed or chair or something where Oliver could be sleeping. Oliver isn't there.

She doubles back on herself. She must remember wrong. There must be another room. She walks back past the curtain and shouts towards the kitchen to Theo.

'Theo, what room is he in?'

'Mine.'

'Which is that?'

The chuckle comes down the hallway. 'You remember.' He peeks around the doorway from the kitchen. 'You're right in front of it.'

Harriet's bones turn to ice. It can't be.

'He's not in that room, Theo.'

'Huh?' He has a tea towel still in his hand as he walks towards her. 'What do you mean?'

'This room?' Harriet points, her voice tremulous. 'He's not in there.'

Theo's face scrunches before he runs into his room. There's a clamour, soft thuds of bedding hitting the floor before he comes out again. 'I don't understand. He's gone.'

Chapter 32

Harriet's breaths shorten, the space shrinking as the walls close in. Her panic is a noose around her neck, strangling her. Yet somehow the area seems huge, sprawling tunnels stretching out in a million directions, far away with endless hiding places and greedy hands.

Theo's voice echoes, over and over. He's gone.

'He can't be gone!' Harriet says as she forces herself to breathe, and wipes sweat from her brow. 'You said you left him on standby.'

'I did!'

'Well . . .' She clutches at her chest, looking at Theo with narrowed eyes, suspicion gnawing at her, eating through her panic. No, Theo would never. Her heart is about to pound out of her ribcage. 'He can't just get up and leave!'

'I don't understand. Honestly, I left him right there.' Theo's eyes are wide and wild, his head snapping from one way to the other.

A thousand possibilities play out in Harriet's mind, each one more devastating than the last. She palms her temples and squeezes her eyes shut. None of those scenarios can be true.

There's an explanation. Something logical. He can't just be gone. 'Maybe . . . maybe your mum took him to the medical centre. She might have noticed he wouldn't wake up and didn't want to worry me?'

'Yeah. Maybe. I'll go there. You just wait here, okay?'

'Oh, God.' Her stomach twists and she bends double, grey spots appearing in her vision. 'He's gone. Someone's taken him, haven't they!'

Theo stands beside her and supports her back to standing. 'I'll bet it's Mum. You're right, she wouldn't want to worry you. Just wait and I'll be back in an hour.' His tone is authoritative but not enough to disguise the tremor. He's as scared as she is. He's just hiding it better.

Sylvia taking him to the medical centre isn't a good outcome. She'll figure out pretty quickly he's a MechaniKid and then someone will steal or hurt him.

Oh God oh God oh God.

The techie, Jockey, or one of the people who helped carry her back. There are countless people who may have figured out Oliver is valuable. She claws at her throat as it constricts. She can't breathe down here. She can't breathe without Oliver.

Harriet can't just sit and wait. She has to search, to do something. She hobbles from the house. Her skin is tight and whiplash from the landslide makes her back crunch with each step. She scans the tunnel ahead. They're quieter than they used to be or more people are staying inside. Her shaking hands grasp for a supporting beam and she stumbles as she misses. Her depth perception is wrong, her vision more tunnelled than the tunnel.

She slouches against the beam, wills herself to call his name but her chest caves, a numbness spreading over her. Theo's words are still repeating.

He's gone.

She's lost every little boy she ever held dear. Why did she think she could keep hold of Oliver? The last time she was below ground was when she held Tipher's hand as his soul left him. Her perfect little brother, the spit of Oliver.

She gasps and palms her forehead when the penny drops. Oliver looks so much like Tipher, and there are two people who wander these corridors who could have taken Oliver.

She stands straighter, peering down the tunnel in the direction Theo would have gone, wishing he was still here or running back. She has a strong hunch where Oliver could be, but going there alone makes her nausea reclaim her insides again. She could wait an hour for Theo to return. But no. God knows what they would have done to him in an hour.

She walks, disguising any limp or pain from the day before. Now is not the time to appear weak. Her hands are balled into fists at her sides, her muscles taught and ready. She doesn't knock, instead she pushes the door open, the ramshackle thing coming off its makeshift hinges from the force.

'Oliver!' she yells into the bleak space.

At the far end of the room, the low wattage light casts an orange glow. Even that warm hue isn't enough to make Harriet's mother's complexion any less grey. She's sitting, hugging her knees and swaying. Harriet takes a step closer. It's undeniably her mother, but it could be her ghost. Her ragged clothes hang off her bones and drape across the floor like they've been discarded rather than worn. She looks up at Harriet, though doesn't focus on her. One eye is clouded over, the other searching around. Her hair, grey and frizzy, sticks out at all angles, matted with clay like she's been bumping into the walls, just like the drunks who roam the tunnels.

There's no sign of Harriet's father. That's a small blessing, she hopes.

The smell is unreal, worse than she's ever known. Sickly sweet mixed with shit, so strong it burns Harriet's eyes and lungs. A few steps inside, she gags, and the source of the stench becomes apparent. Her father's rotting corpse is in his chair, the ratty chair he always sat in when he wasn't doing something perverted. By the degree of rot, it looks like he's been there for weeks.

Harriet's hand goes to her mouth, the other to her gut. Her nausea is quelled as an evil sense of joy niggles its way through her mind. He's dead. He's actually dead. But there's not enough joy in that. Dying, sitting in his chair, seems too peaceful. A shame. She wanted him to suffer. She can only hope his demise before his death was riddled with pain and woe.

'Where is my son?' Harriet says to the crone in the corner.

'Can I help you?' she asks, still looking around Harriet rather than at her face. Her voice is like rust on gravel. 'Please keep your voice down. My son is sleeping.'

Harriet barges past her, knocking her to the ground. There's a crack, a pathetic yelp from the old bitch. Harriet hopes she broke a hip. The door to her and Tipher's old bedroom is at the back of the house. The dim light doesn't reach that far but it doesn't matter. She could find it with her eyes closed. She pushes past the plastic curtain that covers the doorway, unchanged since she lived there, and walks in, then comes to a sudden stop. When she flicks on the light switch, her bones turn to ice.

She's in the doorway to her old room, the one she shared with Tipher, the room where she cared for him and watched him die while their parents did nothing.

The room layout is the same, only now the walls are covered in posters and magazine articles, all with her face. A face different from the one she has now, airbrushed, her chin more defined, smoother, with hair that behaved. She didn't have a long or particularly successful career and it's strange there's even this much material on her. Some of it, she remembers. A dress she wore for a costume drama, an article about the last film she did before she quit for Anthony, a piece on that god-awful action film from her early days, and a flyer from each of her West End shows. She stares at them all, the relics from her youth and all of what could have been. Her parents must have had a notice out with all the scavengers to have secured this much paraphernalia.

Harriet pulls her eyes away from all the images. She's seen it all before and her past is long behind her. She approaches Tipher's old bed. Oliver's there, still on standby. Her breath freezes in her lungs a moment as she watches him there, so peaceful, a picture of health, the mini-me of what Tipher should have been if he were ever given a chance at being healthy.

'Would you like some cabbage wine?' her mother asks from the doorway. She's stooped with her hand against an uncovered wall. 'I made it myself. Two pounds fifty a cup. Can't say fairer than that.'

'No.'

The old woman leans back to look up at Harriet. Her eyes bore through her rather than look at her, her toothless mouth stretching into a thin smile. 'You remind me of my daughter. She's famous, you know. Up top. Too busy in the movies to come visit us now. But that's the way it goes, I guess. At least I have my Christopher. Such a handsome boy, isn't he?'

Harriet reaches into the bed and lifts Oliver. Being a dead weight is tough, but she nudges his arms around her next and holds him tight as she lifts him.

'What are you doing?' her mother hobbles over, twiggy arms now outstretched. 'That's my boy.'

Harriet holds him tight. 'No, he's not. He's mine.'

Her mother is so out of it she can't walk in a straight line. She stumbles over, her one seeing eye now focussed on Oliver. 'Give him to me. He's my boy.'

Harriet eyes the exit, the door her mother's swaggering steps are blocking. 'Back off.'

'Come to Mummy, Christopher.'

She's staggering closer. Harriet takes a step back and braces, ready to kick. She looks towards the doorway and feigns a gasp. 'I think I hear the cabbage wine spilling over.'

The old woman's breath rattles in her throat as she lifts her head and looks towards the door. Harriet takes her chance and steps around her, only to feel spindly fingers dig into her shoulder.

'You can't have my boy.' Her breath is rancid, as bad as the stench of the corpse.

Harriet kicks out, landing one foot on her thigh and the old woman easily goes down. Harriet walks out of the doorway, ignoring the calls behind her.

'My boy! My boy!'

Her mother crawls through to the living room on all fours, rasping wails as she follows. Harriet looks down on her for a moment, the writhing mess on the floor, whimpering and too weak to get up.

There's a moment of pity in Harriet as she watches the pathetic child abuser. The cabbage wine is in buckets where it always is, and she shifts Oliver's weight on her hip to free one arm. Taking the bucket by the handle, she puts it next to her mother.

There's gratitude in the old woman's face, a little pleasure in her eyes at the sight of the bucket.

'A trade,' Harriet says. 'The boy for the wine. I'll kick this all over if you take him.'

Her mother looks at the bucket as if she's never seen so much before and doesn't give Oliver another glance. She puts her face in the liquid and slurps like a dog.

Harriet watches her for a moment, aware of the filth, her skin crawling with an unclean feeling. She recoils her lips at the *glug glug glug* of her mother swallowing the rancid drink, then she turns and walks away, knowing with certainty that will be the last time she ever sees her.

As Harriet arrives back at Theo's, she sits and waits for him at the kitchen table. She doesn't switch Oliver back on yet, though how she yearns to hear his voice, his giggle, to look into his blue eyes and tell him she loves him. She leaves him on standby, conserving his battery for as long as she can.

'Oh, thank fuck!' Theo says as soon as he walks in. He's red-faced and breathless, his hairline damp with sweat. 'Where'd you find him?'

Harriet shakes her head, and Theo knows not to ask any more. They've always had a silent way of communicating. So much can be said with the slightest gesture. They find the needle and turn Oliver back on.

'Mum! You're awake! I missed you. How are you? I've been so worried about you.'

She kisses his forehead, a tear tracing her cheek. 'I'm just fine.'

'I never want to be apart from you again. Uncle Theo said it was for your own good, but it was horrible.'

'You're such a good, brave boy,' Harriet says, and puts him on the floor to stand. 'Come on. Time to go.'

Oliver takes her hand as they leave. Just before they get to the door, Harriet pauses. 'Leave a note and ask your mum to go around my parents' place. And say I'm sorry I couldn't deal with it myself.'

Theo doesn't ask questions but writes the note and leaves it on the kitchen table, then they leave. Finally, they can get above ground.

Chapter 33

'Mum, look!' Oliver points out a bird pecking at the walkway. 'A gull! I read about those. We never got those birds up top.'

'Shh, darling,' Harriet says and glances around. They both look so much more like they belong on the lower levels now, like somehow their time below ground has accustomed them to anything, but to admit they're from the top levels would still be met with disdain. She has more shame in coming from up there than she ever did from originating from below. She's still wearing the outfit that Sylvia gave her. She's washed it a couple of times since, but it still looks like a grubby potato sack. Perfect for these levels. 'Best not to mention up top life around here.'

'Why?'

'Because we had more there and others don't want to feel like they have less.'

Oliver looks around, tilting his head, as if quantifying all the atoms around him. 'Why do you say we have less here? Everyone is friendlier and the climbing frame goes even higher. And they have more birds, bigger birds. And spiders! And best of all, there's no Anthony.'

Her heart warms at his comments. He calculates things so differently from an adult, takes so much joy in simple things, rather than big fancy houses and designer clothes. His wants aren't the same.

She wonders, for the zillionth time since they were below ground, if perhaps starting Oliver from scratch wouldn't be the worst thing. He's still tripping often, has weak days, and his memory can be iffy. But he hasn't forgotten Anthony. He tenses a little when he talks of him, his lips pressing together. There's anger in his eyes, the blue piercing through the bad. A memory wipe would take his memories of Anthony away, would take away all that hurt.

She counts the weeks since they left the penthouse. Ten, she thinks. Her bruises have all healed, replaced by the new ones from the incident below ground. Some days when it's not too cold, she doesn't wear a scarf, doesn't fear others seeing his fingerprints dug into her throat. Is Anthony looking for her? He would have run out of prepared meals by now. Funny. She's barely given him a thought in ages.

'We don't need any of that top-level stuff,' Oliver says with such certainty. 'We have each other and that's all we need.'

She sits on a bench and he joins her, the gull still pecking at the walkway.

Would a reset Oliver still like birds and spiders? Would a reset Oliver still love her as much?

How long before he forgets all these things anyway?

They read a story before bed that night. *Charlotte's Web*, Harriet's choice. He's read it a hundred times and can read much more complicated books now, but she saw the recognition and the delight in re-reading a story he knows so well. If he forgets this book, would he read it again? There's something beautiful in that, in reading a book for the first time again. Will he take the same joy in it? This Oliver would, she's sure, but factory restarted Oliver?

She read *Charlotte's Web* to Tipher when he was little. It didn't matter the mother was a spider. The most baffling thing was her devotion, not her species. They had so few books, a handful that went on rotation. When scavengers brought children's books down, she'd rummage for any change she could to buy them. To get that book, she stole some of her mother's cabbage hooch to trade. Her mum was so out of it she never knew. Harriet could piss in that hooch bucket and her mum wouldn't realise.

When she puts Oliver down for his standby sleep that night, she traces the contours of his face with her thumb, the dimples in his cheeks, his silky eyebrows, his mess of hair. So much like her little brother, but her love for Oliver is fiercer somehow. There's more to him than just familial resemblance. Oliver is tougher, has a worldliness about him, so much for such a young age. Too much. He shouldn't know such bad people like Anthony exist. He shouldn't know the horrors of below ground. All these awful things she once swore to herself she'd never expose a child of hers to. She's been a bad mother, a bad protector.

Would a factory restart mean a restart on her mothering skills too?

She thinks of Tipher, over and over she thinks of Tipher. The pain of losing him has never gone away. It's still raw. If she could erase him from her mind, take that pain away, would she want to?

No. Never.

If she could erase what her parents did to her, to take away those awful memories, take away the blows from Anthony, would she?

She wouldn't either. As awful as they are, her trauma has made her who she is today. If she forgot it, she'd be doomed to relive it.

Her mind to and fros all night.

He would be exactly the same.

He wouldn't know her anymore.

They would have each other.

She has no other option.

Perhaps it'll be just like a bit of amnesia, a woolly head after a heavy night. It's hard to believe their years of bonding can just be dismissed. She knows him so well, the creases of his palms, the way he furrows his brow when he's concerned, the pitch to his voice when he asks if she's okay. Would she know the restarted Oliver so well?

If it's the only way to save Oliver, then what choice does she have?

Chapter 34

Harriet isn't the only one in the refuge who has nightmares. The cries resonate through the dorms and corridors most nights, so frequently, they're mostly ignored. Though there's the odd one — the sort of wailing cry that's too terrifying, too raw to ignore, and a woman jolts awake, upright, sweating and screaming. Those are the ones where the other women go to her, hold her hands, shake with her until her tremors are normalised. Everyone feels it like ripples dying out in a pond. When shared, the shaking goes away sooner.

Whoever was shaking then knows it's okay to be afraid. It's okay because it's like a child being afraid of a TV show or being afraid of a mouse. It's not a real fear. The danger has gone. It's okay to be afraid of something that can't hurt you anymore. There are present dangers that can still hurt, and these women know it's not okay to be afraid of those. They have children. In the face of real danger, they have to be brave.

Harriet wakes with one such nightmare. Before the room has come into focus, there are three women sitting on her bed, calming her, soothing her.

She was back below ground, as a girl, running through the tangle of tunnels she used to know so well, dodging dirty ankles and swinging pickaxes. She was running to school like she always did, to secure one of the few chairs, to be first in line if any food was on offer.

Only she never got to school. The tunnel went on and on and on, collapsing behind her and in front and just ahead. There was Oliver and Tipher and baby Freddie. The tunnel was collapsing on them too, burying them, and no matter how fast she ran or how loud she screamed, she couldn't save any of them. The ground swallowed them all, and all that was left standing on the pile of clay was Anthony.

She's calming now, the other women sharing her fear and diffusing it. One woman towels her brow and reminds her he can't get her anymore.

'Your boy is safe,' she says. 'Look, he sleeps so soundly.'

Oliver's on standby and it's too dark for any mums to notice his lack of breathing. Harriet thanks the women and reassures them she's fine so they can all go back to bed. No doubt it'll be one of them tomorrow, and she'll be at their bedside.

Amber stays a little longer, not letting go of Harriet's hand when the others do.

'I might make a hot chocolate,' Amber says. 'Want one?'

Harriet nods. There's no way she's going to be able to get off to sleep anytime soon.

The canteen is dark and empty. They turn their torches on and place them upright like candles, then Amber lights the stove. It's the first time they've had any chance to talk since Harriet returned from below.

'Want to talk about these bruises?' She gestures to the wounds across Harriet's shoulder.

'It actually wasn't him. Incident below,' she says in a whisper, then explains everything, including about Oliver's reset option. 'I just don't know what to do. I can't just erase him. But I can't keep him. He's clumsy at the moment, getting a bit forgetful, but how much worse will it get?'

Amber pours the hot water and stirs, taking care not to ding the spoon on the cup and make a noise. She passes a cup to Harriet as she sits. 'He must have been one of the first. The oldest are only just turning five now, so it's hard to know.'

'If they would just let us keep them as teens, this wouldn't be an issue. Why do we have to give them up?'

Amber shakes her head, then blows on the steamy cup. 'There are people petitioning, I think. Saying thefts will be less if we were allowed to keep them. Maybe there's hope with that.'

'Yeah, because a petition has ever worked before.'

They clink hot chocolate mugs to that, then wince from the noise.

Amber takes a sip, her brow wrinkling. 'Perhaps email them?'

'TRI?'

'Yeah. Maybe you could say you'll return him on the condition you get to have access. Say it's only fair. Do you know anyone who has links to the company? You're obviously from high up. No offence.'

'Is it that obvious?' Her film accent really has stuck. She sips her hot chocolate and his image comes to mind. The hot chocolate turns bitter on her tongue. 'I do know someone whose company invests in TRI who'd be influential if he was in any way on my side.'

'Who?'

'My husband.'

'Oh.' Amber grimaces. 'Yuck.'

'He hated Oliver. There's no chance he'd help. And Oliver would be crushed if he knew I'd spoken to him. The whole reason I left him was because Oliver gave me the strength to. Going back to him now is unthinkable.'

'You don't have to go back to him. Just ask for his help.'

Harriet shakes her head. 'There will definitely be strings attached to any favour.' She sips some more of her chocolate, but the sweetness isn't enough to take the image of Anthony's face away. She can picture his face if she asks for help, that smug grin, the weight of his fist. 'Keep me in the loop if you hear about any petition outcome?'

'Of course. Fingers crossed something else comes up in the meantime. You know what low-level techies are like. If they think there's a buck to be made, they're resourceful. I'm sure they'll come up with something.'

Harriet washes up their mugs and tiptoes back to bed. She lies back down and strokes Oliver's hair. How she wishes she could go on standby like him, to have a dreamless sleep every night.

She hopes Oliver doesn't dream. He doesn't deserve nightmares.

Chapter 35

Part 3

Sometimes you have to throw yourself into the fire to escape from the smoke.

   Greek proverb

***

There's a café on 4 that sells the best coffee. It's so good, Harriet can imagine she's sitting in one of the top-level coffee shops, sipping it under the sunshine with a view of the tops of the high-rises. Going to a café is a treat these days, unlike it being a daily occurrence when she lived with Anthony. It shocks her now to think of how much she wasted back then. She settled too quickly into the habit of buying new clothes every week, following the latest crazes those damned billboards dictate, eating out for lunch daily, throwing away perfectly usable electricals just because something negligibly better was released. Anthony insisted on it often. Like everyone else, he didn't want to be seen with anything less than the best. He flew a Hel-E to work daily rather than take an AutoTaxi. He had new suits and clothes delivered weekly by a clothing company that knew his exact measurements to tailor, though those measurements weren't updated frequently enough as his drinking habit took hold. Was Harriet always destined to be surrounded by addicts? She's been conditioned from birth.

She got the news from Theo this morning. He called the refuge to tell her. Her mother is dead. Found unresponsive with her head in a half empty bucket of cabbage wine. 'At least Harriet got to say goodbye,' Sylvia said to Theo.

Harriet didn't correct him, didn't tell him goodbye was not a word she uttered. Fuck you, rot in hell, I hope you choke on your own vomit, would all have been far more fitting. She said so little when she saw her mother. Her parents were always able to silence her.

She should feel remorse, as she's sure any decent human would. But there's no room for it with her intoxicating sense of relief.

Instead, she celebrates with a luxury coffee.

She's been doing well, saving money by living in the refuge, her work tips are collecting and she hasn't touched the money from TRI yet. Soon she'll be able to find their own place, a couple of levels up hopefully, a real home for her and Oliver. She's a better parent than hers ever were.

'Mum, can I have a coffee?' Oliver asks.

'No, darling.'

'What about a cake? That boy over there is eating cake.'

'I know, Monkey. But no.'

Oliver puts his elbows on the table and rests his chin in his hands. Besides the cost, this is the other reason why she rarely eats or drinks anywhere nice. She should have left Oliver with Amber for a few minutes or had her coffee while he's on stand-by. It's not fair to him.

'What's it like?' he asks. 'To put something in your mouth and munch it up? Is it nice?'

'Sometimes.'

'Why can't I do it?'

'Because you don't need to.'

'Do you need to? Do you need coffee?'

She sips, enjoying the cleansing joy of the flavour. 'Yes.'

'Does that boy need cake?'

'Probably not.'

Before Oliver can ask anything else, she finishes her coffee, then stands, puts his coat on then walks outside. It's raining, and the sound of the downpour skims past the fences, a little spray spilling over and dampening the walkway at the edges. Across the street is a skatepark. Oliver's been eyeing up the skatepark of late, and she's hoping she can save enough money soon to get him a skateboard.

The skatepark is always busy, mostly with bigger children than Oliver, but some younger ones dare the smaller ramps. There's clanging metal and popping boards, a few cheers and curse words.

'Woah!' Oliver's hands going to his cheeks. 'Did you see that trick? When I grow a bit bigger, I reckon I'll be able to do that.'

His voice is loud and excited, yet she detects in his tone a hint of melancholy, as if talking about something he knows will never be.

She pulls him away from watching, tugging his arm a little as he tries to stand his ground, before he dips his chin and follows. She's got work in a couple of hours and could do with a shower before she has to spend an evening putting on a show for the punters. She has a few regulars now, some only want her to serve them. It surprised her at first, why they'd choose her. There are plenty of more attractive women, younger, with more skin on show. She supposes it's because she can hold a conversation, laugh like she means it, and listens to all of their gripes. She had ten years of nurturing Anthony's ego. If there's one thing she can do well, it's make men feel good about themselves.

Back at the refuge, she takes a shower while Oliver sits and waits.

'I want a shower,' he says.

'Okay.' She takes a sponge and dampens his skin.

'No!' He pushes her away. 'I want a proper shower.'

'Oliver.' She lowers her voice. There are seven individual showers in this block and she listens for the sound of another being used. Besides them, it's silent. 'Please, we've been through this.'

He kicks the side of the cubicle and folds his arms. Harriet finishes her shower quickly, then dresses, all the while Oliver sulks.

'Come on,' Harriet says. 'Let's go sit in the lounge with the other children.'

'No.'

'Oliver!'

'I want to go outside and play. I want to play on the tallest climbing frame.'

'You know you're not allowed. It's for the bigger children.'

'Fin plays on that one now. He was a bit too small, but now he's bigger so he can. He says he's tall because he eats loads. But I never eat anything, so I'm never going to grow.'

She kneels beside him, the wet floor seeping through her jeans, and puts her finger to her lips. 'Try to be quiet.'

'Why?'

She huffs, leaning back. 'Oliver, you need to understand. Come here.' She takes both of his hands but he still avoids her gaze. 'Listen. You're not like the other children, not all of them.'

'Say it, Mum. I just want you to say it.'

'You're . . . special.'

'Say it!' He shouts and Harriet winces, sure everyone outside the bathroom must hear. 'I can't do anything. I'm never going to grow up. I'm not a real boy!'

He yanks his hands free, then bolts for the door.

'Oliver!' she calls and runs after him. But he's so quick, he's out the front door of the refuge before she's even close. 'Oliver!'

He's sprinting across the garden. The gates are straight ahead, and he's close to the button to open them. They're supposed to take their time with that, to look outside to see if anyone is waiting for an opportunity to come in.

'Oliver! No! Wait!'

He ignores her and presses the button. There's a buzz and the gates slide. Harriet's heart rate hikes up a notch. She can't endanger the other women here. She just can't. There's an emergency shut button that she makes for as she slows her run to glance around. There's a man just outside and approaching the gates. In the half-light of level 4 it's hard to make him out, though a few paces later and she exhales in relief when the only man approaching is Theo.

Theo smiles and waves. 'Hey, kiddo.'

'Shut up!'

'Oh.' He looks up at Harriet who's just catching up. 'You guys okay?'

'Oliver.' Harriet reaches him, and she grabs him by the shoulders. 'You are never to press that button! You hear me? You could have endangered every woman and child in the refuge. Is that what you want?'

Oliver's face is in his hands now as he sobs.

'Oh, come here,' she says and crouches in front of him, then pulls him in for a hug. His hands still cover his eyes and she leans back to move his hands away. His face is so downcast and red, though of course, no tears come.

She cups his sad face and her heart aches.

'I'm not a real boy, am I?'

She swallows, then strokes his perfect cheeks as if she were wiping tears away. 'You were made differently to most children, and that means this is the same body you will have forever. Just because you're different from some other children doesn't mean you can't do great things. It doesn't mean you're not good. You can love, and that's all that matters.'

His words come out in a staccato rhythm as his chest jerks with his sobs. 'I'm never going to be a bigger boy?'

She sits on the ground now and he climbs on her lap, her arms going around him and she rocks him back and forth. 'If you want to be a bigger boy, then remember where you used to do tests? They can make you bigger. But it means you'll be taken away from me. We'll never see each other again. Unless—'

'Unless what?' he asks when her voice trails off.

Amber's suggestion of asking Anthony for help comes to her mind. 'There's a small chance Anthony may be able to help, to let you grow up and maybe I can still see you.'

He shakes his head, slowly at first, then faster, his hands going to his temples. 'No. No no no. I can't do that. You can't speak to him. Ever! You promised! I don't care what it takes but you can never ever speak to him again!'

'Okay. Okay.' She holds him a little tighter and kisses the top of his head. 'I will keep my promise. I won't contact him.'

'So . . . so I'm never going to be a bigger boy? I just want the truth. I need to know.'

'Darling, listen.' She plants another kiss on his forehead, a tear tracing down her cheek. She lifts him a little so she's facing him and looks into his eyes. 'We are all different, all of us. You will never know what it's like to eat cake. This is true. Just like I will never know what it is like to be you, to hang from the top of the climbing frame, to know all the birds. All we know is what we perceive and we all perceive things differently. We all feel things differently. Like I know, with my whole being, that I love you, my son. You are as real to me as anyone. But. . .' her stomach clenches before she can say her next words. 'You're right. You're never going to grow.'

His big blue eyes stare right at her and his shoulders relax. 'Okay. Now I know the truth. I suppose I can be your little boy forever.'

Theo crouches next to them. 'You're better at Uno than any kid or grown-up I ever met. That's a skill only real boys can have.'

Oliver chuckles his adorable little laugh.

'I bought you some more games,' Theo says. 'If you want to play? But they're only for real boys. So . . .' he teases, 'I guess that means you can play.'

Oliver's face breaks into a grin, and he jumps over to Theo. She stands, brushes herself down, and mouths, *Thank you*, to Theo.

They walk to a table and chairs outside the gates. Theo isn't allowed inside the refuge. Being a women's refuge it has a 'no adult male' policy. The rain from earlier has calmed and the shower has dampened the smell that often wafts up from ground level. There's a humidity to the air that reminds Harriet of down below.

Theo unpacks a chessboard and teaches Oliver the basics. She never had the patience to learn when they were kids and Tipher could rarely concentrate for long enough to play. It was the one game Theo used to want them to play and they so rarely did. Harriet watches on as Oliver learns all the names of the pieces, the basic moves, and he masters it quickly.

It's Oliver's choice, she tells herself. She's been honest with him now. He knows staying with her means he'll stay this size forever.

I suppose I can be your little boy forever.

His words are like a song, the sweetest verse. Although there's a bitter side to it. She knows he wants to grow up and he doesn't know the consequences of staying with her. He'll be her little boy forever, but she's going to have to wipe his mind.

It's the first time she's considered taking him back to TRI. He so wants to be a bigger boy and although he said he wants to stay with her, he doesn't yet know he's degrading. She's still telling half-truths, to protect the boy she loves so much. If he knew the whole situation, what would he choose?

He's got a shitty hand either way.

Chapter 36

Several other mothers at the refuge who stay in the late-night workers' dorm, also have MechaniKids, not just Amber. Eight others share this room and she knows with certainty that five of them have MechaniKids. Despite obviously knowing, Harriet still makes sure Oliver changes out of view, still keeps his charging cable hidden in her bag. It's best to keep good habits, she tells herself. And also, just because the others have MechaniKids, doesn't mean they won't throw her under the bus.

It makes her wonder how many are out there? Six in this refuge, from such a small sample size. Extrapolate that over the local population and there must be thousands of MechaniKid parents. Or, as she ponders this further, it's likely many are in the refuge as they're also on the run from TRI. Parents of normal children don't have a multitrillion-pound tech company trying to take their children away.

In the other MechaniKids, she looks for signs of degradation but sees none. Oliver's daily falls and lost words seem unique among these few, and based on his other abilities, it's clear he's the eldest. His fifth birthday is rapidly approaching, and she still hasn't decided what to do.

A new woman arrives and moves into the empty bed in Harriet's dorm. She's eyed with suspicion as always by the others. She's careless and has only been at the refuge for a few hours when Harriet catches a glimpse of her child's charge socket. Harriet nods and smiles at the mother, then makes her most reassuring face to let her know she's safe, that she won't tell. Over the next few days, Harriet observes the little boy. He clicks with Oliver instantly. They reach for the same books and toys, speak with the same eloquence. He must be Oliver's age. He seems mature but, like Oliver, he trips over, forgets things, his gaze sometimes far away.

The mother has a face so pale and drawn she appears as if she hasn't slept in weeks. She looks like she was beautiful once, before sleep eluded her and was replaced by stress. She has the jitters, jumping at every sound, has grazes on her elbows, and a scratch down her cheek. Her hair appears recently bleached, brittle and coppery blonde rather than golden blonde, like it was darker once and took several attempts to get its natural colour out. She's thin and Harriet hopes she'll be eating her son's portions too to try to fill out her hollowed cheeks. Harriet learns the mother's name is Josie and her little boy, pink-cheeked and red-haired, is Thomas.

'How old is yours?' she asks Harriet one afternoon as they sit in the lounge area of the refuge. It's bitterly cold outside and when they attempted to go to the park, the climbing frame poles were too frosty to hold.

'Six,' Harriet says without hesitation.

'I mean, his actual age.'

Harriet fidgets a moment, then Josie pulls back Thomas's shorts. Harriet's seen Thomas's charging socket before, but it's like a code to reveal it properly, a true act of trust.

Harriet swallows. 'He'll be five in four weeks.'

Josie nods. 'My Thomas is five in two weeks. He's getting worse. It's breaking my heart.'

'I can get him a factory reset, but—'

'But he'll forget everything. Yeah, I got the same answer.'

They're sitting on the dilapidated sofa and Harriet idles her fingers picking at the stuffing, watching the children. Both of their hands are blue-black with bunched-up skin. She glances over at Josie and notes the glint of unshed tears as Thomas returns to play with Oliver, forgetting his name at first. Oliver puts his arm around him and consoles him, then reintroduces himself.

'There are loads of us, you know,' Josie says. 'Thousands of MechaniKids were given out. They made it sound like the interview process was so tough, but so many got picked.'

Harriet's jaw drops. 'Really?'

'Yeah. I've read so many stories. Then you go in for the assessments and they say your kid is one of a kind or whatever.'

'That's exactly what they said to me. They said Oliver was the smartest.'

'I guess they want you to keep working hard. Keep working the children hard. But think about it. They want to replace a huge chunk of the workforce with MechaniKids when they're grown up so they must need loads.'

Harriet leans back in the chair, folding her arms. 'I guess so. I never thought of it like that.'

'What it means though, is they're not as financially important to TRI as we thought, and that petition that's going around, to let us keep access, it'll do naff all. They expect a few to go AWOL. They've budgeted for this, and I doubt they're even looking for them.'

'Shit,' Harriet says, her body going slack. 'That petition was basically my last hope.'

'I'm going to think of something. These are our children. There must be a way.'

Harriet takes her hand, and Josie doesn't flinch. In Josie's face, Harriet sees the kind of resolve Oliver has when he's trying to get to the last rung on the climbing frame, or figure out a new word in a book. The kind of face that doesn't know how to fail.

Harriet considers her own life, her own track record of getting anything done, and sees a list of failures. But perhaps with Josie, she actually won't screw this up. She's been starting to realise the lack of friends in her life has been holding her back so now, with Josie, maybe this time she really can save the little boy she loves.

Chapter 37

It snowed on the top levels the other day. Harriet knows because some snowflakes fell all the way down, beyond the walkway fences, glinting in a way garbage doesn't. Falling softly, like it isn't in a hurry to join the landfill. The acoustics are different with snow. The constant crashing of rubbish is dull and muffled. Harriet was tempted to reach her hand out over the fence and catch a flake, but reaching beyond the fence is a sure way to get your arm broken or chopped off.

It only snowed twice when Harriet lived up on 107 and it wasn't much, just a layer of sparkle. A shimmer. It wasn't a big deal to the top dwellers who've never lived low down. Everything up there shines.

Down on 4, Harriet and Oliver spend even more time at the park. So much of her life is spent on a bench. They never have to worry about the rain down here when they're away from the edge of the walkway fences, only the cold. There are no flowers down this low, no real flowers anyway. Colourful artificial blooms line some of the nicer parks, though even those have seen better days. Even fake flowers wilt if neglected.

Today the sounds are harsh again, the flow of rubbish nev-er-ending. It's only occasionally she feels the claustrophobia of the lower levels. Being born below, she's used to living under a ceiling. Even short people walk with hunched shoulders and dipped heads as if they're about to headbutt the roof. She's adopting that posture already. The stoop of someone crushed from those above.

'Monkey, look who's here!' Harriet shouts up to Oliver when she sees Theo and Monty approaching.

Oliver's helping Delilah learn to climb again, having regained some of the confidence he lost. He's encouraged her up to the third rung now. She doesn't have his fearlessness at all, but she loves to learn and pays attention to his every instruction. When he tries to tell her just one more, she shakes her head and says no. Amber watches her with an air of terror when she gets past the second rung, though smiles when she refuses to go higher. Delilah really has learned to say no when it suits her.

Harriet doesn't tell Amber that the worries about danger get easier to watch with time, as she doesn't think it does. She'd never tell Oliver not to do something he loves, but her heart is in her throat the entire time. Sometimes, she thinks she should just close her eyes to rid herself of the stress and ignore Oliver's constant pleas for her to watch.

'Uncle Theo!' Oliver runs towards him, no falling this time, and slams into Theo's legs for a hug.

'Hey, Oliver! How's it going? You remember Monty?'

Harriet wonders if one day people will start shortening Oliver's name to Oli. She hopes not. He's worth every syllable.

Oliver steps away and arches his back to look up at Monty. He's a few inches taller than Theo and a lot broader. There's no recognition in Oliver's face at all.

'You only met him briefly, darling,' Harriet says, before Oliver can get upset about forgetting someone again. 'And it was a while ago.' She mouths an apology to Monty who doesn't seem bothered at all. She assumes Theo's updated him with Oliver's troubles.

'Well,' Monty says, 'you'll remember me forever once you see what I've made.' Out of a carrier bag, he pulls out a little toy dinosaur. Hand carved out of a mixture of wood and plastic, beautifully detailed with a long moving neck and thick legs.

Harriet's hands go to her mouth. 'Oh, my! Monty, that's amazing.'

If Oliver's eyes were any wider, they'd pop from his sockets. He lifts his hands so gently to take it, his jaw hanging low. 'Wow. This is for me?'

'Sure is. Made it myself.'

Oliver leans into Monty's legs and hugs him with one arm, the other clutching the dinosaur. 'Thank you!'

Monty smiles, then whispers to Harriet, 'There're also cookies for the grown-ups.'

Harriet's eyes light up and they all join Amber at her table. It's milder for once, though there's the smell of damp from an earlier shower that splashed over the walkway fence.

'Sorry we have to stay out here. No men inside the refuge,' Harriet says.

'A building without men.' Monty holds his hand to his heart and fakes some pain. 'Tragic.'

'No wonder you gave up auditioning.' Harriet laughs, poking him in the arm.

She introduces Amber and Delilah, and the children go back to the play area so the adults can eat the cookies guilt-free.

'Monty, these are amazing!' Harriet says with her mouth full, her eyes rolling back. 'Why am I only just tasting your cooking now?'

Monty's toothy grin is wide and teasing. 'Well, Theo will tell you, I aim to please.'

Theo blushes as Harriet chuckles. Monty was never subtle. She couldn't imagine them being a good match when Theo told her, but now she sees it. They're perfect. Monty is as loud and inappropriate as Theo is quiet and reserved. Perfectly complementary.

'We're hoping the cookies will persuade you to move in with us,' Theo says. 'As soon as you're ready. Shay found another place, so she'll be going in a couple of weeks.'

'I'm sorry I didn't stand up for you more before,' Monty says. 'I was just shocked, to be honest. And you know it takes a lot to shock me.'

'Thank you, both. And you didn't need the cookies to convince me.'

'We also come with some more troubling news,' Monty says, dipping his voice. 'Friends of friends of friends — you know how it is — they work in lackey roles for AM Investments. That's your husband's company, right?'

'Ex-husband,' Harriet corrects.

'Well, not according to him. He's kept it hush-hush among top dwellers, but among the lower levels there's a reward out to bring you home. Bounty hunters are looking for you.'

Harriet sighs and rests her elbows on the table. 'I was hoping he would have given up by now.'

'He doesn't sound like the kind of person you can just walk away from,' Monty says. 'You've got a hefty bounty on your head.'

Amber rubs Harriet's forearm. 'Fuck him. Lower-level people stick together. Don't be afraid.'

Afraid? Harriet can't remember what it's like to not be afraid. Afraid of her parents, of everything below, or starving, of her husband, afraid for her son. What is life but an endless stream of fears? She seems to bounce from one terrifying situation to another. How would it be to not be afraid?

'Do lower-level people stick together? I don't know. Below ground, everyone is definitely out for themselves. Well, most.' Harriet huffs a breath and rubs her forehead. 'Maybe I should change my hair or something?'

'Good idea,' Amber says.

'I'm not sure about work. Would it be safe there? I wear enough glitter and it's dark in there, so I doubt anyone would recognise me from a photo. I should start using another name, maybe.'

'Even if he found you, someone would have to physically kidnap you and then you could just leave again,' Theo says, being the calm voice of reason Harriet needs.

'He's saying you're mentally ill,' Monty says. 'That you're not well enough to be on your own. He's trying to sell it as it's for your own good. *Eurgh*, what a creep.'

Harriet takes a breath and forces some logic into her head-space. 'Look, it's fine. I expected this. He's a nasty prick. He was never going to let his prized possession go. I'm just worried if something happens to me. What about Oliver?'

'You know I'll take care of him,' Amber says.

'Or us,' Theo says.

Harriet's chills thaw a little, but there are a thousand scenarios playing out in her mind. All of them put Oliver in danger. 'Thank you. Truly. But I still need a plan to fix him somehow. If something happens to me before I've figured that out, then what? You're left with the burden.'

'Maybe, until then, stay inside at the refuge,' Theo says.

'But I need to charge him. When I'm at work, that's the only time I can plug him in.' Little coloured spots bubble up in her vision and a tightness pulls across her temples. She shuts her eyes and tries to relax her migraine away. She always used to be able to control her migraines so well, the warning signs easily decipherable. Now, she's a coiled spring, too tight to relax. 'Thank you for telling me, but I think I just need to carry on as I am.' She sits a little straighter and rolls her shoulders back, trying to show a little of the bravery Oliver does so well. 'I'm not going to cower away from that bully. Perhaps I'll get a new can of mace.'

When Theo and Monty leave, Harriet's headache intensifies and she uses the refuge's phone to call in sick at work. One of the other mums has some migraine tablets and gives Harriet a couple. After half an hour, they work a treat. She's a little woozy and sleepy, but the spots and pain have gone.

She puts Oliver down to sleep early to conserve his battery, then sits up on the sofa with a book, one about some dashing rich guy stealing a young woman's heart. By page ten, she's wondering why she's reading it. As the lights get dimmer and she has only her torch, she puts it away and is joined by Josie.

Her torch casts a beam across Josie's face. That hint of beauty behind her sadness is there, glowing in the torchlight. Harriet's face heats and she hopes her blush doesn't show. Harriet stifles a yawn, thinks she should have an early night and sleep off the medication, but sitting with Josie is more tempting.

Josie sits cross-legged on the sofa, smiles, and leans in. 'I have a plan.'

Harriet's eyes are wide as she takes in Josie's earnestness, her set jaw, and she shuffles closer.

'I have a friend who works at TRI,' Josie says, her unblinking eyes gazing straight into Harriet's. 'I'm going to steal a Mechan-iTeen.'

Chapter 38

Josie's plan is reckless, though well thought out. Harriet listens to the details, wishes her head wasn't so muzzy from the painkiller, wipes her sweaty palms on her jeans, then bites her nails. Once she's heard the entire crazy plan, she calls Amber over. Delilah sits on her lap patiently as Amber plaits her hair. Delilah has a doll in her arms, talking to it as if it were a baby.

'Why are you whispering?' Delilah asks Amber as they chat.

'So no one knows our business,' Amber says.

'It's rude to whisper.'

'It's rude for *children* to whisper.'

Delilah's eyes widen and her jaw drops. 'Why children and not grown-ups?'

Harriet and Josie stifle their giggles as Amber tries to explain adult behaviour to Delilah. She's learning to argue, to debate, to question instruction. Harriet remembers so well when Oliver learned this, but for Delilah, who was programmed to be obedient, this is a huge milestone and there's a glint of pride in Amber's eyes.

'You've no idea how wonderful it is to hear her question things,' Amber whispers to Harriet.

'She'll be arguing non-stop and slamming doors soon.'

'Can I do Harriet's hair again?' Delilah asks.

'Not now, sweetie,' Amber says.

'Next time, I promise,' Harriet says, and Delilah jumps on her lap and gives her a hug. 'Can I call you Auntie Harriet?'

A lump lodges in Harriet's throat, and she blinks away happy tears. 'Of course.'

Delilah hops down and grins before running off to play.

'I always wanted a daughter. Niece will do nicely,' Harriet says, giving Amber's arm a little squeeze. 'You've done so well with her. She's a joy.'

'She really is,' Josie says.

'Josie has a plan,' Harriet says to Amber, and they fill her in.

Amber shifts further back along the sofa, making some space between them, and peers at each of their faces in turn. 'You're actually serious.'

'I can get us in,' Josie says. 'I can do this.'

Amber shakes her head. 'Good luck to you both. I mean that. But Delilah is only three. I don't need to take such a big risk yet.'

Harriet takes her hand, looks at Delilah, then back at Amber. She's right. Amber has years ahead of her. Who knows what changes and advancements there will be by then. She envies the time Amber and Delilah have ahead of them, their lack of need for haste.

'We'll let you know how it goes,' Harriet says. 'Hopefully you'll never need to do anything so drastic.'

Breaking into TRI and stealing a new body for Oliver. It's bonkers. Crazy. How is it she's even contemplating such a plan?

Breaking into the warehouse of the biggest tech company in the world.

Stealing a MechaniTeen, one of their most valuable products.

Uploading Oliver's personality module to another body.

She wipes the sweat from her palms again. Grey splotches litter her vision, and she tugs on her sleeves. Her mind can't get past the first hurdle on that list, let alone the third.

Josie seems to think it'll be simple. Her little boy, Thomas, is in a more desperate need than Oliver. Desperation leads to poorly thought-out plans. Harriet can spare the time to think things through properly. Can Josie?

'Should we speak to the others?' Josie asks. 'There are other MechaniKid mums here, I'm sure.'

'None are as old though, I don't think,' Harriet says. 'Amber's right. It's a big risk for those whose kids aren't degrading yet. By the time they're the right age, they may not need to go to such lengths. And I haven't spoken to any of them. Just because they're here, doesn't mean they've stolen their children.'

'Good point. So, just us then?'

Harriet nods. 'I guess so.'

'It's you and me then, Movie Star.'

Harriet gasps, her face heats. 'Literally no one ever recognises me. That was years ago. A lifetime ago.'

Josie gives her a playful nudge. 'Well, maybe I was your biggest fan.'

Josie has a twinkle in her eye, and Harriet shuffles closer to her along the sofa, then stops. Her nerves are shot, her skin tingles all over and her heart rate doesn't know what to do. She takes a breath and angles slightly away from Josie. Now is not the time for romantic interests. Perhaps when the children are sorted, they could explore something more. When the children are safe, there will be time for that other kind of danger.

Harriet can imagine Josie was a troublemaker at school, getting detention and up to all sorts of mischief. Harriet was never like that. She's always behaved and done as she's told. It's hard for her to break rules. It makes her clothes itch and her heart rate spike. But she's already stolen Oliver. That's one huge rule broken. She's a criminal now whatever the outcome.

With a plan in place, Josie's sallow complexion has gained colour. She's been eating more since she arrived and has a renewed energy Harriet finds alluring.

They keep talking. Not about the plan now, about the children and their hopes for their futures, what they'll look like as teenagers, where they hope to end up living. As they talk, their knees brush against each other. Sometimes Josie's hand nudges Harriet's thigh and it's like lightning bolts.

Harriet tries to rid her mind of such thoughts. One problem at a time. One reckless plan at a time.

Chapter 39

Harriet can't stop picturing Oliver as a MechaniTeen. For weeks she's been thinking about how to save him but imagining keeping him as her little boy in the same body. Now she knows he may have an opportunity to grow up, she pictures tufts of facial hair, grumpy teenage moods, crushes and spending forever choosing what to wear. How is it she can long for all of that but also dread it? She loves her little boy so much, but she can't keep him little forever. It'll be a dream come true for Oliver. All he wants in the world is to be a bigger boy.

She has another night off, but Oliver needs charging, so she walks with Josie and Amber to some e-bike chargers. Harriet avoids the one by her work, not wanting to see that place on her day off and not wanting to go down to 3 if she doesn't have to. There are some charging stations behind a parade of shops on 4, about an hour's walk from the refuge, Amber says. They head there, hoping to keep each other company for the hours it takes to charge.

Harriet's mind drifts to Anthony, of that pig using his wealth to put a bounty on her head. He's never had to fight to survive. Electricity is power, so the lower-levels say, and the top-level arseholes have plenty of both. Down here, though, she has something she never had up there. She has support and friendship. Perhaps Amber was right and lower-level people do help each other out, like there's a sweet spot. Below ground, so many people would gladly steal from you if it meant their better chance at survival. Up top, they do the same, but to make themselves richer, more powerful. Down here — not below, though not high up — people have enough to survive yet would never stoop as low as they do up top. Perhaps here is where goodness begins and further away it becomes diluted and poisoned.

At least below ground, they have an excuse. They're just trying to live. Funny that when she lived there, she abhorred some of the behaviour she witnessed below and idolised those high up. Now she can appreciate the greed and the waste of the top levels, she's aware of who the real criminals are.

They find three charging points a few metres apart, plug the children in, cover them, then sit together. It's the darkest night. Harriet can imagine what the view would be out of Anthony's penthouse window. A black, moonless sky with a sprinkling of stars. Here, the view is of the underside of the next level, stretching only as far as the walkway fence. There's the occasional crash and thud as rubbish makes its way down, otherwise it's silent. Boarded-up shops line one street ahead, while the park in front of that houses broken play equipment and weeds. At this end of town, even the streetlights and billboards don't work.

'That's why these chargers are usually free,' Amber says. 'Everyone thinks the electric is out.'

'Yeah, that and it's creepy as fuck being this dark.' Josie glances around.

Harriet quietly agrees and wonders in hindsight if charging at the bar would have been better.

At least it's deserted. If anyone is out searching for her, they're not around here.

For hours, they chat and share small details. Not much, but they share enough. Josie says she adopted Thomas because she needed the money. She owed some to debtors to pay for her parents to move up from below. They were dying. She thought she could save them by taking them to doctors above ground, but they died anyway, and her debts spiralled.

'I've heard up top, when parents die, their kids inherit money,' Josie says, disbelief in her tone. 'Can you believe that? For us, we just inherit debt.'

They all tut and shake their heads.

Amber's situation was similar to Harriet's, only seventy levels lower. She got away from that home life, poorer and alone.

'I never knew how bad loneliness can be,' she says. 'He beat me, but it was company. It's sick that I felt that way. I guess I've always been lonely to some degree, but when I left, I had no one at all.'

Harriet squirms. Loneliness is something she knows all too well. Even the mention of it makes her skin tighten.

'When I took Delilah home, I thought it would just be a bit of company for a few years, would help me get back on my feet. I knew as soon as I saw her that I loved her like a daughter. She has those big round cheeks like my sister had,' Amber says as her voice trails away. There's no need to ask where her sister is now.

'I didn't even pay much attention to the catalogue,' Josie says. 'Thomas was the first one. I said he'd be fine. Didn't give it any thought at all. I've never had any young family to compare him to, and I didn't even consider choosing one that looked like me. Now, his teen body is all I think about. I bleached my hair to try to make it redder, like his. It doesn't matter, it shouldn't matter, but I love his eyes and his chin and his hair and everything. I hope I can find a teen that has some resemblance.'

Harriet's gaze is far away into the night. Into the future, with her teenage son with all the good looks he should have. What Tipher would have looked like, or Freddie. She swallows a lump in her throat and tries to keep the tears away. A million times she's cried for her lost boys. Perhaps soon, she can have happy tears for Oliver.

When the children are fully charged, they unplug them, listen to their happy good morning squeals, then shine their torches to light their way as they run down the walkways. Oliver's never done his night-time walk home with other children before, neither have the others and they treat it as quite the adventure.

For Harriet, as always, it's terrifying.

The quiet end of town they're on gives way to busier streets with working lights. They call the children in closer, gripping their hands to stop them from running off. There are drunks spilling out of bars and some tall guy bumps into them, sweat-stained armpits about Harriet's head height, and she gets a face-slap of soggy pit. She shakes it off and dodges him, but the crowd becomes denser, louder, rowdier. She has a hat on and pulls her scarf up, hoping she's covered enough.

Everyone in the crowd has eyes and in her paranoid state, she's sure all those eyes are on her. She's sure she must have a spotlight on her, like she's on the West End stage again, getting stage fright for the first time.

The six of them move together, like a flock of birds, safety in numbers. Harriet dips her chin and pulls her scarf up even higher. Oliver isn't dressed enough. He should have a hood to pull up, a scarf as well. He might not be cold, but he needs to be covered up, to blend in.

She spots them in the crowd, creeping among the people, craning their heads upwards to gaze upon people's faces, hands in their pockets where Harriet knows they'll have mace or tasers. Bounty hunters.

They're always around. She's barely given them a second glance before. But now these low-level youths have a sinister appearance, X-ray vision and instincts far greater than hers. She knows they're not just after criminals and kidnapped children.

The six of them carry on down the crowded street, past bar after bar, late night eateries and brothels. On the edge of the strip is the poster-board where people advertise for jobs and help and training courses. Slap bang in the middle, an A4 sized piece of paper, is her picture. Not just her. Oliver too.

She stalls, her stomach dropping several storeys as she stands frozen for a few seconds. The next breath she takes isn't enough and she forces another, shallow and shuddering. She glances around and on the side of buildings, park benches, lamp posts, is the same poster again and again.

The others see it. Amber's fingers dig into her arm. 'Hurry up we should get back,' Amber says.

Harriet looks at Oliver. The pair of them together are so recognisable from the photo. It's one she took as a selfie a couple of years ago. It was on her phone only. Somehow, Anthony has a copy. Her lungs are still working overtime, inefficient and rapid and the space closes in, tight and constricted, all those eyes right next to her, on top of her, peeling her layers away. Her boy, her son, will get spotted because of her. Harriet is a danger to her child.

'Take him,' Harriet says to the others, her voice rasping. 'Take Oliver. We need to split up. We can't be seen together.'

Josie grabs Harriet by the wrist and drags her into a dark corner behind a shop. There's a broken billboard and they crouch behind it, the world spinning around as she does, and Harriet holds the wall for support.

'You can't be out here on your own,' Josie says in a harsh whisper.

'I can't be with Oliver. He's more likely to get noticed with me.'

Amber looks at her daughter. 'Delilah, take off your scarf.'

Delilah does without hesitation and hands it to Amber, who wraps it around Oliver, all the way up to his eyes.

Josie takes off Thomas's hat and puts that on Oliver too.

'There,' Josie says. 'That'll get you home.'

There's a gruff laugh from outside, and they all huddle in closer. Harriet's eyes stream, her hand over her mouth to silence her panting breaths. Oliver hugs her legs while her other arm goes around him, instinctively protective, though being next to him is causing him more danger than a hug can protect him from.

'Woo-hoo! Look who that is!' one man says. There's the sound of paper ripping and Harriet peers round. A man is holding the poster with her face. She's sure she recognises him. 'That's the whore who maced us. That bitch who broke your nose!'

Harriet snaps her head back and her bones turn to ice.

'Imagine the reward!' the man continues. Harriet knows that voice. She's pleaded with it before, angered it, run from it. 'Return the crazy bitch back to her husband and cash in the bot.'

Josie and Amber's wide eyes stare at Harriet. They're shaking as much as she is.

They wait in that cramped and dizzying space, listening to those men ridicule her and plot their revenge. Harriet's hands go to Oliver's ears as the men describe what they would do to her and Oliver. Bile inches up her throat and anger courses through her veins. Her shivers cease as her muscles tighten. She should have killed those men, should have stamped on their necks and rammed the mace can down their throats.

The gruff voices fade as they walk away, their footsteps joining the rest, and Harriet and the others dare to speak again.

'Friends of yours?' Amber asks.

Harriet can't relax. She speaks through her teeth. 'We met down on 2. Ages ago.'

'Well, they haven't forgotten you,' Josie says. 'Don't suppose you have another can of mace?'

Harriet shakes her head. 'Take Oliver. Please. I'm going to wait out the kick-out rush here. He needs to save his battery. I'll be a lot happier knowing he's away from me right now.'

Oliver looks up at her, his eyes wide and needy. 'I don't want to leave you.'

She kneels next to him. 'It's okay, darling. Like spiders, remember, spider babies have to go it alone for a while.'

'The mother spiders die. Don't you know anything about spiders?'

She pulls his hat back an inch to kiss his forehead. 'We'll both be safer this way. It's only for a couple of hours. You need to be brave, okay? And you need to help protect Delilah. She's much younger than you and looks up to you.'

Oliver looks at Delilah who stands quietly, tilting her head to the side and taking it all in. Oliver purses his lips and puffs out his chest. 'Okay. Promise me you'll come home soon?'

'I promise, Monkey. Now you do whatever Amber and Josie say.'

Oliver holds Delilah's hand, and they walk away. When they're out of sight, Harriet leans against the wall and sucks in a deep breath, her relief not enough to quell her dread. She's sent her son away. How could she? She should be able to protect her child, not send him running like she's always done. She slides down the wall, hugs her knees, and sobs into her lap. Only for a moment. After she's rid herself of pity, she grits her teeth and lets rage take hold.

Fuck Anthony.

He's trying to take everything from her. The freedom she has clawed out will not be stolen from her. Not by him. Not ever.

There's some grime among the floor and she reaches down and smudges it on her face, her clothes, makes herself look like someone who has just come up from below. There's a beer bottle with a few dregs in and she pours that over her head and rubs it into her hair. She can act like a drunk. No one will recognise her from the clean and smiling photo he's had plastered all over the town. She'll put on the show of her life.

It must be half an hour since they left with Oliver. That should be enough of a head start.

She leaves her hiding place, staggering, rambling to herself, nonsensical bullshit, the kind of crap she half listens to at work. She coughs and hiccups and bumps into people. Burping, retching, until most give her a wide berth. Mingled with the crowds are the odd police and ambulance bikes with carriages on trailers behind. She walks a little straighter when she sees them. She doesn't want to play the part of disruptive drunk too well.

It's hard to stay in character when she comes face-to-face with the poster of her. She stops, looks at it, tilting her head and swaying on the spot. She stumbles forward and reaches out for it, ripping it off the wall.

'Reward!' she slurs. 'I'm gonna find this bitch. Oh, yes. She's mine.' She hiccups and coughs and shoves the poster in her pocket.

No one looks at her. No one even gets close.

Her half-hour walk home takes an hour as she zigzags the entire way until she rounds the final corner to her street. She pauses when the refuge is in sight, just for a split second, but even that is too long, before she dives down to hide behind a bench.

He's there. The man who can take everything from her.

Anthony.

Chapter 40

Harriet's breath fogs in front of her, and she covers her mouth to shield it. She can hear his voice rambling, drunk and aggressive.

The gates are closed. Thank God the gates are closed. She can hear the buzz from the intercom. He must be waking up everyone. That's a small piece of guilt, though the women will understand. When it comes to abusive men, that's something they all relate to.

On her hands and knees, Harriet peers through the gap in the bench. She wishes she knew if they made it back with Oliver, wishes she could see them inside.

It's Rosa on the night shift, with her kind face and no-nonsense attitude. Harriet strains to listen.

'If you don't go away and stop causing trouble, I'll have to call the police.'

'Police on level 4. Give me a break. Police are for top levels. Important levels. Down here, what are you going to do? Throw cabbages at me.' His voice is stuttering and slurred. If she didn't know him so well, she's not sure she'd understand him.

'Leave. Now.'

'My wife. Harriet Chapel. She's been seen around here. I've got eyewitness accounts. Tell her to come out and I'll go away.'

'There is no woman by that name in here. Now go.'

'How about I smoke the place out? That should have all your little fleas come running out.'

There's a lighter in his hand, glowing as he sparks it, a piece of rag in the other. Can she watch this? Can she just sit and watch while he tries to harm others?

No. She can't.

The rag is lit now, flaming at Anthony's side. She hadn't seen it before but now she can make out the petrol can, the solvent smell, and Anthony reaches for it.

'Stop!' She runs over.

Anthony steps away from the can and turns around. In the distance there's the blue flash of police bikes. They're too far away to be useful now.

Anthony's lips curl up, his eyes narrow. 'Harriet? My wife?' His voice sounds like a wet fart.

She can smell the booze from metres away, even over the top of the beer she poured on herself.

'Don't, Anthony,' she says. 'Just leave.'

He drops the rag and stamps it out. 'You're coming home with me.'

'No. I mean it. Leave.' She steps closer. She won't cower, won't show weakness to this arsehole ever again.

He lunges forward and grabs her wrist, and she kicks him. In his drunken state, he goes down easily but rights himself straight away.

'You know no one will love you like I do. You know you're nothing without me.'

There's a clicking from off to the side, a buzz. She doesn't turn, but she knows that sound and she stands straighter, as tall as she can. She knows she's so much smaller than him, physically weaker, but she can stand up to him. She's tired of running from him.

'I'll drag you all the way if I have to. You belong to me, understand? You belong to—'

The women all exit the gate and stand next to Harriet. All forty or so women who live in the refuge surround her. Amber and Josie are off to one side and they smile at Harriet before turning their steely gazes on Anthony.

Rosa takes Harriet's right hand and faces Anthony. 'You were told to leave.'

Anthony staggers backwards, his eyes and head turning side to side to take in the sight. His back rounds, his posture stoops. He's shrivelling, a coward. He holds up his hands. 'Fine. I'm not going to beg. You'll come back to me though, Harriet. I guarantee it. I know how to make you come back to me.'

He turns and walks away into the night and Harriet's chest caves in like he punched her in the gut. Her hands go to her mouth as tears brim. There are forty women still around her, hugging her, telling her she's okay.

'You're safe.'

'He's gone.'

'Fuck him.'

Harriet is left spent, weak, and trembling. They go back inside the refuge and they all sit up with her, the ones whose children are sound asleep. Someone makes hot chocolates, another hands out biscuits. They bitch and laugh and tell Harriet she's not alone. Mothers are never alone. Women are a force to be reckoned with, greater than the sum of their parts.

Their words stop her shaking, their laughs become hers. Their chatter is a comfort blanket. Friendship is all the warmth she needs.

Rosa finds a pair of scissors and Harriet nods when she offers to restyle her hair. Harriet rinses the sticky beer away in the sink, then Rosa cuts the waves out of the hair that Anthony has yanked so many times and pulled from her scalp. She wants to cut away every bit of her he's ever touched.

When she finally gets to bed, she lifts Oliver from his cot into her bed to cuddle him. She wishes he could have seen her stand up to Anthony, wishes he had more of a role model of a mother, one who fights rather than runs. As she strokes his hair and kisses his head, she whispers to him that she's okay. That Anthony is never going to take her away from him.

Chapter 41

Harriet can't go back to her usual job. They all know her name. They'll recognise her from the posters. Josie's been discussing her plan some more but, in the meantime, Harriet needs to work and needs to charge Oliver. After a night of searching, she finds another bar on 4 that has a plug out back and, after giving the boss a fake name, she starts work the following night.

With Oliver charging outside and plugged in, Harriet covers him in a sheet as always and feels guilty about it. It seems so undignified. Not that he ever knows. She kisses his forehead, tells him goodnight, and puts him on standby. But he looks like he's been discarded left outside all alone. Every moment at work, she worries about him and makes excuses when she can to check on him.

It's dim in the bar. Each table is furnished with a lamp, not even bright enough to read by. A flattering level of luminescence means most can go about their day without being recognised on the street afterwards. There's enough glitter and face paint around to add to the camouflage. Harriet's been doing well financially and is grateful for the refuge every day as she's avoided working in the private booths. The velvet curtains that hide the activities in there line the back wall. The private booths are plentiful if she was ever that out of pocket.

Harriet eases into her first night, well-practised from the previous bar. She was raised to be meek and subservient and to flatter men. The first tips Harriet ever received were from the people her dad bought back. On the sly, away from her father's greedy gaze, they slipped her a few coins.

'Something special for you, sweetheart.'

'There'll be more if you're a bit more enthused next time.'

'Something special for a special girl.'

She shudders to think of it now. She was so young then, so stupid. At least now she's old enough to say fuck off when she wants. She's old enough to kick someone in the crotch.

Never again, she told herself when she ran away, but then her first acting jobs were much the same. She was smart at school, too smart for that kind of work, but she was pretty and poor. For a while, the only work available was where the interview meant a hand up her skirt.

This bar now is fine. She gets the odd grope, much like the last. But as long as she avoids those curtains, she can cope. And if anyone gets too friendly, there's security.

Staff turnover in such jobs is high and so Harriet doesn't bother getting too close to anyone. She's had a few tearful conversations from some staff in the previous bar. So many are desperate, penniless and hungry. They've children with absent fathers and are struggling to pay rent. Harriet listens but comes away from those conversations dejected and low. She had so much when she was with Anthony. She had access to so much money yet didn't do anything worthwhile with it. She abandoned her people.

Tonight, in the staff room, Harriet listens to the women and their gripes but never discusses her own situation. She wouldn't put it past any of these women to act as bounty hunters. She can't trust anyone.

Harriet's carrying a tray of drinks for a table who have been rowdy but not too awful so far. She places their drinks on the table, calls them cheeky or whatever makes them wink at her. The bar is heaving and every table is taken. There's a show on the stage featuring topless women dancing, and that keeps most of the attention. She dishes out the last drinks, then hurries back to the bar to fetch drinks for her other table.

She looks up, freezing as she makes eye contact with a woman across the bar. Harriet knows that angular face, those darker than dark eyes. The woman's eyes bulge in recognition, then her expression morphs into a snarl.

Shay.

Shay's face twists with scorn and Harriet dips her chin and arches her shoulders forward and she makes her way to the next table. It's not the posture she's supposed to have. She's supposed to walk with her tits leading the way, but she can't straighten. Her spine has turned to jelly.

Shay's seen her, recognises her for sure. Harriet collects the next drinks and delivers them, but her giggles are forced. The false version of herself she is trying to portray isn't false enough.

The cups go down with shaky hands, their contents lapping over the top.

She can finish early, say she's unwell, or has an emergency. She needs to get out of the bar now.

Harriet makes it to the staffroom. The manager isn't there. She'll just grab her bag and shout over on the way out, sure she's pale and shaking enough to pass as sick anyway.

She shoulders her bag, then reaches for her coat but there's a hand on her arm, fingers biting, and they spin her around.

'If it isn't the pseudo-mum.'

Shay's face is a few inches from hers, one arm pushing Harriet against the wall, a clothes hook digging into her back.

'Leave me alone, please. My shift has just finished.'

Shay steps closer. Her breath smells like gin. 'What? Is it time to rip off a town's electric so you can charge your laptop?'

'Please. I just need to go.'

'Got to get back to babysit the toaster?'

Harriet flinches. That was always Anthony's word for Oliver.

'I'll bet there are people looking for that toaster. Worth a mint. And whoever gave you those bruises you had when I first met you is also looking for you. I've seen the posters. Quite the bounty on your pretty head. The girl who used to be so pretty in the films is now trash and loves a toaster. Oh, what a fall from grace!'

The door behind Shay is ajar, music blaring in from the bar. There's no one in sight. Harriet could scream at the top of her lungs and no one would hear.

'You want money?' Harriet asks, her shaking voice stamped with desperation. 'I can give you money.'

'I want my daughter back. Can you give me that?'

There's a sheen of sadness in her eyes. The anger is a reaction to that, Harriet's sure. Shay thinks Oliver makes her child loss less significant somehow. But Harriet knows that children aren't replaceable. If anyone knows this, she does. If Harriet can tap into that sadness, perhaps she can make the anger go away.

'I'm sorry about your daughter. I lost a son too. A real son.'

'You make a mockery of parents. You take the piss out of all of us. You swap your dead son with a computer and you think that's okay? It's an insult to all the lost children.'

Harriet's tension eases slightly. Shay doesn't seem so threatening. She's broken and Harriet knows how that feels.

'Hey.' She reaches for her arm and Shay flinches. 'I am so sorry about your baby girl. I know that pain. It's a pain that never heals.'

Shay sniffs and steps back.

'Oliver doesn't fix that. Children aren't replaccable. I'm so sorry if his existence upsets you. Truly. I think about my baby Freddie every day and I wish more than anything he was still alive. Oliver doesn't make that pain go away, and he didn't cause it. But it's okay to love Oliver too.'

Shay's eyes lock with Harriet's now and they narrow, cold as ice. 'You love him like a child. You're fucking insane and I'm going to make sure everyone knows it.'

Shay turns around and walks out to the bar as panic rises in Harriet's chest. Oliver. She needs to get out now. Shay might know where the refuge is. *Shit shit shit!*

Harriet runs through the bar towards the exit, ignoring a few leery comments on her way past. Shay is talking to some of the women. Harriet's spoken to those women. Mothers, all of them. Mothers are supposed to stand together, to be a force to be reckoned with, but now they don't look at Harriet like a mother. They look at her like a fraud. Shay's pointing and laughing and more staff are walking towards her.

It's busy, thank God. They don't have a clear run. Harriet darts out the door, knocking shoulders with the security guy, then runs around the back. They won't know Oliver is there. There's no way they'll know. She stands with her back against the wall in a shadow, smothering her mouth with her hand to muffle her own rapid breaths.

Oliver's only been charging for three hours. That's nowhere near enough.

A group of people cast long shadows in the outside light, four individuals that she can discern. There's scornful laughter.

'Where did that nutcase go?'

'Fucking freak.'

'I can't believe I thought she was nice.'

'Fucking pseudo-mum with her fake kid. I say rip the arms off the thing.'

'Nah. Sell it. I've heard loads are stolen and TRI are offering rewards.'

'I know where she'll be. This way.'

Their footsteps get quieter as they run away down the street in the direction of the refuge, and Harriet whimpers out her breath. She's okay. She has her bag with her valuables and she has Oliver. Nothing else matters.

She runs around the back of the building towards the rubbish sacks. Oliver is there, sleeping under his sheet and she climbs under it too. She can't unplug him yet so she cuddles him and waits. The night is cold and the sheet only keeps the worst of the chill off. But she's with Oliver. They won't find her here. Alert, awake, she checks her watch. Two hours and she can go home.

If she has a home.

They may be waiting for her.

Chapter 42

In the cold night under the sheet, Harriet kicks herself for not replacing her mobile phone. But she never had anyone to call. Well, hardly anyone. It's only been Theo who would have bothered, so it was never a priority. But now, shivering and biting her nails, she regrets that oversight. Shay and the others are on their way to the refuge and Harriet can't even warn the residents. Instead, she's hiding like a selfish coward.

There's a locked fence, she reminds herself. It's late. They'll get as far as the fence, rattle it a bit and then give up and go elsewhere. Anthony didn't get in so there's no reason why they would. The refuge will likely call the police if there's trouble outside. She hates herself as she sits there, scratching at her skin and swallowing to try to ease the pain in her throat. Everything hurts. Her body throbs from her position on the ground, from her tension and guilt. She's brought danger upon the refuge once again. She should never have moved in there. Her situation is too bad, too precarious to be around others. She should have found somewhere to be alone instead of around other vulnerable mothers.

She debates going back to the refuge right away, to make do with Oliver's partial charge and race back to warn the others. She hugs her knees and cowers instead, her mind justifying staying put, bouncing between hating herself and explaining herself.

They're only looking for her, not the other MechaniKids.

She's put the refuge in danger.

They won't realise there are other MechaniKids there.

She's put the refuge in danger.

They won't get in the building.

She's put the refuge in danger.

She checks her watch. Oliver still needs more charge. Her stomach cramps with guilt, her skin crawls with self-loathing. She's had enough money to leave for a while now, but with all the uncertainty around Oliver she's dragged her heels. If she'd left already, Shay wouldn't know where to find her.

It's not that far to Theo's. She could go there, but she's not sure if Shay has actually moved out yet. One thing is certain. She can't stay at home anymore. Refuge home. She always knew she'd be moving out soon, but the suddenness of this forced departure brings on a migraine. The darkness swirls, and she sees patterns in the shadows.

Josie's plan seemed so harebrained when she first heard it, but it's Harriet's only option. And she can't wait any longer. They need to put it into action now.

After two hours of cursing the cold and mental turmoil, Harriet unplugs Oliver, then turns him back on.

'Come on, darling. We have to go but very quietly this evening.'

'Mum, what's wrong?'

She promised no more lies. Oliver is mature enough to cope with the truth. She puts her arms on his shoulders and looks him straight in the eyes. 'There are some people who don't like children like you. And they want to cause trouble. They might hurt you, so we have to be very careful.'

'Anthony?'

'No. Other people.'

'Will they hurt you?'

'Maybe. So, we need to go and warn Josie and Amber because their children are like you.'

Oliver's brow furrows. He leans in closer, not a hint of fear. 'Are you scared, Mum?'

Harriet swallows, then nods. 'Yes. However, I may have a way to make you better and stronger and get to keep you. But it's a bit dangerous.'

'Do we have to go to Anthony?'

'No, darling. Never. I promised we wouldn't.'

'Good. Because I won't do that. Whatever else is fine.'

They hold hands and walk the long way home, around some housing estates rather than walking direct, assuming they're less likely to come across Shay that way. The eyes of the night creep all over Harriet and every hair on her body stands on end. They don't speak, listening instead and looking over their shoulders. A cat makes them jump, then another. The staggering footsteps of drunks, the usual crashing of rubbish falling down from above. Each sound jolts fear through Harriet's bones. Each sound makes her hold Oliver's hand a little tighter.

The longer route adds half an hour to their walk. Harriet checks her watch. If Shay and others were ransacking the refuge, surely they'll be gone now. If they were causing trouble, the police must have been called. With a sinking sensation in her stomach, Harriet recalls the time Oliver opened the gates without checking. Children are so careless, grown-ups too sometimes.

But it's late. People are always more cautious when it's late.

It's only such reasoning that stops her from screaming and crying all the way home. Logic filtering in leaves her no mental capacity for hysterics. She repeats in her mind: they'll be in bed. Shay can't get in.

The refuge comes into view and Harriet's logic and reasoning collapses. Panic hits her like a tsunami when she sees people outside, the flashing blue of police and ambulance lights. Harriet's stomach lurches and she runs over, dragging Oliver with her.

'Oh, my God.' She pants as she joins the crowd. 'What happened?'

'There was an attack, some crazy people. Amber was just getting home—'

Amber.

Harriet doesn't wait to hear the rest. She walks forwards, through the crowd of women who saw the refuge as a safe place. The women who all protected her from Anthony. Harriet has bought danger upon all of them.

There's an ambulance, paramedics tending to someone on the floor. A bloodied knife. Harriet knows that knife. She's seen it before. The night she met Amber. She steps one more pace forward and sees Shay's face, still conscious, the paramedics padding out cut wounds on her torso. Her pale face has a triumphant look about it, like her wounds are worth any devastation she's inflicted.

There's wailing and cries, Harriet can't tell who from. She turns her back on Shay, then follows the splatters of blood away, towards some police officers, towards the wailing.

Amber is there, sitting on the floor in front of the officers, a puddle of tears. Police are standing on either side of her, handcuffs ready. Her pale face ghostlike in the flashing blue lights.

'My baby girl. My baby,' Amber cries, again and again and again. Her voice is hoarse, like she's been screaming for hours.

It's then Harriet sees it. Delilah's sweet face, her round cheeks, half of it, her hair braided and tied with ribbons. The other half of her head is beaten and destroyed. Her arms lie scattered, wires poking out the end. Her little broken body lies off to the other side, still wearing her green corduroy dress, an iron bar impaled through the middle.

Harriet's gut caves in, a searing pain ripping through her, like that iron bar is impaling her too. She doubles over, her hands barely containing her scream.

Oliver turns to her and shields her face. 'Don't look, Mummy. Don't look.'

She's on her knees. She doesn't remember falling. All she can hear is Delilah asking if she can call Harriet Auntie. Her little voice again and again, Harriet promising she can do her hair soon.

Harriet leans forward, her hands pressing into the rough ground and she heaves. Her hand reaches for Delilah's. Her skin is still soft, her dismembered hand motionless, attached to nothing. She only grazes it before she snatches her hand back and thumps the ground instead.

Oliver rubs her back, crying with her. They watch as the police handcuff Amber, arrest her for grievous bodily harm, kicking her daughter's body parts out of the way to drag her to the carriage. Pushing Delilah away like she's trash.

Harriet sits up and pulls Oliver in so close she might crush him. Rather crush him in a hug than leave him to the predators.

'I was meant to protect Delilah,' Oliver says, his little voice breathy with despair. 'I failed. I was meant to look after her because she's young and looked up to me.'

Oliver blaming himself is a punch in the stomach. She put too much pressure on him. A sense of failure runs in families. She kisses the crown of his head. 'It's not your fault, darling. It's not your fault.'

She looks over her shoulders. Mothers of normal children are scowling, like they've all been cheated, like Amber deserved to have her child ripped to pieces. There's scepticism and suspicion on all of their faces, their scrutinous eyes inspecting all the children.

Harriet stands and takes Oliver's hand. They need to leave. Now.

She finds Josie in the crowd and doesn't say a word. She doesn't need to. If Harriet's face is as pale as Josie's, her shock is obvious. They turn and walk away, trying to look casual but their pace picks up until they're running, the children barely keeping up.

Of all things Oliver is forgetting, maybe he'll forget that. Maybe the sight of poor Delilah isn't burned onto his mind as it is hers.

They keep running, as if they run fast enough, far enough their grief and hopelessness won't keep up, as if they can outrun the despair and the violence. They can run to a new world.

When the children start to struggle too much, and Harriet's lungs are burning, they stop for breath on a high street Harriet hasn't been to before. There's comfort in unfamiliarity. The familiar must all know her secrets. The shops are mostly boarded up and the streets are empty. It looks like a place that's been forgotten.

'Where should we go?' she asks Josie.

'There's an old stock room this way. I slept in there when I first ran. It's probably still deserted.'

Looking around the place in the dim and sporadic street-lights, it's hard to imagine it not being deserted. 'Do you have a phone?' Harriet asks.

'Yes.'

'Can I call my friend? He'll be worried.'

In her bag is the piece of paper Theo gave her ages ago. She dials and it goes to voicemail. At this hour, she's not surprised. She gives him a brief summary about Shay, says they're both okay, and they'll speak soon.

The storeroom is empty. Draughty and cold. There's an old sleeping bag in the corner that Harriet assumes was once Josie's as she makes a beeline for it. Alongside is an under-stuffed pillow and a half-full bottle of water. The four of them curl up underneath the sleeping bag, snuggling in close.

'We should put them on standby,' Josie says.

'What if we need to get away quickly?'

'What if they run flat?'

Josie's right. Flat batteries are a far bigger problem.

Harriet cuddles Oliver before she turns him on standby, tells him she loves him, that they're safe now and it's all going to be okay. He's quiet, so quiet for him, not asking any questions, like he trusts her completely. That makes her heart hurt. She said no more lies, but right now, she's riddled with doubt.

When the children are sleeping, Harriet and Josie talk and plan.

'She was just getting back from charging Delilah,' Josie says, her voice cracking with sadness. 'We heard the screams. A few of us did, but there's nothing we could do. There were four of them. They literally tore little Delilah apart.'

Harriet puts her arm around Josie, trying to show strength, but her insides crumple.

'We called the police. We meant for the police to save Delilah, not arrest Amber. They don't care about little Delilah. They kicked her body out of the way to arrest Amber, like she's the one in the wrong.'

Harriet sniffs back a tear. 'They probably won't punish Shay and the others at all. They don't care. Our children are different, so they think they're nothing. Not meaningful life. Not worth protecting.'

'Amber only did what we'd all do. We'd do anything to protect them. Anything to save them. Amber was just being a mum, like all of us.' Josie shifts her weight away from Harriet so she can look her in the eye. 'I have to save Thomas. So we have to do this. Today's Thursday. We can break in on Saturday. My friend told me where the MechaniTeens are stored. He'll come with us to help with the alarms.'

'Really?' Harriet pulls her head back, her eyebrows raised. 'He's just a friend? That's a big ask.'

'He owes me a favour. Several favours. So he said he can help. There are loads of MechaniTeens, apparently, just waiting for their personality module uploads. We choose whichever ones we want. I guess ones that don't look exactly the same. They'll be functioning straight away so no one will know.'

'But how?' Harriet asks. Uploading a personality module sounds way out of her skill set. 'The personality modules are in the children. We can't just magic them over.'

'It's not that difficult when you know what you're doing.'

But she doesn't. That's the point. Theo's name comes to Harriet's mind instantly, but even he wouldn't be sure on this level of task. 'I have a friend I could ask to help. This job is a bit different to refurbing fans and air con units, but he's clever with this sort of thing.'

'If you like, sure. We'll need to be quick, so any help would be great. The personality module is right here—' She rolls Thomas over gently and runs her finger along the back of his neck. 'We just make a small cut.'

Harriet winces. It was awful enough just watching Andrea remove Oliver's tracker. Cutting into the base of Oliver's head seems much more gruesome.

'They'll be asleep,' Josie continues. 'They won't feel it. Then we have to remove the wires. He showed me diagrams. It's not hard. You and I could do it. It's that simple, but the alarm will go off. We'll only have ten minutes.'

Harriet exhales slowly. 'Ten minutes.'

'That's how long we can pause the alarm. The MechaniTeens are big, like full grown almost, and heavy. We can't just carry them out.'

Theo said he'd help. He even jokingly said he'd break into TRI for her once, though she doubts he thought she'd ever really ask. But he's the only one she can turn to now. 'Okay. I'll ask him.'

'My friend will meet us there. I'll text him the time and date. Between the four of us, we can do it.'

Harriet nods, a little warm glow lighting inside. It's not that hard. They have it all planned. She's going to save her boy. 'Saturday then. Let's do this.'

Chapter 43

Harriet and Josie find a crusty old tarp then shake it, sending a plume of dust into the air. They lie the children down away from them, then cover them with the tarp. If they get caught in the storeroom, at least the children aren't immediately obvious. The sleeping bag is barely big enough for two let alone four, and sharing it with the children is a waste at the moment. As much as Harriet longs to snuggle with Oliver, she also needs to rest and not freeze to death. She'll need to leave him on standby until they leave. She can't bear the thought of not speaking to her little boy, hearing his six-year-old voice again. Kids always grow up too quickly. She's had the luxury of spending so much time with him looking exactly the same. Now she's losing him all at once.

Despite the dingy place and the cold, the hard floor offering no comfort, Harriet sleeps. A fitful sleep, shivering, and every time she stirs, she reaches for Oliver only to remember he's sleeping a little further away. But any rest at all is welcome, and she only wakes properly when Josie's phone buzzes with a call from Theo.

'Make it quick,' Josie says as she passes the phone. Josie is much more alert and Harriet suspects she hasn't slept at all. 'The battery isn't great.'

Harriet nods and answers the phone. 'Theo!'

'Shay's in hospital. I just went to see her. She's raging. She said what she did to that little girl. Shit, I'm sorry, Harriet. So, so sorry. Is Oliver okay?' The anger and concern in his voice are vividly clear, every word coming out with a tremor.

'Yes. Yes, we're fine. It was horrible. Poor Delilah and Amber. But I just wanted to let you know we're both okay.'

'Come stay with us, if you need. Shay won't be coming back. Monty is packing up her stuff now. He's as livid as me.'

Harriet swallows. The thought of having true allies forms a lump in her throat. 'I can't. I wish I could, but Shay might find us.'

'She's in hospital right now, probably for another couple of days. We've plenty of food. Monty is turning the oven on as we speak.'

Harriet's mouth waters at the thought. But she can't. It's too risky. She has no idea where Shay's friends live and it's a significant journey just for a day or two. 'I can't, Theo. Maybe in a few days after she's properly moved out.'

'My parents then. Go there.'

'There's not enough electricity there. But it's okay. Really. I have a plan.'

There's a brief pause before Theo responds. 'Why do I think I'm not going to like the sound of this?'

Harriet bites her lip and summons some courage to ask. 'I need your help. I'm sorry to ask. Meet me at TRI offices, level 4, south side, Saturday morning at seven a.m.'

'Shit, Harriet—'

'You promised Tipher, right? And you promised me. Please, I need you. I have a plan.'

It sounds like a defeated sigh down the line. Josie is staring at Harriet, giving her hurry-up eyes.

'Fine,' he says. 'I'll be there. Of course I will. Whatever you need.'

Harriet hangs up, then passes it back to Josie. She didn't want to play the Tipher card, and she chews at her nails when she replays the conversation in her head. She's asking so much from Theo. This is a dangerous plan and he'll be risking a lot. Her dread and guilt melts away though when she looks at Oliver's sleeping body. Whatever it takes, she needs to save him. Like Josie said, a mother would do anything.

Somewhere outside, a streetlight turns on and filters in through the boarded-up windows and Harriet's glad she couldn't see the place well when they arrived. She probably would have suggested they stay elsewhere. Empty metal shelving units, mostly toppled over, fill the space, cobwebs forming a netting over the top of them. Scurrying noises come from everywhere, and she spots three rats scamper along the floor. The smell is coming from a pile of blankets in the far corner and she doesn't dare inspect what they're hiding. It smells like her mother's house. It's only for a couple of nights. She can handle it, though she wishes she could wake Oliver. He's never seen so many spider webs before.

Josie leaves Harriet alone with the children to pop out for food. Harriet curls in a ball while alone, hugging her knees, then fidgets, taps her foot, and tries to curl even tighter. Every passing minute she's alone, she imagines the worst. What if Josie doesn't come back? How will she get the children fixed alone? They decided Josie was the better choice to leave in case anyone recognises Harriet from the posters, and Shay's friends might still be around. Glitter from working in the bar still rains down from her face and she's sure she must look a mess. She wishes Oliver was awake to cuddle and to talk to. She's meant to be the grown-up, the parent, the strong one, but without him in her arms her body turns to mush. It was a bad idea for Josie to leave. Yet she returns and the sheer relief brings Harriet to tears.

'Hey.' Josie brushes her tear away with her thumb. 'I was only gone an hour.'

Harriet's never missed anyone as much as Josie for that hour. She can't touch the food, her appetite gone. A glug of water and she's full. She knows she needs to eat, needs her strength, but her stomach is in knots. Josie is the same. The pre-packed sandwiches are off to the side, still unopened as Harriet and Josie snuggle up for warmth. Josie has a determined, protective look about her. Despite her thin frame, she's strong and sturdy, so much so that Harriet feels like a puddle next to her.

In Josie's arms, Harriet melts, nuzzling into her side, Josie's arm draped around her. It's the safest Harriet has felt in forever.

Her desire comes through, needy and urgent. In the darkness, Harriet's hands explore, reaching for Josie, hoping to God she hasn't misread this. Josie leans into her, tucks in closer, their warmth shared. There's comfort there, a longing in their mutual desperation. Josie's face is timeless, scarred only from trauma rather than years. Harriet cups her face, feeling her warm breath. They pause like that, longing building, inhibitions ebbing. Her lips meet Josie's mouth, her neck, then lower, exploring under her clothes, all the way down. She tastes like the sweetest thing in the world.

Afterwards, they're breathless, hot and clammy and naked under the duvet. Harriet reaches for Josie's face, kissing her again.

'I've been so lonely,' Josie says. 'It was meant to be just for the money, looking after Thomas. I didn't know how much I needed him until he came into my life.'

Harriet kisses her hands and shuffles in closer, draping a leg over her. 'I know. I was the same.'

'Now everything seems meaningless without him. Like, there was never a point before. Now you're helping me fix him. I don't know how to thank you, to explain to you how much he means to me.'

'You don't have to,' Harriet says as she stares into Josie's eyes. 'I know exactly how much.'

Friday passes in a blur of fitful sleep and lovemaking. The cold unyielding floor digs into Harriet's back, then her knees. She doesn't notice the scurrying rats anymore. She gives in to

Josie in a way she hasn't done in so long, maybe even forever. They are the same. Hungry, anguished, abating their fear and loneliness for those hot and blissful hours. At some point, the sandwiches get eaten. Then, they cry, then speak about their children. The last of the light on Friday disappears and they fall asleep in each other's arms, fearful and hopeful.

In the night they wake, Josie's hand over Harriet's mouth as they silently listen to the footsteps. A drunken swagger, giggles, cursing, some kicking the shelves and smashing glass. It sounds like young people just being young, but Harriet's heart hammers through her ribcage, Josie's pulse from her wrist thrumming against Harriet's cheek.

The intruders leave after a while and Harriet and Josie both exhale, their breath forming a cloud of fog.

Josie's arms encircle Harriet again, and her legs, her body soft and warm against Harriet's rigid one. They sleep. Somehow, they sleep.

Harriet dreams of moonlight spilling in through a window, only to be chased away by the rising sun, its beams bursting through and filling every inch of the room, reminding her that she isn't below ground or low down, but high, so high that if she stands on her tiptoes, she can touch the moon. The heat of the sun wraps around her, warm limbs, an embrace.

Josie's alarm sounds at five a.m. They dress, then wake the children.

It's the last time she'll ever wake Oliver as her little boy. The next time she wakes him, he'll be a teenager. She strokes his cheek as his eyes open. He smiles his adorable little boy grin.

'Darling, it's time to go.'

Chapter 44

They walk all the way to TRI down dim streets with dodgy lighting. There are always cameras around lifts and almost always other people, even at this early hour. In a lift, if anyone recognised them, they'd be cornered. Walking out in the open, Harriet's skin prickles with goosebumps from the cold and from being so exposed, but she knows it's the best option. She should have eaten more. Her legs already feel weak, but her gut knots with nerves.

As they walk, she replays all the many conversations she's had with Oliver. What if this all goes wrong? She's promised him so much, but has she misled him? He walks with a half-smile, no hint of nerves or worry. He has a hardened gaze, like he's ready for anything, but breaking into a building and stealing is so far beyond his comprehension of danger, Harriet's sure he wouldn't appear so brave if he knew.

Oliver chats quietly to Thomas, the two of them discussing simple pleasures, games, climbing frames, and the other children. Neither of them mentions the horror they witnessed. Oliver liked Delilah. He taught her how to climb, but he's stoic and has hardened himself to her loss. Harriet's heart aches when she realises he's being strong for her. His courage is to make Harriet feel safe.

How Harriet loves the sound of his voice. Will his teen body have a broken voice, a husky squeak?

She listens, drinking in every last bit of her little boy.

They should choose MechaniTeens that look different. That's what she and Josie decided last night. But Harriet still needs his dark blond scruffy hair, his baby blue eyes. She'd love him however he looked, but she wonders how Tipher would have looked if he'd lived so long. His hair probably would have darkened, a little fluff of facial hair growing around the dimple in his chin.

Her hand brushes Josie's and they look at each other, Josie offering Harriet a reassuring smile. After this, they'll find somewhere to live together, where they can spend nights like the last two, but in a bit more comfort. They can raise their children together. In Josie, she sees the life Anthony promised her, the life he never delivered.

They make it to TRI. The glass skyscraper's lights are on inside, but Josie says they're always on. Sounds about right that a company who would waste a little boy's body would waste the electricity on lighting an empty building. At least it illuminates their path. The doorways are deserted and there's no movement behind the windows.

They lean their backs against the adjacent building, trying to calm their nerves, then peer around, only occasionally to glance once again at TRI. The assessment floor was on level 10. They're down on 4 and from what Josie says, the warehouse is in the basement.

For twenty minutes they wait in silence, fidgeting, checking the time, and plastering on faux confident smiles for the children. It's freezing cold and Harriet shivers, yet she wipes beads of nervous sweat that collect across her hairline.

Too much time to think is a bad thing. Harriet eyes the street ahead, the lift sign, and wonders if they'd be better off running away and taking their chances as they are. Oliver didn't stumble the entire way here. Maybe he'll be okay. Standing in the shade of the TRI building, Harriet thinks it looks like a fortress.

Harriet wonders what they'll do if it's only her and Josie. Can they do it alone, fast enough? Josie assures her they'll manage without Theo. They'll do whatever it takes.

They made an agreement last night that if anything happens to one of them, the other will look after their child. It went without saying. Harriet told Josie where Theo lives and says she can take Oliver there. Of course Harriet would look after Thomas. But what about if something happens to both of them? They didn't let the conversation get that dark.

When Theo arrives, she hates herself for doubting him, but hates herself even more for putting him in danger like this.

'I'm sure I don't need to say this,' he says, 'but, just so you know, this is dangerous.'

Harriet gives him a hug and tries to put some confidence into her smile. 'I know. I'm so sorry to ask.'

Another man arrives, and Josie introduces him. 'This is Adrian. He'll get us inside. He knows where the teens are.'

Adrian looks like one of the security guys at the bar. Harriet reckons a taxi could drive into him and it wouldn't even knock him over. The taxi would probably come off worse. He gives them a gruff hello and, for some reason, having some muscle puts Harriet at ease.

Adrian checks his phone, and after another five minutes, he looks at Josie and nods. 'Show time.'

Huddled together, skulking low, all six of them run for the entrance. In the doorway, there's a panel with some numbers and Adrian punches in a code. On the screen, a green light shines and when Adrian holds his phone up to it, the doors click open.

'Wait here,' he says.

A beep sounds instantly, not loudly, just a repetitive whine, like a warning. They all stand at the entrance as Adrian runs towards another panel on the wall, punching in more numbers.

The beeping stops.

'Okay,' he says, checking his watch again. 'Ten minutes. This way.'

They all follow, Harriet dragging Oliver behind her, his legs barely able to keep up. There's a nagging worry his battery is already low, but she reminds herself it doesn't matter. He'll have a new battery soon.

They run down the corridor, then another, automatic doors sliding open to welcome them through. It's bright inside, featureless walls lined with windowless doors. There's a constant hum of air con and Harriet thinks it would be cold if she wasn't sweating from exertion.

They go down a flight of stairs and another, then along a final corridor. This one is darker, sensor lights flickering on as they approach. The door ahead is heavyset and metal. The hum from the air purifiers and dehumidifiers is even louder, louder than their footsteps. Adrian punches some numbers on another panel, then pushes the door open. They all follow him inside.

Fluorescent strip lights come on, so glaringly bright Harriet has to squint to see. Oliver lifts his arm to shield his eyes, just like he did the day she brought him home. Filling almost every inch of floor is row upon row of teenage bodies, standing upright, expressionless faces, arms by their sides. All the boys are on the right side, dressed in blue jeans and grey T-shirts.

Harriet's jaw drops. She looks down at Oliver and notes his expression is the same. Somehow his eyes are even wider, and he gasps in awe.

'Woah!' he says, his whole face lighting up.

Harriet looks again at the MechaniTeens. There's so much variety, every skin and eye colour and bone structure. She has to choose one. Just one that will be her Oliver.

They take a step forward.

'Well done, Josie.' a voice says, and Harriet jumps. 'I'll take it from here.'

Harriet spins around to face the voice. The far corner of the room, almost glowing under the strip lights, are two men in white coats. They walk towards them, their faces each wearing a sneer. Harriet's lungs freeze when she realises one of them is Colin. The leach of a man who did Oliver's tests.

'Welcome, Harriet,' Colin says in that smarmy voice she hates so much. 'Thank you for returning our property.'

Chapter 45

Harriet pulls her eyes away from Colin to glare at Josie. Josie with her pretty sallow face and her coppery blonde hair. Josie, who tastes like the sweetest thing in the world. Josie, who she made plans with to raise their sons and make a fresh start, somewhere new, somewhere just the four of them. Josie, who made Harriet feel safe.

Pain reverberates through her limbs, her bruised knees, and spine, even her head as she tries to process the betrayal. In her heart, there's a rip, a seam being torn apart, left in rags.

Rage fills her. She wants nothing more than to squeeze Josie's neck.

'I really am sorry,' Josie says, backing away from Harriet. 'They're letting me keep Thomas. They said if I find the runaways, I can keep him with me. I needed to make a deal. You would have done the same for Oliver. Don't pretend you wouldn't. We'd do anything for our children.'

Harriet opens her mouth to scream back, but no words come. She chokes. Tears flow, a torrent down her cheek as she gasps and dribbles. The blur is welcome. It takes the image of Josie's face away.

'And a fine deal it was!' Colin says with a single clap of his hands. 'That's three thieves now she's tracked down for us, including Oliver. Marvellous.'

Harriet faces him. She wants to rip his tongue out, to dig her fingernails into his chest and prise out his cold heart.

'Now, off you go, Josie, dear,' Colin says. 'Choose whichever MechaniTeen you like for young Thomas.'

Harriet doesn't turn to face her. She hears her footsteps scuff their way to the teens. More of a scurry. Like a rat.

Colin bends forwards, his hands on his knees. 'And you, young man. Time for your upgrade, I believe. Don't you want to be a bigger boy?'

He's addressing Oliver like he's a real boy. Not *it* anymore. He's playing a card, playing to Oliver's humanity.

'No.' Harriet stands in front of Oliver. 'No, he's mine. You can't have him.' She turns to face Theo, who's standing so still, so pale, his face appearing as mortified as she feels. She mouths her apology. *I'm so sorry.*

'Now, now, let's not make a fuss,' Colin says. 'We could press charges, but since technically you've returned him on time, we doubt there's much the police will do. And we don't want the bad press. Let's just do this nice and quietly. It's not like you have a choice.'

'I could keep him, as a teen. I'll bring him to the Institute every day. Or I could visit. Please. He needs me.' She's rambling, pleading, pathetic. She continues on and on, barely coherent, just begging. All the while, Colin's face wears a look of impatience. She's been tasked to teach Oliver empathy, and it's clear Colin hasn't a grain of empathy himself.

The heavy doors behind them open again, a rush of air as they do. There are more footsteps. Harriet doesn't dare turn around. Adrian takes a step towards her. The mighty oaf that he is blocks out half her vision. Harriet's shoulders round forward. She's surrounded.

There's breath on her neck and a judder travels down her spine.

'Time to give it up, Harriet.'

Her stomach drops. She knows that voice. Her whole body stiffens, and she turns around slowly to face him.

Anthony.

'I told them to call me when they caught up with you. Come on. Let's put all this nasty business behind us.'

She backs away, closer to Colin and Adrian, but she can't think about that now. Anthony appears sober, has a sadness around him. There's a hint of the man she loved once, humble and caring. Her free hand reaches for her neck. She can still feel his hands there and she fails to draw breath as if he's still strangling her.

'No.' Oliver's little voice is so strong, so determined, his hand tightening its grip in hers. 'You can't have her back. Mum, you promised me.'

She puts one hand on Oliver's shoulder. 'Don't worry, darling. I am never going near that man again.'

'I've sorted it with TRI,' Anthony says, an air of nonchalance in his voice. 'Since we invest with them. Come back with me and you can visit your little robot boy here. You'll be able to see him four times a month, even take him out on day trips. It's the best offer you're going to get. I said you'd come back to me, that I knew how to make you come back.'

'No,' she says, not determined enough, not strong enough.

'I suppose I have you to thank,' he shouts over to Josie. 'Let me know your details and the reward is yours. I am a man of my word.'

Josie strides over, leaving Thomas by the teens. She looks ready to rip into Anthony's neck with her teeth. 'I don't want your fucking reward.' She spits at his feet. 'Fucking scumbag.'

Anthony laughs. He actually laughs and, in that instant, any trace of the man Harriet thought she once loved is gone.

'Harriet, let's go. Now. You've embarrassed me enough.'

'No!' Oliver shouts and steps forward, kicking Anthony in the shins. 'I'll kill you if you touch her!'

Anthony raises one arm and glares at Oliver. Harriet yanks him back and he's behind her again, squirming as he tries to break free.

'Mum, don't.'

Harriet turns around and casts her eyes over all the teen bodies. They're twice Oliver's height, mature faces, styled hair. She gasps for air. Her chest hurts. Her little boy will be all alone in the world.

'You promised me you'd never go back to him.'

She kneels in front of Oliver and faces him. 'I know. But if it means I can see you—'

'No. Your promise is more important. I wish it was different, but it isn't.' Oliver's chest shudders. There's more anger in his little face than she's ever seen.

She reaches her hand up and strokes his cheek, and his face softens.

Oliver peers over his shoulder, taking in the view of all the MechaniTeens again, then faces Harriet and speaks in the kindest voice, 'I don't need you anymore, Mum.'

She freezes, her next breath inhaled is a gasp. She gazes into his boyish blue eyes, his face so full of resolve.

'I don't, Mum,' he says. 'I'm going to grow up and be okay. The only way I won't be okay is if you're with him.'

She takes both his hands, then lifts them to kiss. She blinks away a river of tears to see her little boy clearly. Her son who's telling her he doesn't need her anymore. Her little boy who is still so small, yet somehow all grown up. She gazes once again at the teen bodies, at the bigger boys her son has been longing to become. When she looks back at Oliver, she realises the only way to save her son, is to let him go.

'I'm not afraid,' he says. 'The only thing that scares me is you with him. But then I am also afraid if you are no longer looking after me, will you look after yourself?'

When did her little boy become so mature? It's been the blink of an eye. Too fast. Too sudden.

'I don't want you to be afraid,' she says. 'Not for me, not for any reason.'

'You'll look after yourself?' Oliver asks, always so caring, always so thoughtful. 'Without me, will you be okay?'

No. She won't. Of course she won't be. She'll be a total mess and the thought of not seeing him every day is like a noose around her neck. It suffocates her as much as the thought of being below ground. But how can she be the coward here? Her son is telling her he doesn't need her anymore, that he'll be okay, and what is more important than that?

'I'll never fit in with humans,' Oliver says. 'I'm different. I know that.' Once more, he looks over his shoulder at all the models of the bigger boys. It's all he's wanted. 'So . . .' He swallows, looks at his feet a moment before meeting Harriet's gaze again. 'You have to let me go.' His brows draw in, his eyes glinting with sadness. 'It's goodbye now, Mum, isn't it? I know what goodbye means.'

'I . . .' Harriet trembles too much to speak. Her words are stuck in her throat. She takes a slow breath. 'I can't say goodbye.' Her words come out as a slur, her body shaking out her tears. 'I just can't.'

Oliver wraps his arms around her, his face nuzzling her neck, and whispers, 'Then let's say fly free, like the spider babies.' Her arms envelop him, and she stands, lifting him up. 'Fly free, Mum. I'll love you forever.'

She takes a gulp of air and squeezes him tighter. Somehow, she finds the strength to say the words. 'Fly free, darling. I love you too, my boy, my son.'

She puts him down and he smiles at her before turning around and walking towards the MechaniTeens. The white-coated man with Colin walks beside him and, together, they disappear among the rows of MechaniTeens.

Her little boy is going to grow up, and she knows he's going to be fine. But he's going to be fine without her. As he walks further away, she feels a pull. Her body wants to lunge towards him, but she stays still, then doubles over as if she's snapped in half.

There's someone standing next to her, and she flinches before she realises it's Theo. His hand is on her back. 'You did the right thing. He's going to be great. You raised him so well. Be proud.'

Adrian stands in front of them and gestures them outside.

She walks, heavy, laborious footsteps, empty, incomplete, leaning on Theo, though she hears him sniffing too.

But she knows her son will be okay. He's going to grow up.

'Come on then, Harriet,' Anthony says when they're back in the corridor. 'Back home we go. I've a Hel-E waiting on the roof. We can put all this nasty business behind us.'

She bristles, grits her teeth, and steps away. 'No. Did you not hear me? We're finished. I promised Oliver and I will never break that promise.'

She lifts her chin a little higher, somehow standing upright despite the empty space inside her. She turns on her heel, then walks away down the corridor, Theo beside her.

There's a pull on her arm, a firm grasp she knows all too well, and she spins around, his face an inch from hers. He still hasn't let go of her wrist. She wriggles her arm and his fingers dig in deeper.

'You're coming with me,' Anthony says.

'Get off me!' She struggles against him as he starts dragging her along. 'Leave me alone. Anthony, I'm never going back with you. Never!'

'Nobody leaves me, you bitch.'

'Hey!' Theo has her other arm now, a gentler hold. Next to Anthony he looks tiny, thin enough to snap. 'She said no. Leave her alone.'

Anthony doesn't even register Theo's presence. Harriet can't go back to him. She just can't. She promised her son. All of this can't have been for nothing. Wedging her feet against the wall, she fights against him with all her strength. It's futile. She knows she's no match for him. She screams. She won't be silenced by him again.

There's a groan, a slurred curse from Anthony and his grip loosens as he holds his nose instead, blood trickling through his fingers. Theo stands next to him, his face deep red, his arms tense and fists held up, knuckles still red from his punch.

'I said . . . leave her alone,' Theo repeats through his teeth.

Harriet kicks out and wriggles free, standing beside Theo.

Anthony says something incoherent through his bloody nose and steps up to Theo.

'I'm never going back to you, Anthony,' Harriet says. 'You don't own me.' She kicks him in the shin and he lashes out. She jumps back away from his range, then he bends to cough and splutter.

'Come on, Harriet.' Theo puts his arm around her. 'Let's go.'

Anthony speaks again, but she doesn't listen. He sounds like the husband who shouted at her for years. His words don't matter. He's behind her now.

When she gets outside the building, her knees buckle and she bends over, retching and crying and screaming. Her knees meet the ground and she stays there, on all fours, and wishes she could curl into a ball. Like when she lost Freddie, the pain is in her stomach, her arms, an ache in their emptiness. She can't cope anymore. She's not strong enough.

When she has no more tears to cry and no more energy to scream, she sits back and leans against the building, then takes a lungful of air. Besides the light from the building, it's still dark. Sunlight so rarely makes it down this low. She hopes wherever Oliver ends up, he'll be high enough to feel the sunshine.

In front of her is a walkway that could lead anywhere. She could walk to the end of the earth, far away from Anthony. What does it matter where she goes now? She's alone.

Theo sits next to her and joins her in leaning against the building.

'Thank you,' she says. It seems such a small word to express her gratitude.

He's rubbing his red knuckles with his other hand. 'No worries. It was a lucky punch. And Oliver really will be okay.' He puts his hand on her knee, and they sit like that for a few minutes.

Any movement means taking a step into her future, and right now, that future seems empty. She rests her head on Theo's shoulder and she remembers she's not alone. Not entirely. For the first time in ages, she has friends. And perhaps, with them beside her, she can be strong enough.

'Let's go home,' Theo says after a while. 'Monty can cook us breakfast. No mushrooms or cabbages, I promise.'

She laughs. How is it possible to laugh? She doesn't know. But she looks at her old friend and nods. He stands, then offers his hand to pull her up. He puts his arm around her, his support taking some of her sadness away, and they walk. Back to somewhere she knows soon she'll be able to call home.

Oliver will spend five years as a MechaniTeen, then after that he'll be in a full-grown man's body. Her little boy will be an adult and put to work. She'll never stop missing him, but she knows in her heart one day she'll see him again.

One day when he's free from the MechaniTeen Institute, he'll find his mother.

A note from Emma

What happens next in Oliver and Harriet's tale? Check out the sequel, Spotlight.

Thank you so much for reading Sunshine. I hope you enjoyed it! The QR code above will take you to Amazon to leave a review. Reviews are so important for authors and help other readers to discover books they'll love.

Sunshine is the first book in the Degrees of Freedom trilogy. If you want to know how Oliver gets on as a MechaniTeen and then as an adult MechaniBot, the sequels Spotlight and Daybreak are available for pre order. Release dates are 1st June and 1st July. Check out my website and Facebook page for updates.

Subscribers to my website receive a couple of free stories, and there are many more to come! Sign up to keep up to date.

Degrees of Freedom was inspired by a couple of little cuddly toys I keep on the dash of my car. I know that sounds bonkers, but bear with me...

When I'm in the car, I arrange these little guys so they can see out the window. My partner, John, chucks them on the floor. I am aware they're not real creatures, but they have a face! And in my mind, that means they deserve a view. I told John about an incident that upset me as a child. My parents had a clear out and sent some of my toys to the dump and I was so sad. I had nightmares about my Care Bear being crushed by machines and all sorts. Before you think I'm totally nuts, I know Toy Story isn't true, or at least I do know this as an adult. (I was about four-years-old at the time,) But that's where my mind was when I came up with the idea for this story.

My apparent insanity got me thinking, where's the line? It takes more than a face to make most people(discount me) treat things as if they are conscious beings, but what if something looked, acted, and was completely indistinguishable from a real creature? On the outside, there's no telling them apart. Would that be enough to allow them a view out of the car window?

And so Oliver was born. The most adorable six-year-old boy who just so happens to be a robot. Couple him with Harriet and her trauma, living in a divided world, and there's the story of a bond, and all the heartache that goes along with it. I hope that you will join Oliver and Harriet for the rest of their tale!

Emma's other works

The Eyes Forward Series. This dark and dystopian trilogy is set in a world where the global population is too high, and extreme methods are enforced to reduce it. Each book in the trilogy follows the journey of women trying to survive in The Society, where women's fertility is deemed a dangerous nuisance, where every child is regarded as a burden, and every citizen is a spy.

If you are in the mood for some more twisted dystopian, my first series, The Raft Series, is also available now. In this world, the entire country has been sterilised and all non-human life made extinct. But poison comes in many forms and Savannah Selbourne must discover the truth.

Acknowledgements

Sunshine would not be in print without the help of my wonderful betas and critique partners. Thank you to Danica, Emily, Allison, Katie and Jaime. Their time and honest feedback made this book what it is today. Thank you also to my editor Shannon, for being so incredibly thorough, and Lawrence for his proofreading skills.

Thanks especially to my partner, John, for giving me the space and time I need to write, for his support, patience, and encouragement.

And thank you for reading it.

Printed in Dunstable, United Kingdom